SEVER

SAVAGE FALLS SINNERS MC #4

CAITLYN DARE

1

SADIE

"Here you go, sweetie." Victoria hands me a mug of hot cocoa as I sit on a stack of tires, staring at the compound gates.

Everyone else is inside, trying to clear up the mess left behind from the raid. There isn't a corner of the clubhouse left unturned. Chairs and tables are strewn everywhere, drawers and closets emptied out onto the floor. It hurt my heart seeing the place in such a mess, so I came out here to get some air. But it still feels like I'm inside, the walls closing in around me.

"Thanks." I inhale a shuddering breath.

"How are you holding up?" she asks, sitting on the bench in front of me.

"How do you think?" I snap, instantly regretting it when she flinches. "Sorry, I'm just..."

"I know, sweetie. I know." Victoria offers me a warm smile. "But Ray and the guys will be okay. The police officers didn't find anything."

"Yeah..."

She's right. Their search came up empty, but it

doesn't ease the giant knot in my stomach. They were arrested. My dad, Rhett, Dane, and Pike. Hauled away in handcuffs for some serious charges.

Nothing about this is okay.

Not a damn thing.

My foot taps furiously against the tires as I take a sip of cocoa. "I need to do something."

Sitting here, I feel useless. Powerless. Everything I love most in the world is slipping through my fingers.

"Sadie Ray, the best thing you can do is sit tight and wait for the club attorney to do his thing. He'll bring them home, you'll see."

"How can you be so calm about all of this?" I stare at her incredulously.

"Because I know Ray, sweetheart, and he wouldn't do anything to risk leaving you."

Or you. The words pop into my head, but I don't say them.

"He's careful. He covers his tracks. This is all just one big misunderstanding. I'm sure they'll be back before we know it."

I want to believe her, but how can I when I watched them cart my dad and the guys away?

"Hey." Wes appears, wearing a solemn expression. "Any word?"

"Nothing." I glance down at my cell phone beside me as if it might ring at any second.

Deep down, I know it won't. They'll have been stripped of their personal belongings and thrown in a cell with nothing but the clothes on their backs.

My chest tightens as I replay that moment over and over in my head.

"Come here." Wes comes to stand between my legs,

taking the mug from my hands and placing it down to the side. "They'll be okay, princess." His eyes search mine, but I can't find it in myself to smile.

"And if they're not?"

"You can't think like that," he says, dropping his head to mine.

"I'll give you two some space," Victoria says, standing.

"You don't have to leave, Mom." Wes releases a soft sigh, and I realize how difficult this must be for him.

For both of them.

They haven't even had time to adjust to everything and the world around us is imploding again.

"It's okay, sweetie. I'll go see if Dee and Rosita need any more help."

My aunt came the second she heard. Micky is down at the station trying to reason with Chief Statham, but something tells me it's out of his hands.

We watch Victoria leave. The second she disappears inside the clubhouse, Wes wraps me into his arms.

"I can't believe this is happening." My words are muffled by his t-shirt.

Everything had been so perfect on our mini-vacay. We'd talked and laughed and loved. Coming back to Savage Falls, I felt like nothing could come between us.

Darren Creed is dead. Gone. He can't hurt us anymore. Yet here we are, ripped apart again.

"Shh, baby. I got you." Wes hugs me tighter, and I take some measure of comfort in his arms.

At least he's here.

If he'd been taken too, I don't know what I would have done.

"I can't lose them, Wes." My voice cracks, the tears

I've been fighting so desperately to keep inside finally spilling free.

"Don't cry, princess." He wipes them away with the pad of his thumb. "They'll be back before you know it."

But as I look into his hazel eyes, I see a glimmer of uncertainty.

And my heart breaks all over again.

It's been twelve hours.

Twelve hours, and I've barely had a wink of sleep.

Wes tried to encourage me to get some rest, but I just lay there, unable to close my eyes long enough to drift off. All I keep thinking about is Dane in a holding cell, lost and alone. After everything he's been through, it's the last place he needs to be.

"Sadie?" There's a knock at the door, and I push up onto my elbows, Wes rousing beside me.

"Come in," I call out.

The door opens slightly and Victoria peeks inside. "Attorney Johnson is here. I thought you might want to hear what—"

"Yes." I bolt out of bed. "Thank you."

She closes the door, and I start pulling on my shorts.

"Hey," Wes says, his voice thick with sleep.

At least one of us managed to get some.

"What's going on?" Concern glitters in his eyes as I whirl around the room, trying to get ready.

"Johnson is here."

"The attorney?" I nod, and he throws back the covers. "Shit, let me get dressed."

We work in silence until I'm presentable and Wes is

clothed. He pulls me into his arms, gazing down at me. "Did you manage to get any sleep?" I shake my head, and he lets out a sigh. "You've got to look after yourself."

"I can't, not while they're locked up…" Wriggling out of his hold, I take a step back, folding my arms around myself, but Wes isn't deterred by my sudden coolness.

"Sadie Ray, look at me." His fingers glide under my jaw, tilting my face back. "I'm here. You need space, you need to get angry and vent, you need to punch something… I'm here." He lowers his face, touching his head to mine. "I'm worried too, okay? I am. But they're going to be fine. This is club life. It happens. It's—"

"Listen to you, *prospect*," I snicker, running my hands down his cut. "One night wearing this thing and you think you know all about the life."

His lip curves in a playful smile. "I'm willing to learn, princess. Surely that's worth something."

"Yeah, it's worth something."

It's worth everything.

"But you don't have to give up your dreams for this… for me, Wes."

"I know, and I'm not. But this is your life, your family. And I want that. I want a family, Sadie."

"I love you." The words tumble from my lips as I press closer. "And I love how good you look in this thing."

Wes chuckles, and it's so deep and playful that the knot in my stomach loosens slightly. He runs the back of his knuckles down my cheek. "I'm here, okay? Whatever you need, whatever the club needs, I'm here."

I nod, swallowing thickly. I don't know what I did to deserve this, to deserve him, but I'm grateful. And I'll spend every day trying to show him. But first, I really need Rhett and Dane to come home to me.

To come home to us.

"Come on, let's go see what Johnson has to say."

Wes leads me from Dane's room, and we head for my dad's office. Dee, Micky, and Victoria are already inside. Part of me is surprised to see Victoria here, but I guess it's a testament to how deep her feelings run for my dad. Not to mention that this is the life Wes has chosen now.

"Sweetheart." Dee beckons me over and I fall down beside her, burrowing into her side. "It's okay, Sadie Ray," she whispers as my gaze meets Johnson. I've seen him around the club a few times over the years, but my dad always kept me away from this side of things.

Not anymore.

"So, what's the deal?" Uncle Micky says, drumming his fingers against his jean-clad thigh.

"Savage Falls PD doesn't have a case. The raids on the club, Dalton's home, and the warehouse came up empty. I suspect the charges are a ruse for something bigger."

"Like the business with the Reapers?" Micky says.

Johnson nods. "It made local news. Speculation is flying around Savage Falls and Red Ridge about a new alliance. It's no secret the club has enemies high up. Statham and Mayor Nixon might be on payroll, but this goes higher."

"Can you get them off?" I ask.

"It shouldn't be a problem. Without substantial evidence, I'll have them out by the end of the day."

Relief floods me. "Thank God." But my spine stiffens when I see something pass between Uncle Micky and Johnson.

"What?" I sit forward. "What aren't you telling us?"

"They can hold Ray and the others for up to forty-eight hours without charging them."

"But you just said—"

"Sadie Ray, breathe," Aunt Dee soothes, squeezing my trembling hand. "They'll be home before you know it."

Johnson smooths a hand over his salt and pepper hair. "I have every confidence I'll bring them home by tonight. But Micky's right, the PD are known for using the time they have to their advantage, particularly in the case of a person of interest."

"You think they could cause problems?"

"I'm not ruling it out. But as far as the possession charges go, they don't have a leg to stand on."

Well, that's something. Doesn't stop my stomach from churning at the thought of the cop who arrested them playing games and trying to pin something else on them, though.

"I'm going to head straight over there." Johnson stands, straightening his lopsided tie. "The best advice I have for you and your guys right now is to sit tight. And don't rock the boat."

I let out a small huff. More sitting around, waiting. Just what I don't need.

But he's right—I don't want anyone to do anything to jeopardize bringing them all home.

"Thanks, Johnson." Micky holds out a hand. "Call me when you know anything."

"Will do. In the meantime, lay low and keep your guys in line."

"You got it." My uncle salutes, following him out of Dad's office in his wheelchair.

"Should we be worried?" Wes asks no one in particular.

"Ray doesn't keep Johnson on retainer for his good looks." Dee snorts. "He's good at his job, one of the best. He'll get them out of there, you'll see."

"I hope so," I breathe.

Because anything else is not an option.

2

RHETT

My fists ache, my head pounds, and my eyes burn as I continue to sit in the fucking holding cell with Dane and Pike.

We haven't seen Ray since we were first thrown in here and he was dragged off for questioning. We assumed he'd join us at some point, but he hasn't. They're holding him separately, and that does nothing for the dread sitting heavy in my stomach.

Pike doesn't seem to give to a fuck about the situation as he snores on the other side of the cell, his long-ass body taking up the entire bench. How the hell he hasn't rolled off, I have no idea. Even less of a clue how he's chilled out enough to get some sleep.

It might not be his first time in here, like it is for Dane and me, but still. Our compound got fucking raided. How is he not worried?

"Everything's going to be okay." Dane's voice startles me. "They wouldn't have found anything."

Leaning forward, I rest my elbows on my knees and hang my head. If Ray hadn't called, if he didn't get a tip-

11

off that this was coming, how different could this have gone?

My fists curl once more as I think about the phone call I received from him the day before we left our vacation.

"We're clearing out the compound. We're gonna get hit Friday night."

Even sitting here now after the event, chills still run down my spine. Fear that we were imminently about to be ripped away from Sadie only hours after our time together. Dread, knowing that we were lying to her. But that lie wasn't on us. Ray told us how it was going to play out, and we had no choice but to toe the line.

Sadie isn't going to like it, but she knows how the club works. She's going to understand.

Although she's still going to fucking castrate us the second she learns the truth.

"Why the fuck haven't they brought Ray back? Something's not right."

We've been questioned, asked about our knowledge of the club possessing and dealing firearms. Obviously, we have no clue what they're talking about. We're all mechanics. The only guns we own are the ones we've got licenses for.

A smirk curls at my lips.

They didn't believe a word of it.

But that doesn't matter. They found no evidence to back up the bullshit charges they were hoping to throw at us. They'd never find our stock. We just needed to play the game for a few hours and we'd be free men again.

Unless we're missing something.

"They've probably just got more questions for him.

Or they're trying to freak us out. Make us squeal. Fuck knows how those cunts' minds work."

"She's gonna kill us, man."

Dane's amused chuckle forces my head up, and when I look at him his eyes are crinkled with laughter.

"What?"

"It's so fucking weird seeing you care, bro."

"Fuck you," I grumble.

"It's great. I like it. Big bad Rhett Savage pussy-whipped by the princess."

"With a pussy that good, it's hard not to become addicted."

"Amen to that, brother."

"Huh, funny... I thought you were all about the ass these days." My brow lifts and Dane shakes his head, scrubbing his hand down his face.

"You still on that?"

"Bro, you..." I glance over at Pike, checking if he's still out of it. "You kissed another guy. You..."

"Touched his cock?" Dane adds. He shrugs as I continue to stare at him, not understanding his thought process. "It felt good. You know I'm all about the fun."

"Yeah, I know, but—"

"I don't wanna touch yours. Is that what you're worried about? Ten hours in a cell and I'm not about to jump your bones the next time we're alone."

"I'm not... that's not..." I let out a heavy sigh. "I'm just... shocked still, I guess. I didn't see that coming."

"Oh, come off it, you knew the second she asked it of me that it would happen."

"If she..." Dane's brow lifts when I trail off.

"Go on?"

"What if she asked it of you and me?"

"You propositioning me, Savage?" He bats his eyelashes at me, and I can't help but laugh.

"No, I'm really not. Just curious, I guess."

"It's different. I know that you wouldn't want to go there. Pretty, though... I could read the same curiosity in his eyes as I felt. You don't have that."

"Thank fuck," I mutter, scrubbing my hand over my head and wrapping it around the back of my neck.

Silence crackles between us as Pike resumes his loud snoring.

"You gonna do it again?"

"Dunno. I don't want him like I do Sadie, if that's what you mean. But in the heat of the moment, it's... It's just like I said to him. What happens between the four of us is just that. We get to make our own rules, explore things safely. Or at least, that's how I feel when we're all together. Nothing is off the table as long as we're all enjoying ourselves."

"I guess. I ain't fucking kissing either of you, though."

"Good. I know most of the skanks you've kissed over the years."

"Fuck you. We've shared more than enough of those whores."

"True that," he mutters.

A loud bang echoes somewhere down the hall before booming voices filter down, although they're not close enough to actually make out the words.

"W-what's going on?" Pike barks, suddenly sitting up and rubbing his eyes. "Can we go yet?"

"No news," I say. "How the fuck can you sleep?"

"What else is there to do? Trust Prez, boys. They'll keep us until the last possible second just to piss us off, and then they'll send us back, all charges dropped."

"I hope you're fucking right."

"I got this, boys. It's not my first rodeo. You'll be back with your girl before you know it." He winks. "Rosi is always more fun after a stint in here."

We can only hope, right?

Something tells me that when she learns the truth, Sadie's going to be less than up for any kind of fun. Pretty is going to have full access to our princess, and we're going to be banished to the sidelines.

Forty-seven hours and fifty-five fucking minutes we sat in the cell, minus an hour or so for questioning.

I finally managed to get some sleep, but not enough. Nothing like Pike, who damn near slept the whole time like we were on a luxury holiday or some shit.

The loud clunk of the lock undoing on our cell makes my entire body jolt with relief. My mouth waters for a taste of the outside, for anything other than the faint smell of piss and death that lingers down here in Savage Falls PD's basement.

"You're free to go," Statham says with a knowing smirk.

"Where's Ray?" I ask before anyone else has a chance to say anything in response.

"We've still got some questions for him."

"Time's up. You've got to release us."

"Unless you charge him. Have you charged him with something?" Dane adds.

"Some... other things have come to light. Let's just leave it at that."

"Fuck," I hiss under my breath as we file out of the cell we've been locked in for two fucking days.

We get through the rigmarole of signing our release papers and reclaiming our belongings before we're given one final piece of bullshit advice from Statham and sent on our way.

"Oh my God." A familiar squeal hits my ears the second we push out of the main doors to the station, instantly blinded by the sun. It's so fucking bright compared to the dank basement that it makes my eyes water.

I only see the blur that is Sadie as she runs at me.

"Thank God," she cries, launching herself into my arms.

I stumble back, not quite expecting that kind of force from her small body, and crash into Dane.

"Whoa, princess," he says, righting me and then walking around the two of us, sliding his fingers into her hair and dragging her face to his mouth.

He kisses her as if it could be their last night together before he finally lets her up for air.

Her face twists as she licks her lips. "You need a toothbrush."

"And a fucking shower," Dane mutters.

"Come here, princess," I growl, claiming her lips as mine, not giving a shit about the state of my mouth—my desperation for her is stronger. But Sadie tenses beneath my touch, and all too quickly she pulls away.

I shoot her a questioning look, but Pike emerges and walks straight into Rosi's awaiting arms before all of us look at Victoria.

"Where's Ray?" she asks, concern filling her eyes. "I thought you were all free."

"They're not letting him out yet."

"Why? They can't do that," she argues. "They've had their time."

"We don't know," Dane confesses.

"It'll be okay, Mom," Pretty says, wrapping his arm around her shoulder.

She nods, tears glistening in her eyes.

Sadie's warm hand lands on my cheek, and I have no choice but to look down into her green eyes. Only when I do, the concern I'd forgotten about after her exuberant welcome begins to flow through me once more.

"We should go," she says coolly.

Narrowing my eyes at her, I try to read what's going on in her head, but she locks it down almost as quickly as it appeared. "Nothing I want more, princess."

To my relief, she takes both of our hands and leads us over to Pretty, who's still standing with his mom.

"Pretty," Dane says as a greeting.

"How you both doing?"

"There's nothing like sitting in a cell with two other dudes for two days. Couldn't recommend it more."

No one says anything for a good ten seconds.

"Shit must be going down. Savage just cracked another joke."

I scoff. "You all make out like I'm not funny. I thought you'd figured out already that I'm a fucking comedian."

"Yeah, sure you are, bro," Dane mutters.

"You need a lift back to the compound?" Pretty asks Victoria.

"I'll get a ride with Rosi. You guys go do your thing."

The three of us make our way over to Sadie's truck as Pretty says goodbye to his mom. Everything feels normal until Sadie slides into the passenger seat, telling

17

us that Pretty is driving and that we should get in the back.

Her voice is cold, hard, and it makes Dane and I share a look.

She knows.

She knows we lied to her, despite the fact that she might have been glad to see us. That flicker of something I saw in her eyes... that was rage.

She's fucking furious.

Dane winces a little before sitting forward and reaching around the seat to touch her. "Missed you, Sadie, girl."

"Don't," she snaps, all previous pretenses gone.

"Princess, you know how it is. We gotta do what we gotta—"

Her body tenses in anger, but she doesn't say anything.

The atmosphere is thick when Pretty climbs in. He looks at Sadie and then back at Dane and me before a smirk covers his face.

"You're in for a world of pain," he promises, a wicked tone in his voice, before he starts the engine.

3

SADIE

We don't go back to the clubhouse. Instead, Wes drives us to Dane's apartment.

Restless energy courses through me as I grip the edge of the seat, forcing myself not to look at them. When I overheard Micky and Wes discussing the fact that my daddy knew about the raid, that they all knew, my stomach sank.

Of course, I'd immediately dragged Wes back to Dane's room and forced him to tell me exactly what had happened.

I still couldn't believe they'd all lied to me.

My father, I got. He only wants to protect me and shelter me from worrying too much. That's his prerogative. But the guys... I can't wrap my head around that.

I thought we were past keeping secrets from one another after everything we'd been through. But apparently, the rule doesn't apply to them. All week, they acted as if nothing was wrong, loving me over and over and knowing full well that shit was about to go down.

No wonder they insisted I stayed at Aunt Dee's while they cleaned the compound out.

Anger skitters up my spine.

"How'd you find out?" Rhett has the balls to ask. "Because I know Pretty has more sense than to—"

"Does it matter?" I snap.

"Obviously."

"Come on, Sadie, girl. We were only following Ray's orders. You know how—"

"Not. Good. Enough."

"Princess, you can't hold this against us." Rhett lets out a deep sigh. "Shit was about to go down and we didn't want you to worry, not after everything that had happened. You deserved a break. You deserved—"

"You lied to me. You all lied to me. Do you have any idea how that feels after everything?" Emotion balls in my throat, but my anger wins out. "You say it was to protect me, but I was still there, watching you get dragged away. How the fuck was that protecting me, huh?"

Wes veers the truck into Dane's small parking lot and throws it into park. The second he kills the engine, I shoulder the door open and hop out, storming toward the apartment.

"Whoa, Sadie, girl, hold up," Dane calls, but I don't stop, racing up the stairs to the door, only to realize I don't have a key. "Ugh," I cry in frustration, hammering my fists on the wood.

"What did that door ever do to you?" Dane approaches first, Rhett and Wes hovering behind.

"I'm not in the mood, Stray. Just open the door and get me my own key."

He moves ahead of me, smirking. "Whatever the lady requests."

"I know what you're doing," I seethe, "and it won't work."

"We'll see." Dane winks, pushing the door open and slipping inside. I follow, strolling right past him and flopping down on the couch.

The place looks a little more lived in since we all started staying here more often, but it's still a shell. An idea strikes me. It's petty and a little bit silly, but they deserve it after pulling this shit on me.

"What are you thinking, Sadie, girl?" Dane regards me.

"Nothing." I give him a dismissive wave.

"You're plotting something," he insists.

"Am not."

"What's that?" Rhett comes over to us, beer in hand, and sinks down on the end of the couch.

"Our princess has a glint in her eye... if I didn't know better, I'd say she's thinking up all kinds of ways to make us suffer."

"No sex for twenty-four hours sounds about right," Wes grumbles.

"Shit, Pretty. She's been holding out on you?"

He nods. "As soon as she found out the truth, she wouldn't let me touch her."

"You deserved it, asshole." I scowl. "You all do."

"Fuck that." Rhett snorts. "Shoulda just made her take it."

"Seriously, you did not just say that." I shoot upright.

He throws his head back, groaning. "We just got out of lockup, my back is hurting like a motherfucker, Ray is still there, and you're acting like a spoiled brat."

"Bro, she's not—"

"No, Dane, don't defend me. I'm glad I know exactly

how he feels. Maybe I should go act like a brat somewhere else." I march toward the bedroom, indignation burning through me.

"Sadie, girl, don't let—"

Dane's voice is drowned out by the blood pumping between my ears as I storm into the bedroom, slamming the door behind me.

Their muffled conversation barely penetrates the red mist swirling around me.

How dare he?

How dare Rhett act like I'm the one making a big deal out of this?

We're supposed to be a team. Equals. How many times do I have to prove to them that I can handle whatever this life throws at us?

They were only trying to protect you.

I silence the little voice. I refuse to back down on this. I watched them be carted away in handcuffs, not knowing when or if I'd see them again, and they knew.

They fucking knew it was going to go down.

Angrily, I strip out of my clothes and head into the small bathroom. Maybe a hot shower will calm me down. At least they can sit out there and think about their shitty actions for a while.

I take my time under the shower, washing my skin with care. Everything inside me screams to call my guys in here, to let them soothe the giant knot in my stomach the way only they can. But I can't shake the feeling of betrayal.

If I'd known, I could have helped. Maybe I would have come up with a plan that didn't end up with them all getting arrested.

But no. Once again, I wasn't trusted with the truth.

It hurts.

More than it should, given the circumstances.

But I don't want to be coddled or wrapped up in cotton. I want to stand at their sides and fight with them.

Turning off the shower, I reach for a towel and wrap it around my body. I'm half surprised one of them hasn't tried to barge their way in here. But maybe Wes informed them just how pissed I am and told them to give me space.

I slip into the bedroom and find a clean Sinners t-shirt. Dane seems to have a never-ending supply of them, so borrowing another one won't hurt. It hangs off my body, so I gather the front and twist it into a knot just above my belly button and pull on my panties.

Looking around his sparse room, I realize I have two options. I could stay in here and sulk, or I could really punish them.

After all, they don't call me brat for nothing.

Decision made, I pad back into the living room.

"What's—fuck," Wes chokes out as his hungry gaze falls on my half-naked body.

"Princess, I think you forgot your clothes."

"I'm a little warm." I shrug, making a beeline for one of the kitchen cabinets. Reaching up on my tiptoes, I search for something to snack on, fully aware that the t-shirt rides even higher on my body, giving them a full view of my legs and ass.

"Fuck, she's hot," Dane whistles.

"Hot little brat," Rhett mutters, and I fight a smile.

He's onto me. Of course he is. But the asshole deserves it. And he might act immune, but I'm sure I can break him.

In fact, I know I can.

25

Grabbing a jar of chocolate spread, I turn around and hop up onto the counter.

"Princess..." Dane leans back in the chair, his eyes all over my body. "You're playing a dangerous game."

"Me?" I smirk, unscrewing the lid. Dipping a finger inside, I scoop out a healthy amount and slowly start licking it off.

"Jesus, she's killing me." Wes shifts uncomfortably, adjusting the crotch of his jeans.

"Hmm," I purr, swirling my tongue over the tip of my sticky, sweet finger. "This is so good."

Rhett's eyes darken, narrowed right on my mouth as I make a show of enjoying the chocolate spread.

"Cat got your tongue, Savage?" I quip, feeling smug satisfaction swim in my veins.

"We're sorry, okay?" He holds my gaze. "Prez said—"

"This isn't about my father."

"Seriously, you're going to hold out on us? Because we were following orders?" He practically spits the words, his frustration bleeding into the air.

"You don't get it. I thought we were a team."

"We are a team, Sadie, girl." Dane stands and starts approaching, but I hold up my hand.

"Don't. I watched you get arrested. Arrested, Dane. Do you have any idea what that felt like, to watch you get carted away like that?"

"Shit, babe, we're sorry, okay? We didn't know how it would go down. We only knew—"

"It doesn't matter." I shake my head, feeling tears burn the backs of my eyes. "What's done is done."

"You don't need to do this," he says, taking another step toward me. "We can kiss and make up and everything—"

"If you say everything will be okay, I swear to God I'll kick you in the balls."

"Feisty." He chuckles, and Wes and Rhett snort.

"This isn't funny. I'm trying to be serious and you're—"

"You're prancing around in those itty-bitty panties, sucking on your fingers like a porn star, and you expect us to take you seriously?" Rhett stands, folding his arms over his chest. "I hate to tell you, princess, but you've got nobody fooled."

"I hate you." The words spill from my lips before I can stop them.

"But you love the way my cock feels buried deep inside of you." He stalks toward me, slow, sure steps like a predator stalking its prey.

"Stay the hell back, Savage."

"Or what? You'll kick me in the balls?" His lips twist with amusement. "Didn't you get the memo, baby? I like a little pain, and if it means I get in your pussy. Bring. It. On."

"There's something very wrong with you." I shake my head, all too aware that he's destroying my resolve.

Rhett reaches me, snatching the jar of chocolate spread from my hand. Shoving his finger inside, he scoops out a big dollop and pushes it toward my lips. "Suck."

"Fuck you."

"That's the plan, princess. Went over forty-eight hours without being inside you. Don't plan on waiting one more."

"Oh yeah?" My brow lifts as I brace myself on the back of the counter. With a big push, I leap down and take off toward the bedroom. "Guess you'll have to catch me first."

"Fucking crazy bitch," I hear Rhett mutter as Dane and Wes explode with laughter.

We all know how this ends, and deep down, I want it.

I want them.

But I have no objections to making them work for it first. After all, they need to remember that I'm their queen.

And it's time they get on their knees and begged for my forgiveness.

4

DANE

I'm the first to take off behind Sadie. Wes is too busy laughing. His forty-eight hours of torture seems to have affected his mental state while Rhett just scrubs his hand over his head, determination in the set of his body.

Sadie is in trouble for that move. And she damn well knows it.

"Whoa," she says, pressing a hand to the center of my chest and stopping me from entering. "Not so fast, jailbait. You and Savage need to shower before you get any closer."

A deep rumble of laughter explodes from my chest, making her eyes narrow.

"What?" she hisses.

"Don't pretend that you wouldn't let us fuck you right now."

She looks me up and down, an angry scowl on her face. Her fire makes my cock ache. "You're not fucking me. None of you are laying a finger on me."

Ideas flicker in my mind, and I can't help hoping that

she's on the same wavelength, because hell yes to the images that are assaulting me right now.

"What's going on?" Rhett asks, coming to a stop behind me.

"Princess is getting all demanding. She wants us to shower."

"Yeah, well. You both fucking stink, so I don't blame her," Wes mutters, slipping past the two of us and into the room behind Sadie.

"Why's he allowed in?"

"Because he's already spent two days groveling. You've barely had twenty minutes."

"Jesus fucking Christ," Savage growls, turning and marching toward the bathroom. "I don't need this shit."

"Then fucking leave. I don't need your lying ass either," Sadie hisses, her eyes burning holes in his retreating back.

He turns back before he makes his final decision as to whether to go into the bathroom or just storm out of the apartment.

The old Rhett would do the latter, and for a second, I fear he might just fall back into old habits. But the second he meets her eyes, I know he's going to fight for her. And not just because he's horny as fuck.

"It's a good fucking thing I like you, Dalton," he grunts.

I can't help the smirk that pulls at my lips as I look between the two of them.

"Like? I think you more than fucking like me, *Savage.*" She damn near spits his last name back at him. "If you want to leave, if you want to run like a little bitch, then be my guest. I'm sure Dane and Wes are more than capable of making things up to me without you."

My eyes immediately lift to Pretty's over her shoulder. A mixture of desire and fear flickers through his eyes.

The two of us haven't talked about what happened between us on our vacation. I have no idea if he's thinking it was just a one-time—okay, just a vacation—thing, or if he'd like to do it again, maybe even explore a little more.

Hell knows I'm easy.

But it's something we're going to have to address at some point.

"I'm not fucking leaving." Without another word, Rhett storms into the bathroom, leaving only the echo of the slamming door in his wake.

"What are you waiting for?" Sadie barks, her eyes trained on me once again.

"I'm not showering with that angry motherfucker."

"Two nights in jail didn't make either of you that desperate then, did it?"

Her eyes drop to my very tented jeans and her brow rises.

"I'll be five minutes." Spinning on my heel, I march into the bathroom. Rhett's already under the torrent of water.

"What the fuck, Stray?"

"A bit late to be shy now, brother. I've seen enough of your cock to last me a lifetime already. Now get the fuck out."

"She holds way too much fucking power."

"You love it."

A grin tugs at his lips. It's the only response I get before I shed my clothes and drag him out by his arm.

He brushes his teeth while I have the quickest shower on record before reaching for my own toothpaste.

"Fuck, that's better. Pretty sure something died in my mouth," I say to myself, pushing my dripping hair from my brow.

"All fresh for your boyfriend," Rhett quips.

"Shut the fuck up, man. It's getting old."

He mumbles something under his breath before marching from the room with a towel around his waist. I don't bother wasting time by grabbing one of my own. I have every intention of being naked with our princess for the foreseeable future.

I walk out of the bathroom with my semi bobbing between my legs and images of where I want this night to go filling my head.

"Look at you," I purr when I come to a stop in the doorway and find Sadie in the middle of the bed, still wearing my shirt and her tiny panties. The look on her face is straight up fire, and excitement shoots through my veins.

"Shut up," she demands, her eyes narrowing on me.

"Uh..."

Her eyes never drop from mine, but I can read her better than she thinks I can. I see her internal fight, because more than anything she wants to drop them down my body. "Touch yourself and I'll cut it off with your own knife."

My brow quirks, my cock hardening at her threat of violence.

Once upon a time I would've been freaked out by how turned on the promise of pain and blood got me. But not now. Now I own who I am and what makes me tick.

As if she knows damn well what that threat does to me, her brow quirks.

"This is your show, Sadie. Do your worst."

"Go stand next to Pretty," she demands, and I glance over to where he's standing, still fully dressed, resting against the wall.

Moving over, I return my eyes to her. "What's the plan then, princess?"

"Thought I'd give you front row seats to what happens when you piss me off."

Excitement explodes from my belly, my body beginning to burn up as Sadie parts her legs and rests back on her palms.

Turning to look at Rhett, she arches her back, ensuring none of us miss how her peaked nipples press against the fabric of my shirt as she whispers, "Did you think about me while you were locked up?"

Rhett has to clear his throat before he can respond as Sadie shifts her weight onto one hand and trails the fingertips of the other up her bare leg.

"You know I did, princess."

"And you?" she asks, turning to me.

"Every fucking second."

"Were you jealous, knowing that you left me behind with only Pretty to keep me company?"

"Hell yeah," I state as her fingers get higher.

"Did you imagine us... fucking?"

I glance at Pretty, finding his eyes dark with hunger for our girl as he stares at her. "On every surface available at the compound."

"If only," he mutters.

"So tell me, Stray... how badly do you want me right now?"

Her fingers hit the edge of her panties and she continues until she's at the waistband and slips them under.

"Really fucking badly."

"Touch yourself, princess. Tell us how wet you are," Rhett demands.

Her eyes shoot to him. "Do I need to remind you who's in charge here, Savage?"

His jaw tics as he grinds his teeth, a vein in his temple beginning to pulsate.

He really fucking hates losing control like this, even if it is to our princess.

"Lose the towel. And Pretty, get naked. I want to see exactly what belongs to me." Pretty immediately begins moving. "But don't forget, no touching. My hands are the only ones that get to move."

"You're a tease, princess."

"I know. Isn't it fun?"

My eyes hold hers, conveying just how unfun this entire experience is.

I could be balls-deep in her ass while Savage or Pretty take her tight little cunt right now. But no, here we are with our balls turning bluer by the second while she drives us crazy.

"We get it, you know. We were wrong to lie to you."

"See... I really don't think you do. I think you think I'm joking."

"Babe," I breathe. "Trust us, we really don't."

She blinks, her eyes holding mine before she looks at Pretty and then Savage. But it's not until they come back to me again that she finally pushes her fingers lower, her gasp filling the room as she finds her clit.

"Fuck, princess," I growl, my fingers itching to wrap around my aching cock.

"This isn't funny, Sadie Ray."

"Oooh," she purrs, her voice all needy and rough. "Sadie Ray. I must be in trouble."

She pushes lower, her head falling back, her breasts pressing against the fabric as she arches.

"How far are you planning on taking this, princess?" I ask, my cock already weeping to slide deep inside her tight body.

"Until you've all learned what happens when you lie to me. Oh God," she moans, her legs falling wider.

Her loud cries rip through the air, the electricity in the room crackling.

Rhett's body is practically vibrating with his attempts to stay put and do as he's told. Pretty's fists are curling and uncurling as he works his jaw.

"Wes," Sadie whispers. "My panties are getting in the way. Take them off me."

He pushes from the wall faster than I thought possible, pressing his knees on the edge of the bed, his hands reaching for her.

"But don't touch me," she warns. "If you do, you can kiss goodbye to coming anytime soon."

"Fuck, princess. You're killing me."

"I know. You all deserve it. Now, as you were."

Tentatively, he wraps his fingers around the sides of her panties, barely brushing her skin before she lifts her ass from the bed and allows him to pull them down her legs. "Fuck, you smell incredible."

"Make the most of it. It's as close as you're getting."

The second the lace clears her feet, she demands he backs up again.

I don't see him move, my eyes laser focused on her pussy. She's got two fingers back inside her as she fucks herself, her head rolling back as she moans.

She's laying it on thick, I know she is, but fuck if I care. It's working.

"Princess," Rhett growls.

"No one's touched me since we were in that beach house. Do you have any idea how wet I am right now?"

My mouth waters as I think about finding out.

"Make yourself come, princess. I want to watch you fuck yourself until you're screaming," Pretty instructs.

"I'm not doing anything you three want."

To prove a point, she pulls her hand from her pussy and slides it under the fabric of my shirt instead.

"Sadie Ray," Rhett barks.

His entire body is locked up tight. It makes him look even bigger, scarier than he usually does. It shows just how big Sadie's balls are not to even look intimidated by him right now. He could pounce on her at any minute and squish her like a fly.

He won't.

But he could.

"I'm hot. Are you guys hot?"

All I can do is laugh at her ridiculous question.

Curling her fingers around the fabric hiding her body from us, she pulls it up, exposing herself.

"Fuck, you're perfect," Pretty breathes.

"Yeah?"

Her hand skims down her stomach, her fingers finding her clit once more before she moans. Her head falls back and her eyes close.

"She's close," I whisper, not that either of them need to hear it. They know her tells as well as I do. "You gonna torture us by making us watch you come without us, princess?"

"You know it. I want you to see that I don't need you."

Her voice is barely audible as she races toward her release.

She lies back, allowing her to use both of her hands to get herself off. It's the hottest thing I've ever fucking seen —her hips rolling, her fingers working her cunt exactly as she needs it, her skin flushed with pleasure.

"Oh God. Oh God," she whimpers.

Forcing my eyes from her, I quickly glance at the guys. They both nod, reading my thoughts.

The three of us move in unison, surrounding the bed —surrounding her. Consequences be damned.

"Rhett... Dane... Wes," she moans, her eyes squeezed tight as she teeters right on the edge.

If she's aware that we've defied her, then she doesn't show it.

Wrapping my hand around my length, I see the others do the same out of the corner of my eye.

We jerk ourselves hard and fast as she falls, her cries getting louder, more desperate. And right as she hits the point of no return, so do we. Already so worked up from her little one-woman show, each of us crawls onto the bed and shoots our load all over her chest.

The second she comes back to herself, she blinks up at us a couple of times before looking down at her sticky tits.

"Now, that was fun and all, but how about we show you how we celebrate getting out of jail properly," Rhett growls.

5

SADIE

"You couldn't help yourself, could you?" My brow lifts as I run my eyes over each of them. Disheveled and panting, my guys have never looked better. Dane lazily strokes his cock, already growing hard again.

Insatiable.

That's the only word that comes to mind for him. For all of them.

Anticipation crackles in the air as I let my racing heart calm, but with the way they're looking at me, stalking my every move, I know it won't fully return to normal.

It's impossible not to be affected by three gorgeous, virile guys watching you like you're the air they breathe, the very thing they need to survive. And when I think about it, really think about what they did, I know they just wanted to follow my dad's orders and protect me from the truth.

But it still hurts that they lied to me so easily.

What else would they lie to me about?

"Get out of your head, princess," Rhett demands in that deep, bossy voice of his.

"Or what, Savage?" My lips curve.

"Or I'll fuck all those thoughts right out of you."

"No touching, remember," I sass, fully aware that the tables have already turned. I can keep up this façade, keep punishing them, but we all know I'm only punishing myself too.

Rhett's knee hits the mattress as he leans down and grabs my ankles, yanking me toward the end of the bed. A shriek of surprise fills the air, the guys' laughter like a balm to my bruised heart. He drops to the floor and slides his hands under my thighs, lifting me slightly. "Gonna put my mouth on you now." Rhett buries his face in my pussy, licking the length of me.

"Oh God," I cry, overwhelmed by his eagerness, by the way he spreads my folds and dives deep, tasting me.

"How does she taste, brother?" Dane asks, moving around the side of the bed.

"Like mine," Rhett growls. "Ours."

That single word does things to me, and I fist the sheet, arching my back into his fevered touch.

"I think Pretty deserves his reward for putting up with you the last couple of days." Dane's eyes dance with amusement as he looms over me. He glances up, and a shiver goes through me at the heated look the two of them share. "Let him fuck your mouth, Sadie, girl. I wanna watch him come down your throat."

I gush at his dirty words, and Rhett moans with approval. "She's so fucking wet. Our princess likes playing games."

"Your *queen* likes getting off. Less talking and more licking," I snap, still not entirely over their betrayal.

But he feels too good between my legs, and there is something deeply satisfying about having a guy like Rhett on his knees in front of me.

"What do you say, princess?" Dane leans down, sliding his hand over my breasts and up my throat. "Let Pretty fuck this pouty mouth?"

"W-what about you?" I pant as Rhett fucks me with his fingers and tongue.

"I'm good with watching, for now. Pretty, get over here." Dane's eyes light up with mischief.

Wes stumbles over to us, his dick so hard it looks painful. "Ready for her to put you out of your misery?" Dane teases.

"Fuck yeah."

"Suck him, princess."

His demanding lilt sends shivers racing down my spine. I push up on my elbows, licking my lips as Wes leans over.

"Open up." Dane moves behind Wes, leaning around to cup my jaw as Wes feeds me his cock.

"Fuck, that's hot."

My body is a riot of sensation as I lick Wes's shaft, taking him hungrily into my mouth.

"Fuuuck," he breathes, but I struggle to control his movement with Rhett eating me, devouring me.

"Here, let me help." Dane wraps his fingers around the base of Wes's dick. Just the sight of him touching Wes like that does something to me.

"Fucking hell," Rhett mutters, stopping for a second.

"Talk less, lick more," I remind him.

"Needy little bitch," he grunts before spearing me with his tongue. I cry out, almost choking on Wes's cock as Dane jacks him off into my mouth.

"Make him come, princess. Make Pretty scream." He runs his nose down the curve of Wes's neck and bites down—hard—but Wes is too lost to the pleasure we're bestowing on him to care. My heart jumps for joy at the two of them like this.

I don't think they care for each other the way we care for each other, but they have a connection, one I'm all too willing to watch blossom.

"I love watching you two," I moan, my legs quivering as Rhett continues working me with his tongue and fingers.

"Something tells me Pretty likes it too, don't you?" Dane grips Wes harder, fisting the base of his cock as I lick and suck him down.

"Fuck, that feels good... fuck," he pants, thrusting his hips wildly as Dane and I both work him over.

My breath catches as Rhett latches onto my clit, grazing it with his teeth, and I shatter, crying his name around Wes.

"Holy shit, that's feels—" Wes spurts down my throat as Dane milks him almost violently.

But I barely have time to enjoy the taste of him as Rhett drags me off Wes's cock and flips me onto my stomach.

"Missed this pussy," he murmurs, grabbing my hips and slamming inside me.

Wes flops down on the bed in front of me, his eyes hooded and body sated as I reach for Dane and grin up at him. "Your turn, Stray."

"I'm all yours, princess." His fingers bury deep in my hair as he starts to fuck my face.

My guys don't just love me. They completely obliterate me until I'm nothing but a boneless mess.

"Feels good, huh?" Dane grunts, pushing deeper down my throat as Rhett pounds into me.

"Nothing ever felt better." His fingers dig into my hips enough to leave bruises. But the thought only gets me hotter as I push back against him, demanding more. Taking everything.

"Who do you belong to?" Rhett growls the words and Dane pulls out of my mouth to let me breathe.

"Y-you," I cry. "All of you."

"Damn right you do, princess. Now hold on tight. I'm not done with you yet."

―――――――

I wake alone, the sheets strewn around my body. Every muscle inside me aches in the best kind of way. If forty-eight hours apart results in that kind of night, maybe it wasn't such a bad thing.

It still stings that they lied to me, but I feel lighter than I did earlier. I still have plans to get back at them. I just need time to execute it.

The clock on the nightstand says it's early, before sunrise, but now I'm awake, I can't go back to sleep without knowing why I woke up alone. Muffled voices beyond the door catch my attention and I climb out of bed, pulling on a t-shirt and some panties. Slipping out of the room, I find the three of them sitting around, drinking coffee.

"Rough night?" I ask.

"Couldn't sleep," Rhett admits, his dark gaze eating me up as I advance toward him. His hand shoots out, grabbing my waist and pulling me down on his lap.

"Hmm," his chest rumbles as he buries his nose in my neck, "that's better."

"What's going on?" He winces at the defensive edge in my voice.

"Nothing, I swear. I couldn't sleep and all my fidgeting woke Dane. Not sure what Pretty's excuse is."

"You were hogging the sheets."

"Bro, Sadie was wrapped around you like a koala." Dane chuckles.

"Don't tell me you were watching them sleep," Rhett grunts, and Dane shrugs.

"Don't worry, brother. I wasn't watching you sleep."

A smile teases my lips but then the knot in my stomach tightens. "What are we going to do about my dad? Johnson said they couldn't hold you for longer than forty-eight hours."

"Which means someone's pulling some strings. Or breaking protocol," Dane says coolly.

"Johnson will get on it today. If they don't charge Ray with anything, they'll have no choice but to let him go."

"And could they... charge him with anything?" My voice tapers off at the end. I'm not a fool when it comes to this life. I know what my dad and the guys do, the deals they operate. But he's still my dad. The thought of anything happening to him...

A shudder goes through me and Rhett hugs me tighter. "It'll be okay, princess. I promise. They've got nothing on us."

"You're sure?" My voice cracks.

"Yeah. Whatever it is, they're clutching at straws."

Heavy silence settles over us. "You know," I say after a few seconds, my gaze sliding to Dane, "you're going to have to go and see Nolan."

"Yeah." He blows out a steady breath, running a hand down his face. "Later. I'll go later."

"And then?"

"Shit, Sadie, girl. We just got out of lockup. Pretty sure I can still feel your mouth on my dick, and you want to talk about this now?" His brow lifts with mild humor, but there's a shadow in his eyes.

He's not ready.

We all know it.

But Nolan is sick, and if Dane doesn't visit him soon, he might not get the answers he needs about his past.

"I'll come with, you know that," Rhett says, and the two of them share a nod of understanding. "There are some big decisions ahead."

"Damn straight, brother."

"The most important being where we're all going to stay," I blurt out.

"I'm not ready to play house, if that's what you're hinting at, princess," Rhett teases, earning him an elbow to his stomach.

"I don't want to play house. But we can't exactly stay at my dad's. Not if Victoria starts staying there."

"That's happening?" Dane asks.

"Heard her talking to Rosita and Jada about it," Wes replies. "Seems like Prez wants her close."

"Dirty old dog."

"Dane," I hiss.

"Sorry, Pretty. Meant no disrespect."

"You all have rooms at the clubhouse, but I can't stay there all the time."

"So we use this place," Dane says as if it's the most simple thing in the world. "Rhett already has a key, and I can get a couple more cut for you and Pretty."

"I'd like that," I say around a wide smile.

"I'm still not playing house," Rhett grumbles, running his hand up the flat of my stomach.

"You'll be the one missing out then, Mr. Grumpy Pants."

"If we're going to stay here more often, we'll need to upgrade the couch to a sofa bed."

"Why the hell would we do that when there's a perfectly good bed through there?" Dane says, almost offended.

"Because, asshole, I don't want you watching me while I sleep like some creeper."

I glance back at Rhett, frowning, and then explode with laughter.

"What?" he huffs. "I'm serious."

"Fine by me." Dane shrugs, flashing me a suggestive look. "I have no problem sleeping with Sadie and Pretty every night."

6

WES

I should probably argue. I probably shouldn't be this willing to spend every night with Sadie and another guy. But I can't, because the truth of it is, I don't care. Hell, that's a lie. I do care, because I want it. I want this. I want last night. I want it all.

The thought makes my heart race and my mind spin with possibilities of things I've never even considered before. But this, this foursome we've got going on, it's given me more than I ever could have dreamed of, and I'm willing to find out just how much more it can give me. Give all of us.

"We should go and get breakfast," Dane announces, rubbing his belly.

"You're not planning on taking me on another date, are you?" Sadie asks from her spot on Rhett's lap.

"Something tells me we've barely scratched the surface of you forgiving us, so yeah. How do you feel about a breakfast date with your men?"

"I feel good about it." She grins. "I need to shower

first, though. My skin is all kinds of gross after last night. Any volunteers to make sure I don't get lonely?"

She slides off Rhett's lap and slowly backs away from us, sucking her bottom lip between her teeth as she begins lifting the hem of her shirt.

"You're a tease, princess," Dane growls, his hand already hidden under the table. He's such a dog.

"Something funny, Pretty?" Rhett asks, clearly watching us.

"Nope. Just thinking that I'm really fucking dirty."

"I'll say. I know who was touching you last night."

"Fuck you, Savage," Dane barks, pushing his chair back. "You've just forfeited shower privileges." His eyes find mine. "Come on, Pretty. Our princess needs us." He winks and my cheeks burn, much to my horror.

Fucking hell, tell me I'm not fucking crushing on a dude.

"Get naked, princess," I say, shoving that other thought aside while I stalk her toward the bathroom.

"You're right, you know," Dane growls behind me. "You're fucking filthy." His eyes trace every inch of her body as she pushes her panties from her hips.

"Get to work then, boys. And don't forget each other." She winks, and the heat that had just left my face returns full force when Dane grabs my upper arms and spins me to look at him.

"You hear that, Pretty? Our princess is getting all excited again."

"Y-yeah," I stutter, looking into his hungry eyes.

Amused by my nerves, he throws his head back and laughs.

"Fuck, you're too pretty to be a prospect. Get naked," he demands, shedding his own clothes and following

Sadie into the stall, immediately backing her up against the tiled wall.

"Get the fuck out or I'm going without you," a very grumpy, and probably frustrated, Rhett growls through the door sometime later.

I've lost count of how many times he's had to listen to Sadie scream as Dane and I ensured she was thoroughly clean, but clearly, he's hit his quota.

"All right, big guy. We'll be there soon," she calls out, having pulled back from Dane's cock.

She winks at me as she jacks me off, leaning over to lick the precum from my tip before sinking back down on Dane.

Watching her work his shaft in and out of her mouth gets me all kinds of hot and makes my head spin even more than before as I wonder how he might taste.

"Oh fuck," I grunt, that thought the final push I needed to fall over the edge.

Sadie sucks Dane deeper, dragging his release out of him before she pushes to her feet. "We need to go and feed the beast," she says, reaching up on her tiptoes and dropping a kiss to both of our mouths.

"Anyone would think he's missing out," Dane mutters as I grab towels for all of us and wrap one around my waist.

"It does him good, learning to share," Sadie shouts.

"I heard that," he complains.

"You were meant to."

Another twenty minutes and we finally put Rhett out of his misery by leaving the apartment to get food. He and

Dane climb onto their bikes and Sadie and I slide into her truck, although I claim the driver's seat.

"You need to get your ass on a bike, Pretty."

"I know. Dane's gonna take me out and let me ride his."

"I bet he is," she quips, shooting me a heated look.

"Behave, Sadie, girl."

"Oh my God," she shrieks, "you're even starting to sound like him."

My chin drops with realization. "I... uh... fucking hell."

"He's rubbing off on you."

"And I'm the one sounding like him?" I bark out a laugh. "You're one more innuendo away from turning into him."

"He's a bad influence. I love it."

"Yeah," I say, scrubbing my hand over my rough chin. "He is."

She turns to me as I focus on driving. I don't need to look over to know what's about to fall from her lips. I was expecting her to ask when we came back from Sterling Bay, but with the guys getting locked up, her mind was elsewhere.

"Are you... are you okay with how things are... developing? Between the two of you, I mean. I know I kinda initiated it but..." she trails off, for once sounding a little unsure of herself. "I don't want to push you into anything you're not happy with. I just thought it would be hot and—"

"It's okay, princess," I say, reaching over and squeezing her thigh gently. "Honestly, it's not something I thought about before you brought it up. But now... I dunno. It's good. Like Dane says, it's pleasure, and it's just between the four of us."

"Yeah?" she asks, damn near bouncing in excitement in her seat. "Because watching the two of you, fuck..." She fans herself. "Hottest thing I've ever seen."

"Well, I'm glad you're enjoying the show."

"I want you to be too, though. I don't want you to think that I'm now expecting it or something."

"Trust me, I'm enjoying it." I shoot her a wink and she giggles.

"I thought so."

Threading our fingers together, she squeezes tightly, and it makes my heart constrict.

"I love you, Sadie."

"I love you too, Wes. I don't know what I would've done without you these past few weeks with everything such a mess."

"You'd have been fine. You're the strongest person I know. You can get through anything."

"It was touch and go back there for a while."

"Nah, you've got this, princess. You were made for this life."

"I'm starting to think you were too."

"I guess only time will tell."

She chews on her bottom lip. I don't need to ask to know what's bothering her.

"I promise, I'm giving up nothing to be with you, Sadie. We'll figure out the future together," I assure her.

"I know. I can't wait."

A smile pulls at my mouth as I reply, "Me neither."

We follow Rhett and Dane through the gates to the compound, and I pull Sadie's truck into a space a little down from the shop.

"Johnson is here," she says, pointing to a car. "Maybe he has news about my dad."

"Let's go find out," I say, taking her hand and leading her toward the clubhouse, Savage and Stray falling into step beside us.

All eyes turn on us as we step inside.

"What's going on?" Sadie asks Rosita, who's standing with Pike and Jada.

"Johnson, Micky, Dee and Victoria are in your dad's office, sweetie."

Sadie takes off in that direction before Rosita has finished speaking. We all follow, just like we would if she was about to walk to the end of the Earth.

Pussy-whipped? Yeah, fucking completely.

The sound of Micky's booming, angry voice hits us long before we get to the office door. Sadie tenses, her hand tightening in mine.

"Everything's going to be okay," I tell her, but even as the words fall from my lips, I hear the hesitation within them. I have no place in trying to assure her of that. Anything could be about to happen.

"That's not good enough," Micky booms as Sadie barges into the room with us hot on her tail. "It's bullshit. They've had their time. We have every right to file a complaint. They're breaking the rules. He's got fucking rights."

"I know. I know," Johnson says calmly, which seems to only anger Micky more.

"Micky, please," Dee begs. "Getting irate isn't going to help."

"Daddy," Quinn pleads, my eyes finding her for the first time on the other side of Dee as she speaks.

"I'm sorry, but this is bullshit. Get him out of there. You've got one job, and we pay you damn well for it."

"I'm going there right now. He'll be back by the end of the day."

"You promised us that before, yet here we are," Sadie snaps.

"Fucking hell," Rhett mutters as Johnson damn near runs from the room.

I get it. I might be a part of this now, but I sure as fuck don't want the wrath of any of these bikers bearing down on me, even some of the nicer ones.

"Shit, I'm sorry," another voice says, slipping into the room the second Johnson has vanished.

"Crank," Dane says, greeting our new arrival. "Now's really not a good time."

"I know. I'm sorry, but I need to speak to Dane. Urgently," he adds when Dane shows no signs of moving from Sadie's side.

"It's okay," she assures him. "There's nothing we can do right now."

Dragging my eyes from the silent conversation going on between Sadie and Dane, I glance back at Crank to find his attention firmly on Quinn, who's now crouched down at Mickey's side.

I look between the two of them until Crank notices and I quirk a brow at him in question.

He just shakes his head.

"Stray?" he barks.

"Fine."

After kissing Sadie's brow, he follows Crank from the room. A door slams closed only two seconds after they leave Ray's office, telling us that they've gone to Church.

"Johnson's going to get to the bottom of this," Dee says, although her encouraging words don't really hit the mark, because the sense of unease doesn't lift from the room.

"I need a goddamn drink," Micky mutters, wheeling himself out of the office.

Dee and Mom trail after him, leaving Quinn with us.

"Are you okay?" Sadie asks, stepping up to her.

"I hate this. I just want life to go back to normal. No more deaths or arrests or..." She trails off. None of us need a reminder of all the bullshit that's happened around here recently.

Silence settles over all of us, the weight of our reality pressing down on us.

"I'm just gonna..." Rhett thumbs over his shoulder and backs out of the room, but before he gets to the door, another slams so hard the floor shakes beneath us.

"What the—" All of us race toward the exit just in time to see Dane blow down the corridor, leaving Crank in the doorway, watching him with a hopeless expression on his face.

"What happened?" Sadie snaps. "What the hell did you say to him?"

"In there." He tilts his chin back toward the office and we all shuffle inside, allowing him to close the door.

"This isn't public knowledge yet, but I know none of you will let me out of here without fessing up," he says wisely. "I've just received a call from Nolan's old lady."

"Oh God," Sadie gasps, her hand coming up to cover her mouth. "No. Please, no. Not yet."

"I'm sorry. Nolan lost his fight in the early hours of the morning."

"No," Sadie cries again.

I pull her into my body, wrapping my arms around her, my eyes connecting with Rhett's over her head. We both know she's not upset over his death, but we're all achingly aware what it means for Dane.

He never got his chance to hear the truth.

Everything that Nolan knew about his past... it's gone. Died right alongside him.

"I need to go to him," Sadie cries, fighting against my hold. "He needs me. I need to go."

"Okay, princess. Let's go and find him," Rhett says, taking her from me and leading her from the room.

"You two gonna be okay?" I ask, looking between Crank and Quinn.

"Of course. Go and sort out your boy."

But as I rush to catch up with Rhett and Sadie, who are already standing outside, I quickly discover that we're too late.

The spot where Dane had parked his bike when we arrived is now empty.

He's gone.

7

SADIE

"Fuck." Rhett scuffs the ground, anger swirling around him like a dark storm. "Fuck." He kicks a nearby tire, grunting in pain.

"Rhett." I reach for him, but he shrugs me off, running a hand down his face.

"Don't, just don't." Agony is etched into his expression as he stares at the compound gates.

This is the last thing we need—the last thing Dane needs.

"What should we do?" I ask, my heart breaking for the guy who has already endured too much.

Nolan was the only man who could give Dane some answers... and now he's gone.

"He hesitated. He fucking hesitated, and now—"

"You can't blame him, Rhett. Dane wasn't ready. He needed time, and things got so crazy."

"Yeah," he lets out a weary sigh, "I know. But he was finally accepting everything. And now..."

"We'll find him." I step up to Rhett and thread my fingers through his. "Together."

"He could be anywhere."

"Last time, he went to the apartment."

"He won't go there, not this time. This is different."

Because Nolan was the last link to his past.

"Can you think of anywhere else?" The knot in my stomach twists.

"Maybe a bar or a club."

Dread snakes through me, but it's unwarranted. He wouldn't do something reckless like get drunk and try to ride... or worse.

I glance away, trying to not let my thoughts go to a dark place. Dane is confused and hurting. But he would never knowingly hurt me.

"Let's go then," I say, needing to do something.

"Maybe you should stay here." Indecision flickers across Rhett's face as he studies me.

"Stay here? You have got to be kidding me. I'm going," I huff. "If you don't take me, someone else will."

"Sadie—"

"No, don't *Sadie* me. Dane needs us. He needs me." But as I say the words, I know they're not entirely true. If he needed me, he wouldn't have left.

"Don't do that." Rhett grips my chin, staring right at me. "This isn't about us."

"You're right," I whisper. "I just... I just want to be there for him."

"We're guys. We act first, think later. He'll come back to us." But there's another flicker of uncertainty in his eyes.

Rhett's worried too.

And this time, he isn't sure it'll be okay.

We don't find him. After riding across Savage Falls for the best part of two hours, checking every place Rhett can think of, we give up and return to the compound.

"Anything?" Wes and Crank greet us.

"Nothing." Rhett storms past us, heading straight for the clubhouse.

"He okay?" Crank asks.

"Not really." I let out a strained sigh. Wes moves behind me, sliding his arms around my waist, and I sink back into his chest.

"He'll come back."

"I hope so," I murmur,

"I gotta head out," Crank says, his eyes tracking something across the compound.

Not something, I realize. Someone.

"You should go talk to her."

Quinn is talking to her mom and Dad.

"I like my balls attached to my body," Crank chuckles but still doesn't take his eyes off my cousin.

"She could use a little biker in her life. Might loosen her up a bit." My lips twist with amusement. If Quinn ever heard me say those words, she'd kick my ass. But it's true. Sometimes the thing you think you hate is actually the thing you need most.

I should know.

As if she senses us, Quinn glances over in our direction. A ripple goes through Crank. Interesting. But before I can tease him some more about it, he mutters a goodbye and takes off.

"Crank and Quinn, huh?" Wes nuzzles my neck and warmth flows through me.

"If she'll give him a chance."

"Think you have more of a chance seeing pigs fly."

"Yeah, you're probably right. I just want her to be happy, ya know?"

"I know." His lips brush my jaw. "Come on, let's go find Savage."

"When will life get easier?" I sigh, my heart heavy with the events of the last three days.

"Life is messy and hard, but it's not all bad." Wes's breath tickles my neck.

"Yeah, you're right." I think back to all of the stolen moments we've had over the last few weeks, and I do agree.

Even in the darkness, there are pockets of light. And Wes, Rhett, and Dane are mine.

"Aren't I always?"

I twist my head back to look at him. "You're different," I say.

"Good different, or..."

"Good. Definitely good. But just remember you're not them, Wes. And that's okay. I liked you before the cut."

"This isn't for you, Sadie," he says. "Well, partly it is. But it's for me too. I feel right here. Like I belong. Does that make sense?"

"Yeah, it does." I kiss him softly, and somebody wolf whistles across the compound.

"Come on," I sigh, touching my head to his, "we should probably go inside."

"I love you, princess. And I need you to know, I wouldn't be anywhere else."

"Good, because it's too late. I'm keeping you. All of you."

We walk hand in hand into the compound. Rhett is propped against the bar, nursing a glass of whiskey.

"Because that'll help." I roll my eyes at him.

"Hey, sweetie." Victoria approaches. "Any word from Dane?"

"No, he's gone."

Wes pulls me into his side, dropping a kiss on my head. Victoria smiles at us, her eyes brimming with melancholy. "He probably just needs some time. He's had a lot to deal with."

"Any news about my dad?" I ask, hopeful.

"Not yet. But Johnson will get him out."

Rhett snorts. "If he doesn't, the police department will have the Sinners to answer to. We all want him back, sweetheart."

Sweetheart.

I smother a giggle and Rhett glowers at me.

"What? *Sweetheart.*"

"Well, I'll be helping the ladies. Everyone is feeling tense given the circumstances, so we're going to make sure everyone is fed and well looked after."

"Sure thing, Mom." Wes nods at her.

"If these guys become too much to handle," she says to me, "you're more than welcome to join us, Sadie Ray."

"Thanks, but I'm okay."

With a warm smile, she leaves us and goes to find Rosita and Dee, who are fussing over the rest of the guys. I spent so long wanting to spread my wings and cut loose from this place, but I can finally see it for what it is. Family. Unconditional love and support. Even when things seem bleak and insurmountable, when you feel lost and alone, you're not. Because these people—this club— would do anything for each other.

And it makes me so fucking proud, knowing my dad had a hand in building that.

My gaze lands on Rhett's back, the way he's hunched

over the bar, defeat rolling off him like a tidal wave. He doesn't just worry. He carries the responsibility of keeping the people he cares about safe.

Stepping out of Wes's hold, I wrap myself around him and press my lips to his shoulder blade. "He'll be okay."

He goes rigid under my touch, and for a second I think he might push me away. But he doesn't. Instead, he grabs my hands and pulls my arms tighter, relaxing into me.

"I'm right here," I whisper. "We both are." I glance at Wes, and he nods. "Whatever you need, we're here."

We have each other.

If one of us hurts, we all hurt.

And if one of us falls, the rest of us will be right there to help them back up.

Dane isn't alone.

And I'm determined to show him that.

"Six fucking hours. Where the fuck is he?" Rhett grips his cell so tightly I'm surprised it doesn't crack.

"Pacman and Jax did another sweep around town and didn't see anything."

"No shit," Rhett growls at Wes.

"He has to be somewhere," I murmur, still trying to tell myself that he'll come back in one piece. When he's good and ready. But with every hour that passes, the pit in my stomach only carves deeper.

I get that Dane needs space, but he shouldn't be alone right now.

"What are we missing?" My foot taps the bed as I stare up at the ceiling.

Between us, we've checked everywhere we can think of. He isn't in Savage Falls or Red Ridge, unless he's hiding.

"Nolan's death was the final straw," Rhett says thickly.

Where could he be?

Where—

"Oh my God," I bolt upright, "I think I know where he might be."

"We looked everywhere."

"Except the obvious place." I'm on my feet, pacing the room. "Nolan was his last link to his past. Except, he wasn't."

"Huh? I'm not following."

"His cousin. Nolan's cousin is the last link."

"The woman who took him in?" Wes asks, and I nod.

"What if he—"

"No, no way. How would he even know how to find her?"

"Nolan's old lady. She might have known."

"Fuck," Rhett breathes. "You really think he went looking for her?"

"It's the only thing that makes sense. He was almost ready to go to Nolan and find out the truth. She's the only one left who can fill in the gaps."

"I need to call Nolan's old lady." Rhett leaps up and storms from the room.

"She could be anywhere," Wes says.

"Then we go after him."

"Just like that?" His eyes glitter with something I can't quite decipher.

"What?" My brows knit.

"You. The way you love. It's a beautiful thing, Sadie

Ray."

"I'd do the same for you."

"I know, that's—"

The door swings open and my dad stands there.

"Daddy!" I run into his waiting arms. "Thank God."

His deep chuckle soothes my soul. But after hugging him for a second, I rip out of his arms and glare up at him. "You have some explaining to do."

"Ah shit, Sadie Ray. You can't let me off the hook for the night? Micky said we have bigger problems to worry about."

"We do, but that's not the point."

"Make no mistake, daughter, I will always do whatever needs to be done to keep you safe."

"I know, Dad, but I'm not a child anymore. This is my club too."

"Your club, huh?" He pulls me back into his arms. "Waited a long time to hear those words."

"I'm glad you're home safe," I whisper, chock full of emotion.

"Now, Rhett said something about you thinkin' you might know where Stray is."

"I think he went to find Nolan's cousin, the woman who took him in."

"What are we waiting for then?"

"You mean... you're coming?" I gawk at him.

This, I hadn't expected.

"Stray is family. He needs us."

Throwing my arms around my dad's shoulders, I cling to him, so relieved he's here. "Thank you," I whisper.

"Now now, sweetheart." He holds me at arm's length. "Everything's goin' to be okay, Sadie Ray. Let's go get your guy."

8

DANE

I knew it was a possibility. Hell, it was inevitable. I just hoped I'd sort my head out in time to get my answers.

I should have gone before now, but I couldn't do it. I couldn't hear the things I knew Nolan would say to me, the pain and the nightmares it would drag up.

But now the choice has been taken away from me.

And I want it.

I want the pain, the torment. The truth.

My grip on the handlebars tightens, my fingers cramping with the pressure as I fly past the 'thank you for visiting Red Ridge' sign. I shouldn't have gone to their house. Vivienne had enough to deal with. She didn't need me blowing through her home, through her grieving family in my quest to find the truths I craved.

I thought I could move past it. Force myself to believe that not knowing didn't matter, that it didn't affect who I am, where I want to go in life.

But it does.

It matters.

And not just for me. For Sadie. For the guys.

I need the answers so I can finally figure out a way to put it all behind me.

My father is gone. My mother is gone. Thankfully, so is my evil cunt of a brother. All of it needs to be firmly locked in the past so I can focus on my future, my girl. My club.

A shudder rips through me.

My club.

In all the years I've wondered who I actually was, never did I think I'd end up here.

President of the Red Ridge Sinners.

I'm eighteen, almost nineteen. I'm in high school, for fuck's sake. It's insanity.

But it's also my destiny. And there's no way I could walk away from it.

I owed it to Ray, to Grandma Irene, to the entire club who welcomed me into their open arms the day I was abandoned at the compound gates.

If it weren't for them...

I shake my head, opening the throttle and shooting down the open road. The freedom helps, but it's not enough. Pain still lashes at my insides as I remember the wrecked look on Vivienne's face when I turned up and demanded to know where Nolan's cousin was, the one he trusted me with all those years ago.

I should have felt bad—I did feel bad—that she's just lost her husband, but everything inside me was spiraling to the point that I knew if I didn't do something, I'd explode.

Sadie is going to rip me a new one for this. But I also know that she'll understand.

They all will.

I hope.

The drive to the coast is long. A little over four hours. But thanks to the fact that we were all up before dawn this morning, it's still early afternoon when I pull up to a white shutter board house. It looks like the most perfect family home with blooming flowers everywhere and a comfortable looking porch, but the most welcoming part is the ocean that gently laps at the sand behind the property.

Killing the engine, I just sit there staring for a few minutes, imagining what it might be like to live as a little family in a house like that.

Is that where this thing with Sadie is going?

I sure as hell want it to. Something tells me that Wes does, too. It's just pig-headed Rhett we need to get on board.

None of us have grown up with typical families. We all have our issues to deal with when it comes to our pasts, but Rhett seems to have the hardest time admitting to even himself what he really wants.

I see it every time I look in his eyes, every time he so much as glances at Sadie.

Movement inside the house finally drags me from my thoughts and I climb off my bike, my heart in my throat as I walk up the path toward the front door.

Will she remember me? Hell, will she want me here?

I ring the bell before I second guess myself and walk away again. I need to do this. I need to find my answers now I've screwed up finding them from Nolan.

"Coming," a soft female voice calls, and only a few seconds later, footsteps head my way.

Wendy pulls the door open and gasps, her hand coming up to cover her mouth. Nothing is said as we stand there, staring at each other. Her eyes are a little bloodshot and watery as if she's been crying, and it's then that I realize she's lost someone today as well.

She's wearing what's obviously a well-loved apron, covered in flour, and the scent of freshly-baked something wafts from the house, making my belly growl.

"I'm sorry for your loss."

Her head tilts and the warmest smile curls at her lips. "Oh, my sweet boy."

Despite the flour covering her, she opens her arms and pulls me in for the hug I had no idea I needed so badly.

Dragging in a ragged breath, I wrap my own arms around her, a sense of familiarity and safety racing through me.

"Come in. I've just baked cookies," she says, finally releasing me.

I catch her sweeping a tear from her cheek before she turns and welcomes me into her home.

Looking around, I take in her space. It looks like something out of a magazine. All the fabrics and textures clash, but weirdly, it works. I scan the shelves for photos of kids or family, but it's depressingly bare.

I don't have any memory of a man or any kids in her life, but then to be fair, any memories I do have of being here are vague at best.

"Would you like a drink? Coffee? Soda? I don't think I have any beer."

"Coffee is great, thank you."

The second I walk into the kitchen and take in the huge island in the middle of the room, a bolt of nostalgia hits me, and I stop on the spot.

"Are you okay?"

"I... um... I don't really remember... anything. But this room... I don't know," I stutter like a fumbling idiot as I rub the back of my neck.

"It's the best room in the house, that's why." She smiles.

Walking over, I pull one of the stools out and take a seat while Wendy starts the coffee machine.

"Did you see him before he—"

"No," I say sadly. "I didn't get my shi— my head together quick enough."

She's silent as she finishes our coffees before carrying them over and sitting with me.

Her eyes hold mine for a moment. "It's okay," she whispers. "Your past is..."

"A nightmare," I finish for her.

"Some of the years, yes. I'm not going to sugarcoat anything for you, Dane. But everything you've been through has helped shape the person you are today."

"I might be a horrible person," I mutter.

One of her brows lift. "I think we both know that's not true."

"How would you— Nolan," I breathe.

"He kept me informed about how things were with you. I need you to know that the last thing I wanted was to give you up back then."

"So why did you?"

"It wasn't safe. We'd hoped to keep you off the Reapers' radar, but we weren't clever enough, and we knew that as soon as someone figured it out, they'd come for you.

"We wanted you to have a fresh start. A chance."

I nod, understanding their reasons for dropping me off where they did.

"But why the Sinners? Why keep me so close to Darren? Why not ship me across the country or..." I trail off, not really knowing what people do with kids they're trying to protect without putting them straight into the system and probably making their lives even worse.

"Nolan always hoped that you might do exactly what you're doing now. Darren was... he was always a little different. Even as a baby, everyone had concerns about his mental state. Nolan knew he wasn't fit to run the club, but he prayed maybe you would be someday."

"That's a big risk."

"The club was his life. So was his family," she says, sniffling and reaching for a tissue. "He wanted you close. He wanted to watch you grow up, to see you do all the amazing things he knew you were capable of. Even if it had to be from a distance."

I drop my head and scrub my hand over my face as I let everything she's saying sink in.

"Your dad loved you, Dane. You might have been a result of a questionable decision on his part, but he never questioned if he wanted you. He really hoped that Lilian would take you on as her own, that you and Darren could grow up as brothers."

"Best laid plans and all that," I mutter, thinking of just how badly everything went.

"I truly believe he had no idea what Darren and Lilian were doing to you. He never would have allowed it if he did... and after your daddy died, well..."

I nod, although it doesn't really make me feel any better about it.

"They tortured me, Wendy. Locked me in a dark cupboard and... hurt me."

"I know," she says sadly. "The first time I saw what they'd done, I could have killed them myself."

The thought of such a kind and softly spoken woman going to stand up against Darren, even if he was just a child himself at the time, is amusing.

"But the best I could do for you was love you, care for you, try to prove to you that not all people are monsters who set out to hurt you."

"You did," I confess quietly. "I don't remember much, if anything really. But this house... I really remember being happy here. I remember you being kind, taking care of me."

"After everything you'd experienced in your young life, that was the least you deserved. I'm glad I could give you some better memories."

"I've had nightmares for years," I mutter. "But when things got too much, you were always there. You saved me."

Her tears fall freely now as she reaches for my hand and squeezes tightly. "You had such a bright future ahead of you. I could see that from the moment you arrived."

I shake my head, unable to believe she saw that when I was so broken, so vulnerable.

"Nolan said you have a good life with the Sinners."

I can't help but smile as I think about Ray, Grandma Irene, Rhett, Sadie, and the rest of my Sinners family.

"The best. They accepted me as theirs from the second they took me in."

"Nolan was confident they would."

"Why didn't he tell Ray the truth?"

"The more people who knew, the more risk you were at. Nolan had every intention of telling you at the right time, once you were able to defend yourself against

Darren. But I think his own fear and Darren's increasingly irrational behavior always stopped him. Then his health, of course."

I nod, taking a sip of my coffee now it's cooled a little. "I thought you'd abandoned me too," I confess quietly.

"Oh, my sweet boy. If I had my way, I would've never let you go. You were my angel. I would've happily brought you up had it been safe to do so."

Her words cause a lump so huge in my throat that I struggle to even breathe around it for long minutes, let alone speak.

"Do you have any kids of your own?"

She shakes her head, sadness washing over her. "It wasn't in the cards for me. But my time with you was everything."

"T-thank you," I breathe, my voice rough with emotion and gratitude for everything she must have given up for me.

"I don't know what your plans are, but you're more than welcome to stay here for as long as you need to."

I nod, feeling a weight lift from my shoulders. "I'm not sure how long I'll get. I've got people who are probably going out of their minds right now, trying to find me. I heard the news and kind of freaked out."

"That's understandable. But I'm glad you've got people who care, Dane."

I can't help but laugh at the innocent look on her face.

She has no clue what the hell I'm involved in. Something tells me it would horrify her. Although I also think she'd probably love Sadie.

They might be very different, but their fierce protectiveness shines bright.

9

SADIE

The ride to the coast seems to take forever. Rhett drives while I sit between him and Wes. At some point, I fell asleep on Wes's shoulder, but Rhett's road rage woke me up when he was honking aggressively at a passing car.

"Here it is," he eventually says.

"Cute neighborhood." The sleepy seaside town is littered with craftsman bungalows with colorful exteriors and neatly kept lawns.

"Check the address again," he orders, and I pull up the map on my cell phone.

"It should be right around this corner and at the end of the street."

"Overlooking the ocean. Sweet," Wes murmurs beside me.

Nervous energy bounces around in my stomach, making me queasy. Vivienne told us Dane was headed here, but what if he already came and left?

What if he found out something he didn't like?

Another blow in a long line of them.

I let out a heavy sigh and Wes slips his arms around my shoulder, drawing me into his side. "You okay?"

"I'll be okay when we find him."

Rhett casts me a sideways glance, his eyes saying everything I'm too scared to.

Dane is okay.

He has to be.

We snake down the road leading to the row of beachfront properties. Their exteriors are chipped and worn from the sea breeze and salt in the air. But there's something idyllic about this place. I can imagine Dane as a child, playing on the sand, jumping waves and trying to catch fish.

Whether he knows it or not, this was his safe haven.

God, he was so young. My heart aches for the young boy abused by his own brother and stepmom.

"What is it?" Wes asks, sensing the shudder that rolls through me.

"It's just hard to imagine..." I swallow hard. "He was just a kid."

Sadness bleeds into the truck, filling the space around us. Dane doesn't like to talk about what happened back then much. But being here, getting ready to meet the woman who took him in after Nolan discovered the truth... it's hard not to talk about it.

"Come on," Rhett says thickly. "Let's go find him."

He shoulders the door open and climbs out, leaving me and Wes alone. "I'm worried about him," I muse.

"It can't be easy, watching your best friend go through all this and not be able to help."

"Yeah, I know." I twist around to look at him and he smiles, cupping my face.

"You're the glue, princess. You know that, right?

When things get too hard, too much, when they feel like they're falling apart, you hold us together."

"I'm the glue," I murmur.

"Damn right, you are." He leans in and kisses me softly, brushing his fingers along my jaw. "We need you. All of us. Dane will come around. Savage too. And eventually, we'll get to move past all this."

God, I hope he's right.

We deserve things to settle. To have a chance to enjoy our relationship and each other.

But as I climb out of the truck, I can't shake the feeling that things are only going to get worse before they get better.

The rumble of Dad's bike fills the air and the three of us turn to find him pull up alongside the truck.

"Is he here?"

"That's what we're about to find out."

I haven't voiced my concern over the fact that Dane's bike isn't here, desperately holding onto the hope that he is.

Because if he isn't...

Don't go there, Sadie Ray.

We approach the beach house as a unit, Dad walking slightly ahead. He oozes confidence, and the fierce determination in his eyes only confirms his commitment and love for Dane.

"I'm so nervous," I whisper to no one in particular. But it's Wes who takes my hand, Rhett too lost in his own head to notice my nervousness.

We get to the door, and Dad raps his knuckles against the wood.

"Just a minute," a voice calls from inside. And then a woman appears. With kind eyes and a warm smile, she takes the four of us in.

"Wondered how long it would take y'all to figure it out."

"I'm Ray Dalton," Dad says. "This here is my daughter, Sadie Ray, and her guys, Rhett and Wesley."

Her guys.

I fight a smile at that.

If I needed any more reassurance that Dad might accept this—accept us—I just got it.

"I know who you are." The woman smiles. "I'm Wendy. Come in."

"Is he here?" I blurt out.

"He is."

"Thank God." Relief slams into me and I sway against Wes, gripping his arm. His eyes flash to mine, and I see his own relief shining bright.

Wendy ushers us inside, but I don't see or hear any signs of Dane. "Let's go into the kitchen. I'll make a fresh pot of coffee." She lingers behind the men, who all disappear into what I can only assume is the kitchen.

"It's so nice to meet you, Sadie Ray." She smiles at me. "You know, he told me about you."

"He did?" My voice cracks.

"He did." She takes my hand in hers. "He loves you so much, sweetheart. A broken soul like Dane needs the love of a good woman to set him right."

"I..." Tears roll down my cheeks. I'm so emotional all of a sudden.

"Hush now, it's okay. It's going to be okay, sweetheart.

He's down by the ocean. You should go to him. He's waiting."

"He is?"

She nods. "Even if he doesn't realize it, he's waiting... for you."

"You'll tell them where I've gone?" My eyes flick over her shoulder to where my dad and the guys disappeared.

"I'll take good care of them. Now go. He needs you, sweetheart."

"Thank you."

I didn't realize how much I needed to hear those words until now. Because although I would never give up on Dane, I can't deny that part of me thought I'd lost him.

I find Dane sitting by the water's edge, the silvery hue of the moonlight illuminating his profile.

My dark prince.

He doesn't turn at the sound of my approach. Instead, he says to the vast ocean, "Wondered when you'd get here."

"Am I that obvious?" I sink down in the sand next to him and pull off my black Chucks, digging my toes into the cool grains.

"You love me, princess." He nudges my shoulder. "I knew you wouldn't give up on me."

"Lucky for you." It comes out playful, but there's a pained edge to my voice. "Talk to me, Dane. Where's your head at?"

"I... fuck, Sadie, girl. I don't know. I don't know anything anymore."

"That's not true," I say softly, peeking over at him.

"You know that I love you. I love you so fucking much. You know that Rhett loves you too. And Wes and my dad. You've got an entire club who loves you like family. And you've got another club waiting for you to take back what's yours. What always should have been yours. If you want it."

"I didn't even get to talk to him, my uncle... fuck, that still sounds fucking strange."

"Nolan did what he thought he had to do to keep you safe."

"Yeah," he blows out a shaky breath, "and look where that got him. Darren ripped his beloved club apart and went on a killing spree." His eyes finally meet mine, haunted with dark shadows. "And it's all my fault."

"No. No, Dane." He looks away from me, but I grip his jaw, forcing his eyes back to mine. "Don't say that. Don't ever say that.

"Darren Creed was sick in the head. He couldn't stand that you were alive, that you were... good. Because you are, Dane. You're so good, baby." Fresh tears roll down my cheeks at the devastation in his eyes. "And I love you. I'm so fucking in love with you that the thought of you hurting, the thought of you thinking you're not worth it, kills me. It kills me."

"Shh, princess." He hooks his arm around my neck and pulls me close. "Shh."

I grip his cut, anchoring us together.

I can't lose him over this, I just can't.

"I need you, Dane. We all need you. I don't know if you want to lead the Red Ridge Sinners or not. I don't care if you want to run away somewhere and never come back. But I need you. And I'll follow you wherever you go."

"You'll follow me, huh?" His fingers slide under my jaw, tilting my face to his. "Even if I'm headin' straight for hell?"

"Even then." I sniffle.

"I'll never understand what I did to deserve you, princess, but I thank my maker every fucking day."

I stare into his eyes, letting his words wrap around me like a soft blanket. "Your past, the scars you bear... they don't define you, Dane. But the choices you make right here, right now... they do. I know you have a lot to process, but I'm here. I'll always be here."

"Love you, Sadie, girl." He swallows thickly, leaning forward to touch his head to mine, breathing me in.

"I love you too, so much."

So much it terrifies me.

They each own a piece of my heart, and without them —all of them—I won't be whole.

"Wendy seems nice," I say after a few seconds.

"Yeah."

"Did you get some of the answers you needed?" I pull back to look him in the eye.

"Yeah, I did."

"Good, that's... good."

"I'm sorry I took off like I did." Shame glitters in his eyes. "I just... I feel like a pressure cooker. Everything has been building and building and I thought—"

"Hey, you don't have to explain it to me, okay? I get it, I do. You needed space." The word tastes sour on my tongue.

"Not from you, princess. Never from you. I think..." He inhales a shuddering breath, looking past me. "Just couldn't stay away, huh?"

I glance back to find Rhett and Wes making their way toward us.

"Been fucking worried sick about you, brother." Rhett drops down on Dane's other side and slings his arm over his shoulder.

"Sorry, I—"

"No apologies needed." Rhett's eyes meet mine and we share a lingering look. "Whatever you need, we're here."

"All of us." Wes sinks down beside me, pressing a kiss to my shoulder. His eyes snag Dane's and something passes between them. "Fucking relieved to see you're okay."

"Miss me, Pretty?"

No one laughs, the air between us taut like a bowstring.

"It's so beautiful out here," I say, in an attempt to break the tension.

"Better now you're here, Sadie, girl." Dane pulls me closer and the four of us sit there, staring out at the ocean. Dane still has a lot of healing to do, a lot of decisions to make. But he doesn't have to do it alone.

"My dad's here too," I whisper.

"Fuck." He swallows. "Prez came?"

"Damn right he did," Rhett says, his voice thick. "You're family, Stray. One of us. And we ain't ever letting you go."

10

WES

The creak of a floorboard wakes me from my uncomfortable sleep on one of Wendy's couches.

After we came back up from the ocean, she insisted on cooking us all dinner and demanded we stay the night, seeing as it was too late for us to make the journey back. We all agreed. Dane seems content here, and we all want him to have that for as long as possible.

I could easily imagine a younger version of the fun-loving guy we know playing on the beach and trying to be the kid he deserved to be.

My life might have been hell the past few years, but my childhood was mostly full of happiness. I never saw the monster that lived under our roof until I got that little bit older. My father was mean, sure. But I just assumed he was stern because he wanted the best for me.

Not that he was just a flat-out cunt.

It makes me wonder how I missed it back then, all the things Mom covered up to protect me.

A shudder rips through me as I remember Dad's fist

hitting her face. How many other times had something similar happened and I fell for their bullshit excuses of her being ill, or having a migraine?

I lie there, feeling like the shittiest kind of kid, when another creak sounds out.

Cracking an eye open, I spot a dark figure moving toward the back door of the house that leads out to the deck. We all sat there until late last night, drinking the beer Rhett insisted on disappearing to buy when Wendy didn't have any.

I'm not sure if it was the beer he really wanted or just a few minutes of peace. He's struggling with this Dane thing. Everyone else might see Rhett as this big, bad, scary biker who doesn't give a shit about anyone or anything. But that's so far from the truth.

Now I'm on the inside, I can see that Rhett loves just as fiercely as Dane. Dane just happens to wear his heart on his sleeve, whereas Rhett is terrified of showing weakness.

Glancing at the couch opposite me, I find Sadie alone, deep asleep. Pushing up onto my elbows, I spot Rhett in the chair, looking about as uncomfortable as I feel, but his chest is moving up and down at a steady pace.

Wendy looked a little awkward when she told us we had to stay but then confessed to only having two bedrooms. Having clearly understood the dynamic here, she offered us hers. She really is a guardian fucking angel for that. But we all refused, more than happy to allow her a good night's sleep.

Getting to my feet, I follow Dane as he slips outside and pulls the door closed behind him. He doesn't hear me coming, and by the time I join him out on the deck, he's standing at the railings, watching the waves crash up on the beach.

My heart aches for him. He might have gotten some of the answers he's needed from Wendy, but none of them will make the pain of his past any easier to bear.

I don't say a word. I just step up beside him, letting my upper arm lightly brush his.

"Shit, did I wake you?" he whispers without looking at me.

"Nah, I wasn't really asleep. That couch is uncomfortable as fuck."

"The other one isn't much better."

I chuckle. "I'm sure having Sadie's ass pressed up against your cock helped."

"Did a bit, yeah," he admits.

"You want a drink or something?" I ask.

"Sure."

Silently, I slip back inside and find two cans of soda in the fridge. When I return, he's sitting on the swing seat, still staring out at the ocean. "Here you go," I say, handing one over and dropping down beside him.

"Thanks."

Silence settles between us. It's not uncomfortable, and I'd be lying if I said I didn't feel the crackling of something else between us too.

"You wanna talk about it?" I offer.

Dane scrubs his hand down his face, rubbing at his rough jaw. "I dunno. I'm not sure where to even start with it all."

"You know I won't judge, whatever it is."

Finally, he looks over at me, his gray eyes meeting mine. I suck in a quick breath at the darkness within them. It's a look I'm used to, but in the past, it was only ever directed at Sadie. Since that night on vacation, things have changed between us. And I'm not in any way opposed to exploring whatever it might be.

He chuckles. "I know that, Pretty. You've proved your loyalty time and time again."

"Oh yeah?" I ask with a hint of a smirk.

"Yeah. Even without the cut, you're one of us. You know that, right?"

I nod. "Yeah. I want this, though. It feels right. What about you?"

"You talking about the club, Pretty, or—"

"The club. *Your* club."

"My club," he echoes. "It's fucking insanity that anyone thinks I can run a club."

"With the family you've got around you, it's not that crazy. You've got the perfect opportunity to rebuild it exactly as you and Crank want it. You're not just inheriting it. You're completely restarting it."

He nods, running my words around in his head. "But how's it going to work? You two in Savage Falls, me at Red Ridge. How do we make that... this," he says, gesturing between the two of us, "work?"

"We... uh... all get a place on the border, halfway between the two? But that's a ways off yet, don't you think? We've kinda gotta finish school yet."

"Yeah, we really should go back there at some point. We don't want that asshole Evan thinking he won."

"I'm pretty sure he knows he lost. The last I heard, he's still walking funny."

Dane barks out a laugh, a wide smile pulling at his lips. "I can't believe you were friends with that asshole," he scoffs.

"Describing us as friends would be pushing it," I

mutter. "Football was... well, forced on me from a very young age," I admit. "Thankfully, I was good at it. Christ knows what would have happened if I wasn't. He probably would have cycled me through every sport that exists until he found something I excelled at. Heaven forbid I wasn't gifted at something."

"He's a cunt," Dane mutters.

"Yep."

"I don't know how your mom stuck it out for so long."

"For me," I whisper, feeling the weight of the guilt pressing down on my shoulders.

"I was a lucky motherfucker really, wasn't I?" Dane asks. "Since the day I turned up at the Sinners' gates, I've had everything I could ever want."

"Nolan wanted you cared for, and he made it happen. Not all of your family was shit, just like mine. A couple of bad eggs shouldn't ruin our trust, our faith in people."

"Oh yeah," he mutters. "I've found plenty of good ones."

"Those two in there would move mountains for you."

"I'd do the same in return. They're my world."

"How did I find myself in the middle of this?" I ask, more to myself than Dane, pushing my hair back from my brow and staring out at the ocean.

"Same reason we're here. Sadie's magical pussy."

I can't help but bark out a laugh. "Yeah. It's pretty fucking addictive."

"Never thought I'd be a one-woman man. Not in the early days of discovering what club life was really like. But I knew Sadie was always special. She was my first friend at the club. We connected before even Rhett and I did. I guess I should have known she was something special. Probably should have saved myself for her or some shit."

"I think she prefers you with a little experience."

"I have more than a little. No fourteen-year-old should have been doing the things Rhett and I were back then."

"Kinda gutted I missed it."

"Would scar you for life, Pretty," he quips. "What about you? When did you first let one of those Savage Falls cheersluts bounce around on your cock?"

"How'd you know it was a cheerleader?"

"You gonna try convincing me it wasn't?"

"Nah, it totally was. Got wasted at a party a couple of weeks before my seventeenth birthday." I can't help but laugh at the memory. "It was fucking terrible. We were so drunk... had no idea what we were doing. Fun times," I mutter, although as I think about it a little more, it really, really wasn't.

"Well, gotta say, Pretty, I'm glad you honed your skills before finding us."

"Oh, don't worry. You've sure taught me a few things."

A smirk pulls at his lips, and he shoots a wicked look my way.

"Oh yeah?" His eyes drop to my lips for a beat and my stomach clenches with nerves.

Surely, he wouldn't. Not when it's just the two of us.

Of course he would. This is Dane fucking Stray I'm talking about. When it comes to sex and pleasure, he dives in feet first and thinks later.

"Yeah," I say, refusing to take his bait, teasing him a little and getting way more of a kick out of it than I should. "That day you walked in with candles and a lighter for Sadie, I almost shit my pants."

"I know, I saw the look on your face. She fucking loved it though, didn't she?"

Images of Sadie writhing on the bed, her wrists bound, candle wax hardening on her breasts fill my head, and I have to reach out and rearrange myself in my pants.

"Oh yeah, good memories. I'd never do anything to hurt Sadie. Any of you," he adds. "I hope you know that."

I nod.

"I push because I trust you all, and I know you do me. It's a fucking heady feeling. Even fucking better, watching you all fall."

My pulse thunders in every inch of my body, blood whooshing past my ears as he stares at me with those dark, lust-filled eyes.

"Will you do something with me, Pretty?" he asks, clearing his throat.

"Um..." I hesitate, my nerves getting the better of me.

"Come on, be crazy with me."

He sits forward, but he makes no move to touch me or do anything.

After draining his soda, Dane stands, briefly looking out over the ocean, and then turns back to me. "Stand," he demands, and I'm powerless but to do as I'm told, abandoning my own can on the deck at my feet.

"Ready?" There's a wicked glint in his eye and a smirk twitching at his lips.

My brows narrow as I watch him try to contain his amusement.

"Three," he says, making my heart race. "Two." I swallow nervously. "One. Last one in the sea is a little bitch," he cries, dragging his shirt over his head and dropping it to the steps that descend to the beach below.

"Oh shit," I bark, racing to follow him, because fuck yeah, I'm all-in for this.

By the time I'm on the sand, he's down to his boxers, which also get shed before he runs straight into the water.

"Yes, Pretty," he calls, turning to find me wading in with him.

"This isn't as warm as it looks," I mutter, a shudder ripping through me as I duck my shoulders under.

"It's fucking great," Dane announces, splashing about like a kid with a wide smile on his face. "I remember this feeling," he says, suddenly sounding happy and content. "I remember feeling free here. Like anything was possible."

I come to a stop beside him where he floats in the water, the moonlight reflecting on the water droplets covering him.

"It is," I say, unable to rip my eyes away from him.

"Yeah," he mutters, standing once more and turning to me. "And what is it exactly you want to happen?"

"I... uh..."

"Because we've got an audience, and something tells me she'd really love for us to put on a fucking show right now."

11

___

SADIE

W hen I woke to find Dane and Wes missing, curiosity had gotten the better of me. I'm not sure what I expected to find... but it wasn't this.

The two of them look so fucking hot, waist deep in the ocean, the moonlight reflecting off their gorgeous faces.

Their eyes track me as I walk down to the shore, the cool breeze lapping at my thighs thanks to the t-shirt Wendy loaned me to sleep in. Electricity hums in the air, and I can feel their simmering connection even from all the way over here.

If I hadn't chosen this exact moment to come and find them, what would they be doing right now?

The glint in Dane's eyes tells me I would have liked it, whatever it was.

"What are you doing out here?" I ask, sinking my toes into the wet sand.

"Getting wet," Dane smirks. "Do you want to get wet with us, princess?"

His words have a direct line to my libido, desire pulsing through me.

"I was worried."

His expression falls. "Shit, Sadie, girl, I didn't..."

"It's okay." I wade up to my ankles, the water sending a shiver through me, making my nipples pebble.

Both of their eyes drop to my chest, and I lift a brow. "See something you like?" I tease.

"Always." Dane grins.

"Are you naked under there?" I ask, knowing full well that I passed their clothes on the way down here.

"Why don't you come find out?" Wes drawls, his eyes fixated on my chest.

Typical guy.

"It's cold, and I'm not sure I want to get wet. You'll have to persuade me." I bat my eyelashes, enjoying this game we're playing.

Things were intense today. But by the time we all turned in for the night, Dane seemed lighter. More at peace with things.

That's all I want for him.

The fact that I found him and Wes out here in the middle of the night suggests he's feeling much better about everything.

"You want us to persuade you, princess?" Dane locks eyes with me. "It would be my pleasure." He slides up behind Wes and wraps an arm around his waist, whispering something in his ear.

Wes gulps but gives a small nod, his eyes still fixed on me.

"Pretty has something for you." Dane glides his hand down Wes's abs, going lower and lower until it disappears under the water. But I see the flare of lust in Wes's eyes, as the way his breath catches in his throat as Dane jacks him off.

"Fuck, that's hot." I purr, inching further into the ocean.

"He's so fucking hard for you," Dane drawls. "Maybe a little hard for me, too."

"Fuck, Stray. *Fuck!*"

"I want to see," I whisper, and Dane responds by nudging Wes forward until their lower bodies are above the surface. His fist is wrapped right around Wes's cock, pumping him hard.

"See what you do to him, Sadie, girl."

Arousal gushes between my legs and I slide a hand up my stomach to touch my breasts.

"Where should I make him come?" Dane's eyes are so dark it sends a shudder through me. He's in control here, but he's giving me the choice.

Because in the end, it's always about me.

"Inside me." I wade closer. "I want him to come inside me."

"Fuck," Wes hisses as I reach out, pressing a hand against his chest. "I need you, princess."

"I know." I cover Dane's hand with my own, leaning in to kiss Wes. Our mouths crash together, all teeth and tongue and sheer desperation.

Dane releases him, pressing the three of us closer so he can grab my thighs and help Wes lift me. My legs go around Wes's waist as they slowly impale me on his cock.

I cry out, so full of him I can't breathe.

"How does he feel?" Dane asks.

"Amazing. So good." I roll my hips, needing more. Needing them both. "But I want you too. Please."

"Yeah?" he asks, eyes wide with hunger.

I nod, moaning loudly when Wes rocks up into me.

"Shit, man. I'm not gonna be able to hold off much longer. If we're doing this, it needs to be now."

Dane comes around to stand behind me, fitting my body between them as if it's exactly where I'm supposed to be. He spits on his hand and jerks himself a couple of times before sliding the tip of his dick between my ass cheeks.

"You good?" He runs his nose along my neck, nipping the skin there.

"Yeah, I'm good."

"This might hurt a little. Hold her tight, Pretty."

Dane pushes forward, slowly working himself inside me. I'm so full of them, my lungs feel tight, like I'm a coiled spring ready to snap.

"Move," I breathe, trying to wiggle against them both. "I need you to—ahhh."

They both slide deep, stretching me until I feel like they might split me apart. But it feels so good I don't care.

I wrap an arm around the back of Dane's neck, urging him deeper.

"Having you full of us is the best fucking thing in the world," he growls. "I can feel you, Pretty. Feels so fucking good."

There's something so erotic about this moment, the two of them loving my body, working together to bring us all to that point of sheer ecstasy. Our moans melt into the night sky as they ride me in perfect synchrony.

"Fuck, I can't..." I stutter, barely able to catch my breath over the intense waves of pleasure battering my insides.

They're like a storm, a violent whirlwind I'm not sure I'll survive. But oh, what a way to go.

Wes grips my thighs and Dane's fingers dig into my waist as they guide my body up and down between them.

"Rhett's going to kill us for this," Wes chuckles, groaning when I clench around him.

"Savage will get his own back. Just enjoy the ride, Pretty. I know I fucking am." Dane's mouth latches onto my neck, sucking hard.

"More," I cry, so close to the edge.

His hand slides up my body, collaring my throat as he pounds into me. "Ours, princess."

"Y-yours." My legs begin to tremble, the wave crashing over me.

"Fuck, she's coming," Wesley pants, his cock jerking inside me as he reaches his own release.

"Holy shit," Dane groans, pulling me hard against him as he comes. "You are amazing. Both of you." He reaches for Wes's shoulder, and the connection between them buzzes around me.

"I hope one of you is going to carry me back to the house, because... wow, my legs are like jelly."

They slowly lower me and I dip down, swirling the water around my body, letting it clean me.

Wes and Dane duck down too, splashing me as they go.

"Hey," I complain, but then suddenly I'm cocooned by two inked arms.

"Love you, Sadie, girl," Dane whispers against my ear.

I let out a content sigh and rest my head back against his shoulder. "Sorry if I interrupted your fun."

"Never." He pecks my cheek. "Whatever is between us is because of you. You'll always come first, princess."

Wes nods, a shy smile tugging at his mouth. "One hundred percent."

Later that morning, I wake to the smell of bacon and coffee.

"Hmm, what time is it?" I crack an eye open.

"A little after ten."

"Ten?" I bolt upright, frowning at Rhett. "Why the hell did you let me sleep until ten?"

"Figured you might need it after your little moonlight swim." His brow quirks. "Heard things got... intense."

"Dane has such a big mouth."

"Actually, I woke up and saw the three of you."

"Oh." My cheeks burn, and something passes over his expression. "What's the matter, Savage? Jealous?" I smirk.

"Watch it, princess. Just because we're in a stranger's house, doesn't mean I won't drag you somewhere quiet and punish you."

My breath catches.

"You're so fucking dirty." He chuckles, helping me up. My arms go around his neck and he pulls me closer. "And tonight, your pussy is mine."

"I'm sure that can be arranged." I kiss him. "He's going to be okay, you know."

"Yeah, I know." Rhett's eyes glaze. "You and Pretty give him something I never knew he needed."

"You give him a lot too, Rhett. He loves you like a brother."

"Don't worry, princess." He cups the back of my neck, forcing me to meet his steely gaze. "I'm not jealous. I just so happen to like our dynamic."

"Me too." I grin.

"Okay, kids," my dad's voice booms. "I don't need to be seein' the two of you—"

"Daddy!" I gasp, pulling out of Rhett's hold. "We're talking."

"Well, do it with a little space between you, or my breakfast will make a reappearance, and nobody wants that."

"Oh, I don't know, Ray. I think it's cute that Sadie has found three guys to dote on her." Wendy flashes me a conspiratorial wink. "You don't have to rush off. I can make lunch and—"

"Appreciate the hospitality, Wendy, but we need to get back to Savage Falls."

"Of course." She smiles. "Well, at least let me feed Sadie Ray some pancakes before you go. A little energy for the road."

"Thanks," I say, heading for the kitchen counter.

"We'll be outside if you need us." Dad motions for Rhett to follow him, and the two of them disappear, leaving me with Wendy.

"How did you sleep?"

"I... uh, good, thanks."

A knowing smile plays on her lips, and I silently pray she wasn't also up in the night, looking out at the ocean like Rhett.

"Dane has grown into a fine young man," she says, pushing a plate of pancakes and a glass of juice toward me.

"He has." I nod.

"And he thinks the world of you. Only took me a second to see that."

"I care about him very much."

"I'm so glad he has you and the guys. What he went through... he deserves to be loved. He deserves a family."

Emotion lodges in my throat. "I'll never hurt him, I swear."

"Oh, sweetheart, I know you won't. You love those boys, something fierce, don't you? I won't pretend to understand it, but God works in mysterious ways, and he obviously brought the four of you together for a reason. Just... promise me something,"

"Anything," I say.

"You'll visit again. Bring Dane and the guys. Hell, you can even bring your daddy."

"That would be nice."

"It sure would."

"Wendy?"

"Yes, sweetheart?"

"Thank you," I whisper. "Thank you for looking after Dane when he was a kid." A tear slips down my cheek, and Wendy hurries around the counter to me, pulling me into her arms.

"Now now, sweetie, there's no need to cry. He's going to be just fine. How could he not when he has so much love around him?"

"You really think he'll be okay?" My voice cracks.

I want to believe her, I do. But part of me is terrified that maybe I'm not enough. That maybe we're not enough to save Dane from his past.

"Trust your heart, Sadie Ray." Her expression softens. "It won't steer you wrong."

12

DANE

I sweep Sadie up in a bruising kiss before allowing her to get into the truck between Rhett and Wes.

Rhett tried to convince me to ride with her, that he'd take my bike, knowing just how much I need her right now. But I refused. I've got some things I need to do, and although I'm not running this time, I need to do them alone.

Ray's bike rumbles to life on the side of the road as I turn to Wendy. She might be smiling at me, but the tears in her eyes and the slight tremble to her bottom lip tells me how she's really feeling.

"Thank you, for everything," I breathe, pulling her into my arms.

It's not enough. Nothing ever will be for the peace and love she provided me with all those years ago, and I don't think she'll ever truly appreciate how grateful I am for her.

"You're welcome, my boy. You're always welcome."

"We'll come back, okay? I promise. Now I know, I—" Releasing her, I shove my hand through my hair.

"It's okay, Dane. You have nothing to be sorry about. I'm so glad you're happy. Look after your girl, yeah? And do Nolan and your daddy proud. They were both very good men."

Another wave of emotion washes over her as my stomach knots. "I will," I say, forcing my voice to come out. "I'll be in touch."

"Safe journey," she calls as I walk to Ray to tell him my intentions. He nods, waving for Rhett to go ahead as I climb on my bike.

With one final wave at Wendy, the two of us trail behind, side by side—until we finally get to the intersection that leads to either Red Ridge or Savage Falls. The truck, Ray... they all turn left to go home. But when I move, it's in the opposite direction.

Even with the space between us, Sadie notices. My skin tingles with her stare and I can almost hear her in my head.

"What's he doing? Where's he going?"

Over the past few weeks, I've been asking myself the same questions. The bombshell about Nolan being my uncle, Darren being my brother, was one that I never could have predicted. But now, after spending the night with Wendy, learning more about who I am, about where I come from... It's made this decision so much easier.

The gates to the compound are open when I pull up, something I'm sure I wouldn't have seen in the lead up to Darren's massacre. A smile plays on my lips as I ride in and park beside Crank's bike. Brothers look my way. Some give a small wave or a nod in greeting.

They all know who I am now.

I'm not just another nameless, faceless Sinner.

I'm a part of them. A part of this.

My blood is laced through this club. My not-so-distant ancestors built it, just like Sadie's and Rhett's granddaddies built the Sinners.

All eyes are on me as I climb from my bike and march toward the clubhouse. Everyone is waiting on me to make a decision, and although they've all assured me that there's no rush, I know they're all desperate to know about the future of their beloved club. I get it—if this were happening to my club, then I'd be dying to know if it had a chance or not.

I pull the heavy door to the clubhouse open and step inside the weirdly familiar surroundings. I might have only been here a handful of times, but seeing the guys in cuts, their old ladies, breathing in the familiar scent of leather, beer and whiskey... it's like coming home. Even if this club isn't my home.

Not yet, anyway.

"Stray," Crank announces, pushing from his bar stool. "How are you doing?" he asks, pulling me in for a man hug and slamming his fists down on my back.

I get it. The last time he saw me, I wasn't in a good place.

"Yeah, I'm... uh... good. Sorry about that, I kinda lost my head for a moment."

"S'all good, man. So, what can we do for you?"

"I was... uh... wondering if we could have a chat. In private," I add when the stares of all the brothers I turned my back on burn into my skin.

"Sure thing. You want a beer?"

"Nah, just a soda would be good."

"Diesel, get our boy a soda, yeah?"

A can comes flying over a few seconds later and

Crank gestures for me to head toward the back of the room.

"So, what's up then, Prez?" he asks, his voice teasing as he drops into what used to be Nolan's chair behind his massive walnut desk.

"Yeah, about that..." I mutter, cracking my can open.

"You made a decision."

I nod. "I'm in. If you still want me."

A smile twitches at his lips. "Yeah?"

"Yeah. I think it's time for me to step up. I owe it to Nolan. To my father."

"Hell yeah," he says happily, only confirming my feeling about this being the right thing to do. "This is gonna be fuckin' epic, Stray."

"Yeah, I think it might. There are just a few things, though," I admit with a wince.

"Whatever it is, we can figure it out. It's our time, bro. We can make things happen how we want them to."

I nod, glad he's willing to accept that my new role is going to come with stipulations. "I'm going back to school with Sadie," I say.

"Okay."

"And I'm going to live in Savage Falls. For now, at least."

"Okay."

"You're sure? I know that I'm kinda taking the top role and then leaving you here with all the shit."

"The role is yours through blood. You deserve it, and it's what your father and Nolan would have wanted. We'll find a way through all this. You've only got a few months until you graduate. We've got the help of both clubs to get us back up and running again. Everything will work out as it should."

I blow out the longest breath at hearing him say that.

"You know, I always thought it would be me and Savage at the gavel, but something tells me that me and you," I say, pointing between us, "we're gonna kill this MC shit."

He throws his head back on a laugh. "I'm sure there will be more than a few kills involved along the way."

Rubbing my hands together, a wicked smile plays on my lips. "I sure fucking hope so."

"You're fucked up, Stray. Pretty sure that's why this is gonna work so well."

"Takes one to know one." I wink.

With another laugh, he pushes from the chair and walks over to the closet in the far corner, pulling it open. "So, I guess you're going to need this then, Prez," he says, pulling out a brand new cut and throwing it over to me.

I catch it and flip it over.

Red Ridge Sinners.

Well, fuck me. Maybe I didn't think this through.

My mouth goes dry as I stare down at the confirmation of my decision.

"Been keeping this safe for you, too." Stepping up to me, he holds out a patch.

My hand trembles a little as I reach for it.

President.

Ho-ly shit.

"Too late to change your mind, bro. We're in this for life now."

"You mean you don't have some fucked-up initiation tasks planned?"

He shrugs. "We might come up with somethin', but right now, I think you've probably been through enough."

115

"You have no idea how much I appreciate that," I whisper.

"We're gonna have to party, though. Friday night. Bring your girl, your guys, and we'll do it Red Ridge style."

"Quinn?" I ask, testing the waters.

"S-sure, if she wants to come."

He tries so fucking hard to play that comment off innocently, but he fails by a long fucking stretch.

"Right. If you wanna keep pretending that you don't want her, then I can too."

"She's Micky's daughter."

"And Sadie is Ray's," I counter. "Maybe my balls are just bigger than yours, *VP*."

His chin drops as I push to stand.

"I guess I should go home and get my sewing kit out, huh? Only just stitched this one on," I mutter, pointing to my member patch that Ray gave me only a few days ago.

"We've got a bright future ahead of us, man. We'll figure this shit out together, so keep your head, yeah?"

"Appreciate it, man." I hold my hand out for him, but he pulls me in for another hug.

"Anytime, brother. You're one of us now."

"Savage Fall and Red Ridge, one big happy family. Who'd have thought it?"

"Certainly not Darren fuckin' Creed," Crank mutters, reaching for his abandoned beer. "Rest in hell, motherfucker." He lifts the bottle and drains the contents. "Onwards and upwards, brother. You wanna hang for a drink?"

"Not right now. I've got things I need to do."

"Fair enough."

"We're going back to school tomorrow, but I'll come

around after. Micky is free, so we can get our heads together."

"Sounds like a plan, man. Take it easy."

All eyes follow me through the clubhouse. I'm still wearing my Savage Falls cut, but there's no mistaking what I'm carrying.

"Yo, Stray," someone calls before I escape through the door. "You coming over to the dark side, brother?"

A smirk pulls at my lips before I lift the cut. "Pipe down, motherfuckers. There's a new boss around here, and he don't take shit from no one."

A ripple of laughs, congratulations, and applause goes through the compound.

"Welcome to the Sinners, brothers. We're celebrating Friday night, so get ready to drag out your worst behavior."

I leave to the sound of excited agreement.

Life around here has been shit for too long, and it seems everyone is more than ready for this new start.

Climbing back onto my bike, I ride out of the compound feeling a hell of a lot lighter than I did when I rode in. The decision that has been nagging at me since the day I learned the truth about who I was has been made.

I'm sure there are going to be tough times ahead when I'm going to regret it. I'm nowhere near old enough or wise enough to really appreciate what I'm embarking on, but I know I'm surrounded by the right people. And I know as much as everyone else that a club isn't made by one person. By the prez. It's made by everyone.

We're family. And our family just got a hell of a lot bigger.

We might be divided by a border, but that's where our differences end now.

We're Sinners.

All for one and one for all.

I don't drive straight back to Savage Falls to deliver the news to the guys. Instead, I swing by a store and head to the house I very briefly visited yesterday to make one very big apology.

"D-Dane?" Vivienne sniffles when she opens the front door to me.

To be honest, after the way I turned up here yesterday, I was expecting her to ignore me and to have to leave the flowers on the step.

"Hi," I breathe somewhat nervously.

"Would you like to come in?"

"I'm actually not staying. I just wanted to give you these and say what I should have yesterday."

"Oh?" she says, taking the flowers from me and sniffing them.

"I'm so sorry for your loss. I screwed up, not growing a pair and coming to talk to Nolan. I owe him my life, and I should have sorted myself out sooner. It's something I'm going to regret forever."

"He understood, Dane. Did Wendy give you the answers you needed?"

"Most of them, yeah. It was nice to see her. Thank you for pointing me in the right direction."

"You're more than welcome."

I stand there, hesitating.

"These past few weeks, months even, have been tough, on you especially, and I just wanted to tell you that I have every intention of having Nolan's name live on with the club."

"Oh?" she asks, her eyes lighting up at the mention of his name.

Reaching for the cut, I hold it up and she gasps. "I may never identify as a Creed, but I'll ensure the club lives on and is run in a way he'd be proud of."

"Oh, Dane," she breathes, throwing herself at me. "He was so proud of you," she sobs on my shoulder, making a lump form in my throat. "Welcome to the family."

"Has anyone heard from—"

"Here he is, Prez," Pacman calls from over by the window.

Wes squeezes my hip, pulling me closer as I stand between his legs.

When I saw Dane take the road toward Red Ridge, I had a sneaky suspicion of where he might be heading. I think Rhett felt the same, given that he didn't turn us around and take off after him.

"Was wondering when you were gonna show up," my dad says the second Dane appears.

He drags a hand through his hair, but something catches my eye. "That's not your Sinners cut," I say, moving toward him.

"No, princess, it isn't." Dane turns slowly, and I gasp, clapping a hand over my mouth at his brand-new Red Ridge Sinners cut.

"You said yes."

"Yeah." He meets my wild gaze. "Decided it was time to step up."

"Oh my God." I throw my arms around him, and he catches me, the sound of his laughter like music to my ears.

The rest of the place erupts with raucous cheers, everyone excited—and no doubt relieved—that Dane has decided to take his place with the Red Ridge Chapter.

"I'm so proud of you," I whisper as he holds onto me as if he might never let go.

"Don't think this means you'll be getting rid of me, Sadie, girl. I'll be needing myself an old lady." He pulls back, winking at me.

"I'm too young to be called that."

"Fair point." A smirk plays on his lips. "How about my queen, then?"

"Thought I already was." I pout, and he hooks his arm around my neck, kissing my head.

"You got me there."

"Okay, Sadie Ray, cut the guy loose and let the rest of us congratulate him," Pike bellows, and I step aside to let Dane have the spotlight.

My heart is so full, watching him, but I can't deny the knot in my stomach. Everything is going to change now.

What will this mean for us?

As if he hears my thoughts, Dane glances back at me, his eyes silently asking me if I'm okay. I nod, because what else can I do?

He's made his decision, and it's the right one. I know that. But Prez of the Red Ridge Sinners... that's a big deal. A huge responsibility.

Watching him get swallowed up by his brothers, I make my way back to Wes and Rhett.

"He deserves this," Rhett murmurs, sipping on his beer.

"I know."

Wes slides his arms around my waist and pulls me back between his legs. "You're worried," he whispers.

"Not worried. Just... it doesn't matter, it's silly." My gaze darts away from him.

"Sadie Ray." He pinches my side. "Nothing will come between what you two share, you know that, right?"

"I know."

God, I sound like a broken record, but this uncertainty is disarming. Me and Wes going off to college is one thing, but this—Dane stepping up to become President of the Red Ridge Chapter—is huge. "He loves you."

"I—" I stop myself, nodding instead. I know he does. I feel it every time he looks at me. So I have to trust that. I have to trust that the bonds between us will be enough to survive whatever the future throws our way.

"This won't change anything," Rhett says, crowding closer. His eyes narrow slightly, burning with promise. "I won't let it."

Another nod.

Does he feel it too? The shift in the air?

Then Wes says four little words to Rhett that remind me that the changes don't end with Dane becoming President of the Red Ridge chapter.

"It'll be you next."

Their deep laughter and heavy footsteps on the stairs outside give them away. I glance around Dane's apartment, hardly able to contain my grin.

After Dane got back to the clubhouse and made his

announcement, I dragged River and Quinn into town to do a little shopping so the guys could celebrate. Dane had protested, wanting me to stay, but the truth was, I needed some space.

Looking around the apartment, I realize I may have gone a little overboard, but they still owe me for lying to me. And we did kind of decide we would all stay here more, so it seems only fair I get to help style the place.

"Honey, we're ho—" Dane bursts into the room. "What the fuck?"

"Surprise." I smother the laughter bubbling in my chest.

"Holy shit." Wes moves around Dane, who's still gawking. "What did you do, princess?"

"I figured since we're going to be staying here more often, the place could do with some home comforts."

"Why the fuck is everything bubblegum pink?" Rhett growls.

"It adds a certain feminine touch, don't you think?" I smirk.

There's a bunch of fluffy pink throw cushions on the couch and chair, a pink shaggy rug, a couple of pink mugs on the mug tree, and I even bought a super cute pink and black framed motivational poster for the wall that reads 'princess,' complete with a crown.

"Fucking hell, I need a drink." Rhett moves toward the refrigerator and grabs a beer.

"Didn't you drink enough already?"

He throws me a dark look and then glances around the room. "Seems not."

"Wait until you see the bedroom—"

"Seriously?" Dane hisses, storming through the place. "Sadie Ray Dalton, get your ass in here," he bellows.

"Shit, princess, what did you do?"

"Oh, you know." I twirl a finger around my hair. "Added some color."

"Are you looking to get punished?" Rhett growls, and heat splashes inside of me. But then I remember why I did all this and roll back my shoulders.

"Actually, I did this to remind you that I'm here. That I'm a part of this group. So the next time you want to lie to me, perhaps you'll think twice."

"Shit, Sadie, not this again." He blows out a long breath.

"You." Dane appears, looking less than happy. "In here, now."

"Yes, Prez," I purr.

Wes chuckles as I make my way over to Dane. He grabs my hand and yanks me instead. "I love you, Sadie, girl. But I can't sleep in this shit."

"But it's so cute," I say looking at the pink sloth bed covers.

"What are they even?"

"Sloths."

"You covered my bed in *pink sloths*."

"*Our* bed."

His eyes flare and he stalks toward me. "What did you just say?"

"I said, *our* bed."

"Say it again." He hooks his arm around my waist and draws me close.

"Our bed."

"Fuck." Dane drops his head to mine. "I love hearing you call it that. Our bed. And it is, isn't it? We're actually doing this? You, me, Rhett and Pretty."

Pressing my palms to his chest, I ease back slightly to

look him in the eyes. The bitter scent of whiskey assaults my senses, but it's the love and adoration glittering in his eyes that steals my breath.

"I thought you were upset earlier," he whispers.

"Dane, I would never—"

"Shh, princess." His lips caress my skin. "The guys talked to me. They explained where your head's at."

"They did, huh?" My brow quirks.

"Yeah. They only care. We all do. But you need to listen to me when I say you have nothing to worry about, okay? I already told Crank I'm seeing the year out at school. Even told him I'm staying in Savage Falls for now."

"You did?"

"Fuck yeah. You think I'm going to up and move there and leave you here? No fucking chance, baby. I need you, Sadie Ray. I don't know how many times I have to say it, but I—"

My lips crash down on his as I start to climb his body. Dane slides his hands under my thighs and lifts me, carrying me to the nearest wall and pressing me against it.

One of his hands wraps around my throat, pinning me there as he grinds his hips into me. "You want this, princess?" His smile is wicked, matching the dark glint in his eye.

"Always."

I'm vaguely aware of the guys out in the living room, chatting and drinking beer. But if they can hear the two of us, they don't interrupt. Maybe they know we need this.

That I need this.

My eyes flick over to the door, but Dane grabs my jaw, wrenching my face back to his. "Don't worry about them. This is about you and me, Sadie, girl."

"Yes," I breathe, trying desperately to rub myself on him, needing to relieve some of the blistering tension inside me.

But Dane stays just out of reach, teasing me.

"Your little plan might have backfired, baby." His lips rub over my lips, my jaw, and down the slope of my neck. "Because your pink girly shit is only going to remind me of you. It's going to make me want you even more than I already do. And I want you all the fucking time." His hand dips between us, finding my lace panties. "You're fucking soaked for me, aren't you?"

"Yes... yes."

"Better give my girl what she needs, then." His mouth skates across my cheek and his teeth find my earlobe, biting hard. I cry out, lost to the sensations crashing over me.

He snaps his belt, works his jeans down over his hips and hooks my underwear to the side. "Ready?" His gaze snags mine, and I see everything I feel shining back at me.

His life is about to change again, but he won't leave me behind.

He won't leave us behind.

With one smooth stroke he fills me, pressing me into the wall until there's nothing between us.

"Jesus, you feel... I love this fucking pussy." He grins. A sloppy, goofy grin that melts my heart.

"I love you too," I sass, clenching my inner muscles around him. "Now fuck me, *Prez*."

He winds his hand into the hair at the back of my neck and lowers his mouth to mine.

"It would be my fucking honor."

Wes and Rhett both look up when Dane and I join them in the living room after an hour of fooling around followed by a quick shower.

"You two work it out?" Wes asks, and Rhett mumbles, "Seriously? At one point, we had to turn the TV up to full volume to drown out her screams."

"Asshole." I flip him the bird, heading to the kitchen. Dane slaps my ass as I walk off.

"What are we watching?" he asks, dropping down next to Wesley.

"Just some documentary about lions. Did you know that the females of the pack run things, not the males? It's fascinating stuff."

"Fascinating, yeah," Rhett grumbles.

"Let me guess," I call over, "you can't comprehend a woman being in charge?" My brow arches.

"They don't call the lion the king of the jungle for nothing," he retorts.

"True." I grab a bottle of water and make a beeline for him, climbing onto his lap and curling up against him. His arms automatically go around my waist, anchoring me to him.

"But you know what they do say, *Savage*." I lean in, flicking my tongue over his lips. "Behind every successful man, there is a woman."

Dane and Wes stifle their laughter.

"When we think of lions, we think of the lion king."

"You're so hung up on that word." I roll my eyes. "And yet, it's the females who hunt and raise the cubs and protect the pack. The males are just along for the ride."

"Hell yeah, we are." Dane whoops. "Especially when they ride as good as you, princess."

"What am I going to do with the three of you?" I chuckle, snuggling closer to Rhett.

"Well, for starters," Wes says, "tomorrow we have to go back to school."

"Ugh, don't remind me."

"We can always play hooky," Rhett suggests.

"Like we haven't already done enough of that. No," I sigh. "Wes is right. We have to go back. I want to graduate. I want..."

"Say it, princess. You want to go off to college and leave us."

"Rhett, that's not fair."

"It's just a joke," he shrugs. But his expression says otherwise.

And maybe he's right. If Wes and I go off to college, where does that leave the four of us?

I haven't given it too much thought because life has been moving too fast. But with Darren Creed behind us, and the threat gone, we can finally focus on the future.

A future that might very well see the four of us separated.

14

———

WES

Walking into Savage Falls High after being away for so long is weird. The interest that falls on the four of us as we approach the main building is even weirder.

I'm no stranger to being the center of attention—that comes part and parcel of being on the football team and a sidekick of the most popular boy in school.

Only, everything is different now.

I'm no longer a part of that crowd. I have no idea if I even still have a place on the team.

I've missed weeks of practice and our first games of the season. We even missed homecoming, something that didn't even occur to me until long after, thanks to the drama that's been surrounding our lives recently.

If you'd have asked me only months ago how I'd feel missing out on these huge traditions that make up our final year of high school, I probably would have said I would've been bothered, but the reality is that I actually don't care.

All that matters these days is that everyone important to me are alive and safe.

Reaching out, I take Sadie's hand, twisting our fingers together.

"You okay?" she whispers, sensing my slight unease about restarting my life here.

"Yeah, I'm good, princess. You're by my side, what could possibly be wrong?"

"You heard from any of your friends, Pretty?" Dane asks, glancing over at me from Sadie's other side.

Rhett trails behind like usual, always on full protector mode. To start with, I always thought it was because he didn't want to be seen with us, but I'm quickly learning his ways, how his mind works. And right now, he's making sure that Sadie is protected from every angle.

Every day, I see more and more just how much he really does love her. He might not say it often like Dane and I do, but he shows it in all the ways that count.

"At the beginning, I had a few messages, but nothing recently. Pretty sure they've kicked me out of their group chats."

"You okay with that?"

"I really, really am. I was never one of them. I always felt like I was on the periphery and didn't quite fit in."

"Well, you've taken that to the extreme now," Dane says, his eyes dropping to my cut.

I wasn't sure if I should wear it or not. I have no idea how it's going to be taken by everyone. But then I figured that it's my life now, and I'm more than serious about it. I'm happier than I've ever been. Mom is happier than I've ever seen her. And it's all because of the club, because of Sadie and Ray and the guys.

Eyes follow the four of us as we walk down the

hallway toward where mine and Sadie's lockers are. Whispers ripple through the small crowds of people. But the four of us walk with our heads held high and our shoulders back.

"Who'd have thought it, Wesley Noble swapping one ball for a pair of bikers' instead," some fucking dumbass comments.

Dane growls as if he's about to jump to my defense as Sadie's hand tightens in mine, but it's not enough. I manage to slip it free and bolt for the fucking cunt who's stupid enough to bad-mouth me in front of the entire school.

Pressing my forearm against his throat, I back him up against the bank of lockers. He stares at me with wide, shocked eyes as my heart thunders in my chest.

I've never really been a fighter, but I'm starting to learn that that was because I didn't have anything worth fighting for.

Now, though... now, everything is different. I have everything to fight for.

A life I love, a girl I adore, and two guys who have quickly become my brothers in all the ways that count.

"Did you want to say that again to my face, Brandon?" I growl low enough that only he can hear it.

He tries to swallow, the muscles of his neck tensing against my arm, but I'm pressing too hard for him to manage it.

"I-I—"

"Not worth it, Pretty," Dane says behind me.

I hold Brandon's eyes for a beat longer, but just as I'm about to release him another voice booms down the hallway, ensuring that I back away from him.

"Miss Dalton, Mr. Savage, Mr. Stray, and Mr. Noble.

My office. Now," Principal Winston barks, a ripple of apprehension following the demand.

"Come on." Sadie's hand slips into mine once more and we move as a unit toward Winston's office.

I've only been in there a handful of times before, and none were because I needed a warning, which I'm suspecting is exactly what we're about to walk into.

"Please, take a seat, all of you," he says, closing the door behind us. Sadie, Dane, and I follow orders, but as per usual, Rhett lingers by the door. "It's good to see you all back, and I'm relieved that life has settled down for the four of you. I understand it's been somewhat of a stressful few weeks."

"You could say that, sir," Dane agrees.

Winston nods. "Well, as glad as we are, I feel that it would be a sensible time to lay down some new foundations, if you will."

"We're not here to cause trouble, sir," Rhett speaks, his voice deep and holding a warning that I'm sure Winston hears loud and clear.

"I'm not suggesting you are. But as you've already experienced this morning, others might be. What you've all been through recently is anything but a secret around town. People talk, as you well know. And my top priority is to protect my students. All of my students."

"Spit it out, sir," Dane jokes. "We've got classes to get to."

"I need you to keep your club business out of my school."

"You want the cuts and any other... paraphernalia gone, I assume," Rhett finishes for him.

He nods. "I think it's for the best."

"People will still talk whether they wear their cuts or

not, sir," Sadie tries arguing. "The school doesn't have a dress code, so I don't know how—"

"It's fine, Sadie, girl," Dane assures her, clearly just wanting to get this over with and get on with the reason we're really here—to fucking graduate, so we can embark on our futures.

"While you might be right, Sadie, I'm sure the board would happily agree that we also don't condone such obvious displays of gang membersh—"

Sadie's chair legs screech across the old, tiled floor. "Our club is not a gang," she spits, her small hands balled into fists.

"I-I know, I just mean that—"

"We get it. No one is going to forget who we are, with or without cuts on," Rhett spits, twisting the doorknob at his hip and wrenching the door open. "Let's go."

We stand to leave, and I'm also at the door, the others already out of the office, before he calls me back.

"Yes, sir?"

"Coach would like to see you in his office."

"With all due respect, sir, I think it's more important I just get to class."

Not letting him get another word in, I slip from the room and close the door behind me.

"This is bullshit," Sadie hisses, making Winston's assistant's head snap up.

"The bell is about to ring. I suggest you four start moving toward where you're meant to be."

"Come on, princess. I'll walk you to English lit," I say, aware that Rhett and Dane are heading in the opposite direction for their morning classes.

We leave the admin ladies behind right as the bell does ring. The second we're out in the hallway, Dane drags Sadie from my side and pushes her up against the wall.

"You need an escape from class, all you've got to do is message me and I'll meet you in the girls' bathroom in a heartbeat, princess."

"The one with the mirrors?" she asks, her voice raspy with desire.

"Hell yeah. One day, the four of us should probably have some fun in there."

"In the girls' bathroom?" I ask, wondering if Dane's freaky fetishes have finally tipped over into complete crazy town.

"Yeah, man. The fucking mirrors... you get to see everything. It's fucking insane."

"We need to move," Rhett growls.

"Yeah, yeah, hang on," Dane hisses. "Love you, Sadie girl." He drops a knee-weakening kiss on her before taking a huge step back, making no attempt to hide the fact that he has to rearrange himself before nodding at Rhett as if he's now ready to embark on his day.

"See you later," Rhett says, giving Sadie a much more chaste kiss before nodding at me and taking off down the hall behind Dane.

"Ready?"

"I guess. Is it just me, or do you no longer feel like you belong here?" she asks as we make our way to our lockers, just like we were when we first entered the building.

"It's not just you, princess."

"Just a few months, right? Tell me it'll be worth it."

"It'll be worth it. We won't let anyone hurt you here, Sadie."

"I'm not scared of anyone here, Wes. I just... I don't know. With everything that's happened, I kinda feel like

I've outgrown it, you know? We've all grown up so much in just a few weeks. We've embarked on our own lives, made some life-changing decisions. This," she says, holding her hands out from her sides, "feels a little insignificant in the grand scheme of things."

"I know what you mean," I mutter.

"You need to talk to Coach. He might help you decide what you want to do."

"I'm not sure I have a decision to make where football is concerned."

"Of course you do. I've seen you play. You're incredible, Wes. As good as any of those college players we've watched on TV."

"You've watched me play, princess?"

"Once or twice. Quinn has dragged me to a few games over the years."

"Fucking knew you always wanted me," I growl, nuzzling her neck and reveling in her unique cherry scent.

"Nah, I thought you were an uptight jock."

"Well, I hope I've managed to prove you wrong." I drag my tongue up the length of her throat, making her shudder.

"Yeah, and then some. Wes," she moans, her head falling back against the lockers. "We need to move."

"I know. I just need a minute," I confess, stilling with my lips pressed against her throat.

"Are you really okay? I know it's weird being back here, but it must be even stranger for you. It's like you've come back a completely different person."

"No," I say, pulling my head free and staring into her eyes. "I haven't come back as a different person. I've come back as me. The real me."

A smile twitches at her lips as she stares back at me, her hand lifting to cup my cheek. "I love you, Wesley Noble."

"Good. Because I love you too, Sadie Ray Dalton. Now, let's get to class and learn some shit. We've got futures to make."

"Together?"

"Always, princess. You're stuck with me now."

A smile pulls at my lips as she opens her locker and sorts her things out.

It might feel all kinds of weird being here, but what I just told her is true. I've been hiding this version of me for way too long, afraid of what people, my father, might think.

Well, I'm done caring. Savage Falls High can either like this me or not. I really don't give a single fuck.

Pulling my girl into my side, I drop a kiss to the top of her head and step toward the next chapter in our lives.

15

SADIE

School isn't the same.

Before meeting the guys, I had my sights set on acing senior year, graduating, spreading my wings and getting the hell out of Savage Falls.

Everything is different now.

I can't imagine leaving them, being ripped apart by time and space. Wes and I could apply to Colton U, sure. It's closer, only a stone's throw away from Red Ridge and Savage Falls, really. But if I'm being honest with myself, I don't want us to be apart, not even for a second.

I know Dane has the club now, he has responsibilities, and Rhett too, if my dad puts his money where his mouth is and makes him VP. They won't be able to come to Colton whenever they like and play house with me and Wes, not now.

And I get it. I get that the club was theirs long before I came along. But when I look into the future now, I see the four of us. Together.

Right now, though, it's a pipe dream. A fantasy. Wes

has already given up so much, I can't ask him to give up college too. And I want the college experience, I do.

I just don't know if I want it enough anymore.

"Hey, you okay?" River bumps my shoulder with hers as we sit in the quad eating lunch.

"Yeah, just thinking..."

"If it's about my brother, you can keep those thoughts to yourself." She chuckles, taking a bite of her apple.

"So what's happening with you? I feel like we haven't talked in days."

"That's because we haven't." There's no malice in her voice, only gentle understanding. "But I get it. You've had a lot going on."

"It doesn't excuse neglecting you, though." I smile, but it feels forced. "Sorry, I've been a crap friend."

"No, you've been dealing with a lot. And I'm okay. I have Quinn and Jax."

"Ah, yes, Jax... how are things there?"

"Things are... confusing. He's like my best friend. We talk about everything. But every time I..."

"You what?" I ask, curious.

"Every time I try to get closer to him, he completely shuts me down. I think he's friend zoned me."

"What? No way. This is Jax we're talking about. The guy worships you."

"I wish that were true. I know he likes me, I feel it every time he looks at me. But he won't act on it." She picks absentmindedly at her packet of chips.

"Want me to talk to him?"

"What? No!" Panic floods her expression. "Promise me you won't. I don't want... just don't, okay?"

"My lips are sealed. Jax is a good guy, Riv. One of the best. But he's young and impressionable, and he's probably shitting himself over Rhett pulling the big brother card."

"Ugh, don't remind me." Her eyes roll. "I just wish he'd let me make my own decisions now. I'm not a child anymore."

"No, but you are his little sister, and he spent a long time trying to keep you away from this life."

"I love this life, Sadie. It's everything I never had. Family. Friendship. A sense of belonging. It was just me and Rhett for so long, and he was never truly there, ya know? My mom was always high, off her face on whatever drugs she could get her hands on. Ray coming around always made things better, but then he'd leave and... sorry, you probably don't want to hear about this."

"It's okay." I swallow. "You can talk to me."

"Home never felt like home. But moving here, meeting you and Quinn and Dee and Rosita and Jada and all the other women, I feel a part of something, and I've never had that before."

Her words make my chest feel heavy. "Well, you do now," I say. "I know things have been scary the last few weeks, but it isn't always like this. And now things with Darren Creed are... over, we can all relax a little. In fact, I heard there's going to be a party Friday to celebrate Dane's promotion. You should totally wear something sexy and put the moves on Jax."

"P-put the moves on him?" She gawks at me.

"Yeah, you know. Try to seduce him."

"Oh, I'm not sure—"

"You like him, right?" She nods. "And you want him to make a move?" Another nod. "So you've got to make it impossible for him to resist you."

"But Rhett—"

"Leave Rhett to me." I wink.

"You really think I should go for it?"

"Yeah. Jax likes you. And life's too short to not go after what you want."

"Yeah, you're right. You're totally right." River sits a little taller, nodding to herself.

I'm going to be in so much trouble when Rhett finds out about this, but River deserves to be happy. She deserves to find a guy who will treat her like a princess. And Jax is a good guy. Rhett can't dispute that.

I just need to gently persuade him to let her grow up a little.

Good thing for me, the art of persuasion is my forte.

———

"This is a surprise," I say, stepping up to Wes as I leave my last class of the day.

"Rhett and Dane had to skip out in fifth period."

"They did?" I frown.

"Yeah, something about—"

"Club business." He nods, and I ask, "You weren't needed?"

"Nope. Besides, someone had to stay behind and look out for you."

"Seriously, you think I need babysitting?" I drop my eye to my waistband, where my knife sits tucked away. I haven't felt the need to carry it with me so often lately. But coming back here today, I found myself grabbing it before we left the apartment.

"Please tell me that isn't what I think it is?"

"What?" I shrug. "A girl has to be prepared."

"You think we'd let anyone hurt you?" He crowds me

against the locker bank, sliding his hand above my head and caging me in.

"And what about if anyone tries to hurt you, huh?"

"So, it's true then?" a familiar voice says, and Wes inhales a sharp breath as he turns to meet Evan.

"Walk on, Henley." Wes moves a little to shield me from Evan's sight, but I step around him to face him head on.

God, it feels like forever since I saw him. So much has happened. Sometimes, I feel like a completely different person. And yet, he looks exactly the same—with the addition of a couple of scars, one along his jaw and one on his eyebrow.

Scars I know my guys put there.

A smug smirk tugs at my lips. "Evan," I drawl. "So nice to see you in one piece."

"God, Sadie Ray." Nyla steps up to Evan and wraps her perfectly manicured hand around his arm. "Do you have to be such a bitch?"

"As opposed to what exactly? A cheap, plastic Barbie?"

Wes snorts, and a warning growl rumbles in Evan's chest.

"Oh, this is cute. Ken Doll is coming to Barbie's defense. You know, you two deserve each other." My voice is all sugar and sweetness.

"You know, Noble." Evan takes a step forward. "I used to think you were something. That you were going somewhere. But now look at you, slumming it with the trash."

One second Wes is standing beside me, and the next he has Evan pinned up against the wall, his arm across his windpipe. "You want to say that again, asshole?"

"Wes, he's not worth it." I spot a teacher at the end of the hall. "Come on, Pretty, let the asshole go." I squeeze his shoulder, trying to snap him out of it.

"Stay the fuck out of our way," he seethes.

"Or what, *Pretty*? what the hell are you going to—" Evan gurgles as Wes presses his forearm harder.

"This is the last time I'm going to say it. Stay. The. Fuck. Away. From. Us."

"Mr. Noble, Miss Dalton, what is—"

"That's our cue, babe." I grab Wes's arm and yank hard, motioning toward the doors.

"Welcome back, Henley." Wes shoots Evan a sly wink before hauling ass with me.

"Mr. Noble, don't you—"

We spill outside in breathless laughter. "Shit, he's still coming," I say, spotting the teacher heading straight for us.

"Come on." Wes grabs my hand, and we make a run for the truck.

"You have the keys?"

"Sure do." He retrieves them from his pocket.

We make it inside just as the teacher bursts through the door. He spots us, a scowl on his face, his hands poised on his hips.

"Jenkins isn't happy," I chuckle as Wes backs the truck out of the parking spot and takes off toward the gates.

"Yeah, well, Jenkins can kiss my ass."

"Who are you, and what have you done with Wesley Noble?"

"Didn't you get the memo, princess?" He shoots me a cocky sideway glance. "Noble has left the building. I'm Pretty now."

"Oh my God," I breathe through the laughter heaving my chest.

"Evan is such a fucking asshole. I can't believe I was ever friends with him."

"It was convenient."

"It was a fucking sham." He grips the wheel tighter. "My whole life was about keeping up appearances, making *him* happy." He spits the words.

I scoot closer, resting my hand on his knee. "He can't hurt you or your mom anymore, Wes." My heart cinches. "My dad would put a bullet in his skull before he ever got to lay a hand on either of you."

The words should terrify me, terrify us both, but they don't. Because it's true. There isn't a single thing my dad wouldn't do for the people he loves.

"Yeah, well hopefully he took Ray's words seriously and will stay away." Wes stares straight ahead as he drives towards the other side of town. But there's something in his eyes, a flickering uncertainty that makes dread curl in my stomach.

He isn't convinced we've heard the last of Grant Noble.

A thought hits me.

"Wes, you don't think your dad had something to do with the raid, do you?"

Because Grant has connections, friends in high places. Friends who have made it clear time and time again they'd like to see the club in ruins.

He blows out a long breath. "I think it's a real possibility."

"But my dad said it was just the new commissioner reminding him that they're watching."

His haunted gaze flicks to mine. "Let's hope he's right."

Because that's the last thing we need—another war. One with Wes's arrogant, self-serving, narcissistic father.

God, when will this ever end? My head drops back against the headrest, and I let out a weary sigh.

"Hey." Wes's hand slides over mine and he threads our fingers together. "I didn't mean to upset you."

"I know. I just... will it ever get easier?"

"It will," he says, smiling. "It has to."

If only he believed his own words.

"Where are we going?" Sadie asks as I sail past the turn that will take us back to the apartment.

"I'm not ready to share you again yet."

"Oh?" she asks, her hand sliding dangerously high up my leg. "I thought Rhett and Dane were busy at the compound.

"Maybe. I'm not risking it, though. I miss you."

"We've barely been apart," she points out.

She's right. We've been inseparable for weeks, but I need some time, just the two of us, and the guys being called away is perfect.

As I pull the truck to a stop on the side of the road, she looks out, her brow wrinkling in confusion. "So you're bringing me to the store?"

"No. This is just a pit stop."

Dropping a kiss to her cheek, I jump from the truck and jog toward the store to grab what I want.

"Well, this is mysterious," Sadie says when I rejoin her and start the truck.

"I like to keep you on your toes, princess."

To my surprise, she doesn't immediately open the bags to find out what I bought.

"So where are we going?"

"It's a surprise."

Sadie looks over at me with a smile on her face, but whatever it is she wants to say, she holds back.

"What is it?"

She shakes her head. "I'm just glad that you're happy, Wes. I know I didn't really know you before, but—"

"I am happy. And I didn't need that run-in with those assholes in school today to confirm that I'm exactly where I should be now."

"Did Coach catch up with you?" she asks, twisting her fingers with mine.

"Yep," I sigh.

"And?"

"He gave me the long speech I was expecting about throwing away a successful football career if I choose this path. How I'm wasting my talent."

"You don't have to give anything up, Wes. I'm sure there's a way to—"

"Sadie," I sigh. "I love your positivity and your need to fight for me. But honestly, I'm not doing anything I don't want to do."

"But you're going to play again, right?"

My grip on the wheel tightens as my body tenses, and she's perceptive enough not to miss it.

"Wesley?"

Shaking my head, I say the words I never thought I would. "No. I'm no longer a Saint."

"What?" she cries, turning to me, her face twisted in

concern. "No, I won't let you give this up. You can't. Football is your future, your dream."

Chewing on the inside of my cheek, I turn off the main road onto the street that leads us to our destination.

It's not until I've parked and killed the engine that I turn to her. Tears pool in her eyes and she worries her bottom lip.

"I thought football was my future. My dad convinced me it was, and I didn't ever get a chance to consider anything else. I've seen other options now."

She smiles sadly at me. "You told Coach you didn't want to play anymore?"

"Umm... not exactly. Come on, let's get out."

It's not until I speak that she actually looks out the window. Despite her concern over my future, a soft smile plays on her lips.

"Wow, it feels like forever since we were last here."

Snatching her hand, I brush my lips over her knuckles. "The first time you kissed me."

"Man, I was pissed that night," she says, thinking back.

"And look where it got you," I laugh.

"Come on, I want to kiss you under the arches again, Pretty."

As I climb from the car, I think back to the miserable shell of a person she found here that night. I put on a solid front, I knew that. Well, I think I did. No one ever called me out on it until Sadie, so I just assumed that everyone fell for my act and thought my life was as amazing as I made out.

I feel like an entirely different person now, and it makes me realize just how true those words were that I said to Sadie earlier.

The old Wesley Noble is well and truly dead. He vanished that moment I fled my house with Mom to get away from Dad. But I'm pretty sure I never would have found the person hiding beneath the lies and fake smiles if it weren't for Sadie. And maybe even the guys.

They've all shown me that there are other ways of handling things. That hiding, suffering silently, watching those you love slowly lose themselves, isn't how life needs to be.

My father has controlled too much of my life. It's time I took back ownership. And so what if I have to leave a few things, a few people behind? I've got something much more important to hold on to now.

With the bag tucked under my arm, I wrap my other one around Sadie's shoulder and pull her into my body, dropping my lips to the top of her head.

"Hmm... and here I was secretly hoping for more than a kiss."

She laughs, and it helps the weight of everything that's been pressing down on my shoulders lift a little.

We settle ourselves in the exact same spot as the last time we were here, and she stares down at the bag as I open it between us. I pull out an array of snacks, most of which are of the cake and candy variety.

"My favorites," Sadie announces, reaching for a packet of Twizzlers and ripping the top open.

Twisting one up into a knot, she throws it into her mouth and chews as I grab a sandwich. "So, you were saying," she mumbles around the candy.

"I've lost my place on the team. Even if I wanted to play—"

"Y-you what?" Sadie screeches, damn near choking on the Twizzler in the process.

"It's fine, Sadie." I sigh. "I was expecting it. I've missed training for weeks. All the games. I wasn't expecting them to let me back in and pick up where I left off."

"B-but—"

"I let them down when I chose you. When I chose this," I say, pointing to the cut I put back on before we left school.

"I fucking hate this. I feel like I'm holding you back."

"From playing a game with a bunch of pricks who don't like me and wanted to hurt you? This is how it's meant to be. I don't regret it, not for a second."

"But—"

"No," I say, reaching over and pressing my fingers to her lips. "No more arguing and taking the blame for all this. I knew the consequences, and the choices were mine to make."

She huffs in annoyance, but she knows I'm right.

Football is in my past. Sadie and the guys are my future.

"I can't believe he just kicked you out. You were the best player on that team."

A smile curls at my lips. "You really were watching me, huh?"

"I mean, I know shit all about football really, but you always seemed to know what you were doing. And," she adds before I can say anything, "your ass always looked killer in those pants."

"Ah, now the truth comes out. You were just there to fulfill your twisted fantasies."

"Well, not really, because now I'm not going to get up close and personal with those pants and have you fuck me in the locker room after a game."

Reaching down, I tug at my sweatpants.

"See, look what you've done," she says with a pout. "Now I'm not going to finish senior year with my bucket list checked off."

I laugh at her, loving that she's able to spin this to make the whole situation less painful.

"Oh yeah? Tell me more about this bucket list," I demand, abandoning my food and leaning closer to her and nuzzling her neck, drowning in her scent.

"Well," she says, with a laugh, "I've had to modify it a little seeing as I've now got more than one boy to make use of. And I've already had sex with Dane in the girls' bathroom."

"Okay, so bathroom. Check. Locker rooms... where else?"

"Classroom, obviously. Parking lot. Around the back of the library. You know, that place where everyone always gets caught."

"Because Ms. White is a total prude who doesn't understand teenagers."

"Do you think she's ever had sex in her life?" Sadie asks, sounding almost concerned about Ms. White's lack of action.

"No. Never."

"Poor woman. Can you imagine?"

"Says the girl with three guys getting her off at every possibility."

"Every possibility?" she asks, quirking a brow at me. "I don't seem to be anywhere near heaven right now, Pretty."

"You're spending time with me, of course you are."

She laughs. "How did no one figure out before that the club was exactly where your oversized ego belonged?"

"No fucking clue, princess."

Wrapping my hands around her waist, I lift her from the ground beside me with little effort and place her on my lap. "Better?" I ask, wrapping my hand around the side of her neck and dragging her toward me so I can capture her lips.

"Hmm," she moans into our kiss, scooting forward on my lap so she's sitting right on my growing dick.

"Never think I've settled for this life, Sadie Ray," I say sincerely. "What I've got now is so much better than football. I chose you before, and I'll choose you every time."

"Fuck. I love you, Wesley Noble, with or without those tight football pants."

"Pretty sure I've got some I could wear just for you one day."

"Yeah?" she asks, her face lighting up.

"Might even let you play with the balls."

"Fucking hell, you goof."

Gripping her hips, I hold her still as I grind against her, making her laughter turn into a needy moan. "Need you, princess."

"Always."

Dipping my hand under her skirt, I find her soaked panties and push two fingers inside her.

"I love you, Wes," she says, her body trembling as her eyes hold mine. "I'm so glad you chose me."

"It's about time. Where the hell have you two been?" Stray barks when we stumble into the apartment an hour or so later, still riding high from our time at the Arches.

"Oh, you know, just having a little fun with our girl."

"Without us?" Dane asks, placing his hand over his heart as if we've hurt him.

"Get over yourself, you big baby," Sadie says, walking over to him and crushing her lips to his.

"Dinner's ready," a deeper voice says from the kitchen.

"Whoa, Rhett cooked?" I ask, only now noticing that the table's set for dinner. "Tell me he's wearing that frilly pink apron Sadie bought."

"Fuck no," Rhett booms, stepping into the room with plates. "I ordered in, and I already told Sadie the terms for having that fucking pink thing anywhere near me."

I shoot Sadie a look, and she smothers a chuckle, which only spikes my curiosity more.

"I'll get the drinks," I say, following Rhett back to the kitchen to grab the rest of the food.

With four glasses of water in my hands, I come to a stop in the kitchen doorway and run my eyes over the three of them as they laugh around the table.

Yeah, there wasn't ever really a choice here.

"Come on, Pretty. You've already kept us waiting long enough," Dane calls, forcing me into action once more.

I sit down with a smile on my face, and it doesn't even falter when Rhett turns to me and says, "Sorry to hear about the team, man."

My brows pinch. "How'd you hear about that already?"

Rhett and Dane share a look that makes my stomach knot.

"What?"

"What happened?" I glance between Rhett and Dane as they both sit silently, wearing expressions of regret.

"Seriously, guys," I press when they don't answer.

"Shit, Pretty, we didn't—"

"Just spit it out." Wes clenches his fist on the table.

"When we were at the compound... your mom got a call."

"My mom?"

"Yeah, from your old man."

An icy chill goes through the room as Wes goes rigid beside me. "He called her?"

"Yeah, he... uh... he wanted her to hear the news firsthand."

"No," I gasp, piecing together everything they're not saying.

"He did this?" Wes leaps up, the chair legs scraping across the floor tiles. "You're telling me that piece of shit got me pulled from the team?"

"Easy, man." Dane jumps up too. "He's just trying to

get a reaction, let you guys know he still holds some power."

"Fuck," Wes hisses. "FUCK!" His fist shoots out, smashing against the wall, a sickening crunch going through the air.

"Shit, Pretty." Dane rushes to his side to inspect the damage. Wes's knuckles are split wide open, blood trickling down his fingers.

"Here, let me look at that." I leap into action, going over to the sink to fill a bowl with cold water and grab a towel.

"I'm fine," Wes argues, but Dane grips his shoulder and shoves him toward me. "You need to clean that up and ice it."

"Feels better though, right?" Rhett asks.

Wes snorts. "It would feel a hell of a lot better if it was his face. I can't believe he called her... fucking asshole."

"What did you expect?" Rhett finally comes over, leaning his hip against the counter as I gently clean the blood off Wes's busted hand. He barely flinches, anger pouring off him in thick waves.

"Ray has everything he wants. You came over to the dark side, Pretty. Your old man wasn't just going to let that go. He might not be able to get what he truly wants, but that doesn't mean he can't still hurt you or your mom."

"You and Ray should have just put a bullet in his skull," Wes spits. "He deserves it."

"Wes," I whisper, coaxing him to look at me. "You don't mean that."

"Don't I? I don't care about football, Sadie Ray, I don't. But knowing he called her, taunted her with this... it makes me fucking sick to my stomach." He lets out a weary sigh as I finish cleaning up his hand. "Fuck, that hurts."

"Suck it up, Pretty." Dane slaps his cheeks. "You're playing with the big boys now. A little blood never hurt anyone."

"Either help or go away," I scold, carefully drying Wes's hand, ready to wrap it.

"We could still go after daddy dearest, make him pay once and for all," Dane suggests.

"We can't." Rhett blows out an exasperated breath. "Grant Noble is too well connected. Made it pretty clear that if anything happened to him, he's taken precautions."

"He did?" I ask. "You never told me any of this." Irritation ripples down my spine.

"Because it doesn't matter." Wes shrugs, raking a hand through his dirty blond hair. "For as much as I'd like to see Ray take him out, watching me and Mom walk away and into the arms of the club is a far worse punishment."

"So, we go to Principal Winston or the school board. They can't just throw you off the team because—"

"No," he says flatly.

"N-no?"

"I'm done, princess. I won't fight to stay on a team I don't even want to be a part of anymore. Like I already told you, football is in my past. It just fucking kills me that he did that to her."

"But what about college?" I ask, my heart aching. Nothing about this is fair, but people are scared of what they don't know, and I've been fighting the same prejudice half my life.

"I can still go to college. I just won't be playing football." There's a finality in his voice that makes me glance at Dane. He gives a subtle shake of his head. Leave it.

So I press my lips together, trapping the words I so desperately want to say.

"I should go see my mom," Wes adds.

"I'll come with, Pretty. Keep you company."

"I'm not riding bitch on your bike." Wes throws him a knowing look.

"We can take the truck, spoilsport."

"I'll come too. I—"

"No, you stay here," Wes rushes out, a little too quickly, and dejection stings me. "It's late, and we have school tomorrow."

"Oh, okay." I fold my arms over my chest and take a step back, worrying my bottom lip. But if Wes notices, he doesn't let on as he grabs the truck keys and makes for the door.

"Keep my side of the bed warm." Dane drops a kiss on my cheek. "We won't be long."

I nod, too overwhelmed to talk.

I'm used to Dane and Rhett shutting me out but not Wes. Never him.

"You okay?" Rhett steps up behind me, sliding his arms around my waist and holding me. I sink back against his chest, letting out a small sigh.

"I'll be fine," I lie, watching Wes and Dane disappear out of the apartment without so much as a backward glance.

"Sadie Ra—"

"I'm fine, Rhett." I shuck out of his hold. "I said I'll be fine."

"You should try to get some sleep," Rhett says from the door. After Wes and Dane left, I took a hot shower—alone —and then crawled into bed clutching my cell phone, waiting for Wes to text me.

He hasn't.

"I want to be awake when they get back."

A deep frown crinkles his eyes, and my heart sinks.

"They're not coming back," I whisper, the words shredding my insides.

"Stray thinks Wes and his mom need some time and we should probably give it to them." He comes into the room, dropping onto the edge of the bed.

"You think I don't know that?" I snap, guilt punching through me. "I'm sorry, I just... it's not a nice feeling, watching one of you repeatedly walk away from me."

"Princess," Rhett tsks, "we fucking love you." He takes my hand, threading our fingers together. "But there's gonna be times when we have our own shit to deal with. It doesn't mean we're shutting you out or betraying you."

"I just want to help. I just want to be there... for all of you. I love you so much, Rhett, and I'm terrified that something is going to rip us apart again."

He scoots along the bed, taking my face in his big hands. "Nothing is ever going to come between us. We're in, princess. We're all fucking in. I don't even know when it happened, but it did. You, me, Stray... Pretty... there's no going back for us. But this life... you know what it means."

"You know, it's funny. I never felt like I had much to lose before all this. Sure, I had my dad, Quinn, my family... but I was so eager to shake the club's hold over my life..."

"And now?" His voice is thick as he gazes down at me the intense way only Rhett can.

"Now I have too much to lose." I pull from his grip and trail my fingers up his arm. "It makes me feel... vulnerable, knowing that if I lose any of you or if something happened..."

"Shh, princess. Nothing is gonna happen to us. Darren Creed is dead. Grant Noble knows he can't go up against the club without some serious repercussions."

I sit up, leaning in to run my nose along Rhett's jaw. "You've all turned me into a sap."

He pulls away, cocking a brow. "You have met me, right?" A smirk traces his lips. "I didn't see you coming, princess. Not for a second. And I fought it. Fuck, I fought it so much. But I need you, Sadie Ray. You don't just own my balls, baby girl, you own my fucking black heart, too."

"Rhett Savage," I chuckle. "That might just be the nicest thing you've ever said to me."

"Good, now get over here and ride my dick."

"Annnnd there he is, everyone."

"Joke. I'm joking. Well, unless you wanna..." His eyes drop to his crotch.

Desire swirls low in my stomach. It's so hard not to be affected when Rhett looks at me with such reverence, as if I'm the center of his entire world.

Without words, I climb onto my knees and slide over his lap, locking my hands around the back of his neck. "Hi." I smile.

"I didn't come in here for this." A frown crinkles his expression.

"I know, but maybe I need this." I always need this.

Leaning in, I trace my lips over his mouth, peppering his face with little kisses.

"Sadie Ray," he starts, his hands clamped tightly on my hips as if he's ready to push me away... or pull me closer.

"I need you," I confess, rolling my hips against him.

He lets out a pained groan. "You're not playing fair, princess."

"And you're playing hard to get." I smirk, gripping his chin between my fingers.

"I'll give you hard to get." Rhett lifts and flips me, pinning me to the mattress. My hand slides over his shoulders, my eyes tracing the ink curling around his thick biceps.

"You are annoyingly hot, Rhett Savage."

"Damn right, I am."

"So cocky." I roll my eyes.

"I love you, princess." His expression softens. "You know that, right?"

"Rhett, I... I know." Emotion clogs my throat, so I pull him down closer, our mouths crashing together, hard and unyielding, neither of us willing to concede as our tongues fight for dominance.

This. This is what I need when things get too much.

"Fuck me," I whisper against his hot, wet kisses. "Show me how much you want me."

His eyes darken, a growl rumbling up his throat. Pushing his hand between us, Rhett snaps his belt, pushing his jeans off his hips.

"You, Sadie Ray... it's only you." He slides his hands under my ass and lifts me, slamming inside of me. I cry out, clutching onto his shoulders as he lets me have it, as he shows me with actions, not just words, how much he needs me too.

How much he loves me.

And when we're both breathless and sated, in that quiet moment right after we lose ourselves to our carnal instincts, I feel strong.

I feel safe.

I feel like nothing will ever come between us.

"Can't believe you didn't want to be my bitch," I say once we've pulled out from the parking lot outside our apartment.

Anger still comes off Pretty in waves, and other than pulling off into a dark lane where no one can see us, I have no idea how to help but with humor.

He grunts in response, his fingers curling into fists as he sits there, his body pulled tight with tension.

"Sadie will have your balls if you fuck up her bandage."

Although he doesn't respond, he stops, clearly agreeing with me. "I hate him. I hate him so fucking much, and I have no idea how to deal with it," he says after the longest silence.

"There's no right answer for this kind of shit, bro. You've just got to do what feels right. You need time, take it. You need to fight, I'm right here. You wanna fuck, I'm sure Sadie would be all-in. I know I am," I say, shooting him a wink.

"We can't solve all our issues with sex, Dane," he hisses.

"Can't we? It's been working for us so well this far."

Wes glances over at me, a wrecked expression on his face.

"It's not always like this," I assure him. "Club life is usually... more fun and less bloodshed."

"I'm starting to like the bloodshed," he admits quietly.

"If you really want him dead, all you gotta do is say the word. We'll figure it out."

He sighs, the breath full of pain and hatred. It's something I'm all too familiar with.

"It'll get better. We'll get through this, just like we did with my shit."

He nods, but I'm not sure he believes a word of it as we pull through the compound gates, coming to a stop beside Ray and Pacman's bikes, and Quinn's car.

To my surprise, he doesn't immediately reach for the door.

Sensing that he needs something, I reach over and wrap my hand around his thigh, squeezing. "We're in this together, okay?"

He nods but says nothing, finally reaching for the door and slipping from the truck.

Everything is normal as we step into the clubhouse. Pitbull is behind the bar, wiping down the counter. Quinn and River are sitting at our usual table at the back of the room with Diesel and his sister, Kat.

They all look up as we head deeper into the room. But as I take a step toward them, Wes beelines straight for his mom, who's sitting with Rosi and Jada.

The second she sees Wes, she hops up and rushes

over to him, her eyes full of unshed tears. "I'm so sorry," she breathes as Wes engulfs her in a bear hug.

I immediately understand what he said earlier about the look Grant fucking Noble puts on her face, because all the progress she's made over the past few weeks seems to have been washed away with one phone call. Her face is pale, deep frown lines marring her brow. She smiles at Wes, but it's forced. The sight makes my stomach twist.

"What's going on?" Quinn asks as I take a seat beside her.

"Grant Noble thought it would be a good idea to stick his nose into our business."

"Great," she mutters. "You've met Kat, right? Diesel's sister."

I lift my chin in greeting. "Yeah, we've met."

"How's it going, Prez?" Diesel asks with a smirk.

"It's good. Looking forward to whipping you lot into shape."

He shakes his head, a teasing grin on his face. "You think you Savage Falls lot are so much better than us."

"Well, yeah. That would be because we are," I shoot back. Yo, Pitbull," I call, earning our prospect's attention. "What's a guy gotta do around here to get a beer? Pretty needs one too," I shout, nodding to where he's still standing with his mom.

"You can get back, if you want," Pretty says, coming over to where I'm now sitting with River, Quinn and Pitbull. "Sadie is probably waiting for you."

"You not coming?" I ask, my brows pulling together in concern.

"I... uh..."

Conflict wars across his face, the pull between his mom and Sadie ripping him in two.

"I'll catch you guys later," I say to no one in particular as I stand, clap my hand on Pretty's shoulder and guide him away from the others.

"We'll stay," I tell him, knowing that's what he needs right now.

"But Sadie," he argues.

"Sadie is with Rhett, and I'm sure he's more than glad for some alone time with her. There's nothing wrong with needing your mom, Wes."

"I hate the look he puts on her face even when he's nowhere near us."

"Where is she?" I ask, noticing that she's vanished from the clubhouse.

"With Ray, out back."

"Let's go then."

Ray has the best room at the compound, which I guess he deserves, seeing as he's the boss, and he's made himself a little backyard that the rest of us don't get to see very often.

"Well, what are we waiting for?"

"You can go, Stra—"

"Shut the fuck up, Pretty."

He does as he's told, and we walk down to Ray's room side by side. He falls silent once more. His anger has lessened, but he's still struggling.

The scent of Ray's cigars hits me the second we step into his room.

"Stray," Ray booms when he spots me. "To what do we owe the pleasure, Prez?"

I shake my head, hardly able to believe the words.

"Just keeping your prospect in check."

Something weird ripples through me as it hits me that Pretty is Ray's prospect. I look between the two of them as Wes drops into the seat beside Victoria and takes her hand in his.

"You sure you're okay, son?"

"Yeah." I fall down into the chair beside him, lifting my beer to my lips, my eyes flicking between Wes and Victoria.

In that moment, I don't care about the repercussions. I want to personally find that motherfucker and put a bullet through his brain for ever laying a finger on the pair of them.

I startle when I look back at Victoria and find her watching me. Despite her obvious distress, I don't miss her curiosity when I smile back.

Dammit. The last thing I want is to cause Wes any more issues right now.

"So what's the plan, then?" I ask Ray, turning to him and giving Victoria and Wes some privacy.

"I'm not sure." He scrubs his jaw. "We need to wait and see if he plans on leaving it at that, if his need to ruin his son's future is enough for him."

"You think it will be?" I ask, disbelief coating my words.

There's no way this is enough for a man like Grant Noble. He spent his life trying to bring down the very club that has taken on those he wanted to protect from it.

Putting an end to Wes's football career is nowhere near the end of this.

175

"No," Ray replies tensely. "I'm just hoping we can get a read on the situation before he makes his next move. He thinks he's smart. But we're better."

"I hope you're right."

He nods, sitting forward in his seat as the firepit in the middle of the small space crackles between us. "They don't deserve any more shit. They've been through enough."

"Agreed."

"I need another drink," he says, standing.

"I can go," I offer.

"Nah, you're good. I want a word with Pretty, anyway. Son," he says, capturing Wes's attention, "let's go get your mom a refill."

Wes stands and follows Ray out, leaving just Victoria and me alone with the fire.

"Thanks for bringing him," she says after a few seconds.

"No problem. I'm just sorry you've gotta deal with that asshole."

A humorless laugh falls from her lips. "It's my own fault for falling for his bullshit all those years ago."

"None of this is your fault. You couldn't have predicted any of this."

She lets out a sad sigh.

"And anyway," I add, "it brought you back here. Where you belong."

She nods sadly, her hand lifting to wipe away a stray tear. "You're good for him, you know. All of you."

Heat hits my cheeks, but as much as I might want to avert my eyes to stop her seeing just how her words affect me, I can't.

"We're just glad we can help. Be here for both of you."

"I didn't realize how miserable he was before you all came into his life. I hate that I didn't see that his smiles weren't genuine. That the future I thought he wanted was actually being forced on him."

I open my mouth to respond, but I quickly find that I don't have any words.

"I always thought football was his life. What does that say about me?"

"Football was his life, Victoria. It was all he knew. But that doesn't mean that it's all he is."

"I know. I know," she sighs. "I just hate that it's been ripped away from him."

"He really doesn't seem that bothered about the football part of all of this. He's more concerned about you."

"I feel like I've completely failed him, Dane. I—"

She chokes on her words, and I jump from my seat across from her to be by her side and take her hand. "I'm so glad he's got you. I don't know what he would have done if it weren't for you, Sadie, Rhett and the club."

"He's strong, Victoria. He would've been fine."

She looks at me, really looks at me. It creeps me out a little, because I can't help feeling like she can see too much, but I hold steady and let her search for whatever she's looking for.

"You really care about him, don't you?"

"I... uh... he's turning out to be a very good friend, yeah."

She smiles at me, but the twinkle in her eye tells me that she can read between the lines. "I love my son, Dane.

I love him no matter what. And if there were something more here..."

"Victoria, I don't think—"

"I'm just saying that you'd always have my blessing."

"I appreciate that, I do. But that's not what's going on here." I don't think. "I care about Wes. But this thing we've got going on... It's about Sadie. She's the glue that holds us together. She's..." I trail off, a soft smile playing on my lips as I think of her.

"She's the one who's stolen all your hearts." I nod and she adds, "I know. I see it anytime the three of you look at her. You're so lucky. All of you. Never let go of that, Dane. Never think the grass is greener elsewhere. Let me tell you from experience, it's not."

"I don't plan on going anywhere. Sadie is it for me. Just like she's it for Wes."

She sniffles.

"We know it's unconventional, but it works for us."

"If it works, then who is anyone to judge?"

"I'm glad you and Ray found each other again," I tell her, squeezing her hand in support as footsteps head our way.

"Stray, why is my mom crying?" Wes asks, although there's no actual accusation in his tone. Quite the opposite.

"I'm just being a sap," Victoria answers for me.

"Here," I say, standing from his chair. "I'm gonna go and chill in my room. We'll stay here tonight. Spend some time with your mom. She's pretty awesome."

"Okay."

With a nod at Wes and then Ray, who's standing a little behind him, I leave them all to it.

My room feels almost unfamiliar when I step inside.

For years, this place has been home, my apartment just a place for one day in case things went wrong. But since Sadie, everything has changed.

I shower before crawling into bed. I lie there for the longest time in the dark, running through the events of the past few weeks, all the things the four of us have been through in our short time together.

I don't realize I've drifted off until my door opens a while later, the bright light from the hallway outside filling my room. Squinting, I watch as Wes slips into my room, closing the door behind him.

"Hey, you okay?" I ask.

"Yeah, I'm good," he slurs, stumbling as he crosses the room.

"You drunk, Pretty?" I ask, pushing up on my elbow to watch him.

"Lil' bit. It's Ray's fault."

"Sure."

"I'm just gonna..." he points at the couch while he wrestles with his hoodie.

"Don't be an idiot, Pretty. Just get in the fucking bed."

Falling back into my pillow, I get comfortable once more as he attempts to decide what to do.

After a few seconds, there's some more rustling before the sheets are pulled back and he slips in with me.

"What are you—"

"Sleep, Pretty. Just sleep," I mumble, already drifting off again.

SADIE

Wes isn't in school the next day. Or the next. And despite the few text messages to tell me he's okay, spending some time with his mom, I can't help but feel like there's an ocean between us.

"Holy shit, River. You look... wow." I stare at her, hardly able to believe my eyes. The leather mini skirt hugs her thighs, showcasing her long legs. And the Harley-Davidson cropped tee reveals a sliver of her flat stomach. Quinn has curled her blonde hair and braided some off her face, adding a ton of smoky makeup. She looks... hot.

"Rhett is going to flip."

"Yeah, well, big brother can get lost." She shrugs, worrying her bottom lip. "I'm fed up with being treated like Little Miss Innocent."

"You look anything but innocent tonight, Riv." I smile, and she grins back.

"Do you think Jax will like it?"

"Jax will freaking love it. He won't be able to keep his hands off you."

"That's kind of the plan." She blushes. "But enough about me," she comes and perches on the edge of the bed, "how are you, really? Have you spoken to him yet?"

"Nope, but I'm fine." The words taste like ash on my tongue. "Wes and his mom have things they need to deal with, and I—"

"Come on, Sadie," Quinn snorts. "You're not fooling anyone. You've been moping—"

"I am not moping," I snap indignantly. "I just... I just wanted it to stop, you know?" My eyes drop, unable to stand their pity. "We've all been through so much, I guess I thought it..."

"You thought it was all over."

"Yeah, something like that."

"Wes loves you, Sadie Ray. You know he does. And my brother and Dane." River squeezes my hand. "But they're guys. Sometimes they're gonna shut you out."

She's right, of course she is. But it doesn't stop the way I feel.

"I'm being silly, I know." I brush River's hand away and climb off the bed, going over to the mirror.

I'm dressed to the nines in a skintight black t-shirt dress with a flaming heart on the chest and my trusty black boots. My makeup is heavy and my hair is swept over one shoulder and pinned in place. I should feel good, sexy and strong. The guys won't know where to look when they see me.

So why do I feel so... off?

"Relax," Quinn says, meeting my eyes in the mirror. "Pretty isn't going anywhere. You just need to clear the air tonight. And I'm sure that outfit will work."

She smirks, and I whisper, "Bitch," right back at her.

"And what about you, huh? Going to finally let that

gorgeous specimen of a man dust off your vagina?" I lift a knowing brow in her direction, and she fumes.

"There will be no dusting of any of my intimate parts."

"Such a prude." I roll my eyes, snickering at her.

"I'm too good for a biker."

"Keep telling yourself that."

And then River surprises the hell out of us by saying, "Well, I hope to be completely manhandled by a biker tonight." She flicks her hair off her shoulder and struts out of Quinn's bedroom like she owns the place.

"Okay, who was that and where did River go?"

"Honestly," I reply, "I have no idea. But something tells me tonight is going to be hella interesting."

The party is already in full swing when we finally arrive at the Red Ridge compound. Dane had wanted us to go together, or more specifically, me to go with them. But I'd declined, insisting he spent some time with the guys, his new club.

That will take some getting used to, but since making his decision, it's like a weight has been lifted and he's back to his old self again. And that's all I want for him—for him to be happy.

It's all I want for any of them.

"You're here, thank God." A girl I vaguely recognize rushes over to us the second we enter the bustling compound.

"Oh hey, Kat," River says with a smile. "You remember Kat?"

"Diesel's sister, right?" I ask, and she nods.

"The one and only. I'm so glad you came. This place is already getting crazy and the club whores are out in full swing." She casts her eyes over to a group of older girls, and I instantly recognize them for what they are.

"Oh goodie," I drawl.

"Don't worry, Sadie Ray, your guy already put Hannah in her place."

"He... what?" I gawk at her.

"Yeah, Hannah's thing is welcoming new members, if you catch my drift. Had big plans for Dane before—"

"Excuse me," I say, brushing past her and heading straight for the clubhouse. People call out and wave to me, Sinners and ex-Reapers alike, but I don't stop, fueled by anger and a violent wave of jealousy.

The second I spot Dane, the knot in my chest loosens a little bit, but then I remember Kat's words and everything inside me goes taut again.

"Sadie, girl," he grins, spotting me. Music blares out of an old sound system, reverberating inside of me. "Fuck, you look—"

"A word," I grit out, not caring that we have an audience.

"Someone's in trouble." A guy with gauges in his ears —Bones, I think—claps Dane on the shoulder, laughing. "Good luck with that."

"Nothing I can't handle."

The guys all howl with laughter as Dane follows me over to a quiet corner of the room. "What happened?" he asks, eyes glittering with concern.

"Who's Hannah?"

"Hann—the club whore?" Realization dawns on his face and he explodes with laughter. "You're not seriously worried about..." He trails off, noticing my murderous expression.

Before I know what's happening, Dane has me crowded against the wall, his hand pressed next to my head as he leans in.

"Jealous, princess?" He runs his nose along my jaw, nipping the skin there. "Because I have no problem with showing everyone who I belong to right here."

"Dane," I breathe, flattening my hands to the wall as his lips trace down the slope of my neck. "I..."

"What is it?" His eyes snap to mine.

"I feel like I'm losing my goddamn mind," I confess.

"What's... Pretty." His expression falls.

I glance away, hating that it's so obvious.

"We talked about this, Sadie, girl. He's fine. He and Victoria just needed some time to work through things."

"Easy for you to say, you've been with him." I glance away, not wanting him to see the hurt in my eyes.

"Princess, look at me." Dane grips my jaw. "This isn't about you—"

"I know," I snap defensively. "I know, okay? I just..."

"You're worried we're going to lose him." Pressing my lips together, I nod.

Emotion floods me, and I'm relieved Dane is shielding me from prying eyes.

"Hey, look at me, Sadie, girl." He touches his head to mine, inhaling sharply. "Wes is one of us now. He's in, babe. All fucking in. And even if he wasn't, you think I'd ever let him leave us now?"

A faint smile traces my lips at that. "He's not going anywhere, princess. He needs us as much as we need him."

"I can't lose you, Dane." I fist his cut, anchoring us together. "Any of you."

"You won't, I promise. I'm Prez now, I have the power." He grins and I smack his chest.

"You big goofball."

"You good?" His expression turns serious again.

"I'm good. But fair warning, if Hannah or any of the other club whores so much as think about touching what's mine... I won't be held responsible for my actions." My lips twist in amusement.

"You're so fucking hot when you're jealous." He collars my neck gently, sweeping his thumb down my throat. "You should probably stake your claim, just so they're absolutely clear about who owns my balls." Dane smirks, the challenge in his eyes too good to resist.

I pull him closer until the hard planes of his body are pressed against the soft lines of mine. My breath hitches when I feel him hard and ready at my stomach. "Someone's happy to see me," I tease.

"Someone's always happy to see you. Now kiss me, princess. Show them who I belong to."

Our mouths crash together, all tongues and teeth and a giant fuck you to anyone who thinks they can come between us. I love this guy. I love him with everything that I am, and no one will ever take him away from me.

"You're mine," I breathe into the kiss, not wanting to break away for a second.

"Always." Dane kisses me deeper, dirtier, sending the room into a frenzy as people hoot and holler around us.

"Think they got the message?" He breaks the kiss, inhaling a ragged breath.

"For now," I sass, kissing him once more. "Go do your thing, Prez. I'm going to find the girls."

I'm about to skip around him, but he grabs my wrist. "You sure you're good?"

"I'm good."

"He'll be here. Pretty will be here."

I nod, not trusting myself to speak. I hadn't even realized he wasn't here yet.

Giving our rapt audience a saucy smirk, I walk straight out of the clubhouse and into the cool night air.

Telling myself that I'm fine.

Even if it is a lie.

———

There's no time to dwell on Wes missing from the party. Dane insists on introducing me to everyone while Rhett stands close by, growling at any guy who tries to get too handsy.

"You need to relax," I say to him as we watch Dane take shots with Crank and Diesel.

"I can think of a few ways to ease the tension. Interested?" He runs a hand over his junk, and I roll my eyes.

"Pig."

"Like you haven't been giving me and Dane come-fuck-me eyes all night in this ridiculous little dress." Rhett hooks an arm around my waist and pulls me between his legs.

"You noticed my dress. Could have fooled me." I smirk.

"I'm more interested in what's under it." His hand grips my knee, sliding up the inside of my leg. Shivers skitter down my spine as I bow into him.

"Rhett, people are watching."

"Let them watch."

"My dad is right over there."

"Fuck." His hand drops like I'm on fire and I let out a soft chuckle. "Later." I lean in and kiss his jaw. "I want you both later."

"Not all of us?" Something catches his eye over my shoulder, and I turn slowly to find Wes standing there. He runs his eyes down my body, leaving a trail of heat in their wake.

I step forward on shaky legs. Why is this so hard?

He's here, isn't he? And Dane said he wasn't going anywhere. So why am I so torn up about it?

"You came," I say when he reaches me.

"You thought I wouldn't?" His brows crinkle.

"I... I didn't know what to think."

"Can we talk? Somewhere private?"

"You can use my room." Dane appears at his side. "Here's the key." He pulls the rope necklace from around his neck and hands it to Pretty.

"You two go talk... work things out." Something passes between the two of them, the air charged with anticipation.

"Come on." Wes takes my hand and leads me down toward the back of the room.

"How do you know where you're going?" I ask.

"Dane brought me out here yesterday. Gave me the tour."

"H-he did?"

"Yeah." Wes doesn't say anything else, leading me down a long hall not dissimilar to the one back at the Sinners' compound. Except when we reach the end, he turns a corner and we come to a single door.

"Prez's executive suite." He smirks, sliding the key into the lock.

"What are you up to, Wesley Noble?" I ask, sensing that there's more going on here than I realize.

"Come on." He grabs my hand and pulls me inside.

"Oh my God," Sadie breathes as she steps into Dane's room.

She might think that I haven't been here all night, that's far from the truth.

I was here, and I've been busy.

I know I've somewhat abandoned her the last couple of days, but seeing that look back in my mom's eyes after she spoke to Dad wrecked me. Not to mention the fact that Ray had business to deal with, which meant he had to leave the compound and I was terrified to leave her alone.

Grant Noble would have to be an even bigger idiot than I've ever given him credit for to try to get to her in the compound, but he's already proved that he's got people in the right places, constantly reminding us of his lingering presence. And if I'm right about him being behind the guys' arrests, then it's clear that he can get inside those gates if he so wishes.

"I've missed you, princess," I breathe, coming up

behind her and wrapping my arms around her waist, pressing my nose into her curls and breathing her in.

"You did all this for me?" she asks softly, taking in all the flickering candles, the pink fairy lights, and most importantly, the biggest bed I've ever seen in my life. It even puts the one in the beach house to shame.

My cock stirs at just the thought of what we can get up to in it.

"I know I've neglected you."

"No, Wes," she says, spinning in my arms and looking up at me with her huge green eyes. "Your mom needed you. I was being a brat. I just... I missed you, and I felt like you'd shut me out."

Reaching up, I tuck a lock of her hair behind her ear. "I'm sorry. I never want to do that. I was just so angry."

"I know. I just wanted to be there."

"You can't always be there," I say softly, brushing her bottom lip with my thumb. "We're a team, remember? You need to trust the others to be there when you can't be."

"Dane?" she breathes.

I nod, thinking of him dragging me to the shooting range the next morning to get out some of my anger before he took off for school. "Yeah."

Her eyes flash with heat at my words. "Tell me more about that, Pretty. How did he help relieve your frustrations?"

I can't help but bark out a laugh. "Not in the ways you're thinking, princess. I can tell you that my shot is getting better, and I've spent a good bit of time making sure I don't lose my six-pack that you're so fond of now that I'm not training every day."

"You worked out together?" Her brow lifts, her interest piqued. "Sweaty and shirtless?"

I chuckle at her little fantasy. "How about you join us next time? Find out for yourself."

"I think I can definitely free up some time in my schedule for that. So nothing else has—"

"No, princess. Not without you."

"I'm not sure if I'm relieved I didn't miss it, or bitterly disappointed."

"Always with you," I whisper in her ear. "It's always about you."

"You know," she says, running her hands up my chest, resting them over my shoulders so she can thread her fingers into my hair, "it's Dane's birthday soon. I've been trying to think of the perfect gift."

Something tells me that she's not suggesting we buy him some new socks, and I'd be lying if I said a little ripple of excitement didn't zap through me.

Nudging her nose, I brush my lips against hers as I whisper, "Maybe we should discuss some options for the birthday boy. Make his day real special."

"I like your way of thinking, Pretty."

"But less about him. I'm fucking dying without my Sadie fix, princess."

"Yeah?"

"Yeah," I confirm, finally claiming her lips exactly as I've been dreaming about for the past few days.

Our time together at the Arches was good, but our quickie out there barely scratched the surface of my need for her.

My tongue plunges past her lips, meeting hers as I walk her back toward the giant bed. Skimming my hands down her body, my fingers wrap around the hem of her dress before I drag it up, revealing what she's hiding beneath.

"Fuck. I've died and gone to heaven," I mutter as I stare at her sexy black lingerie.

Lifting my hand, I run my finger along the lace cut of her bra, loving how her entire body trembles at my touch.

"You like?"

"I fucking love, princess. Almost too good not to share."

She stares at me, daring me to call them.

"But I won't. Not yet." I smirk. "You're mine right now. And only mine."

Grabbing her thighs, I throw her back onto the bed and shrug out of my cut, dragging my hoodie off in one quick move. I lose my boots before lifting my knee to crawl on with her.

"Whoa, more please," she demands, her eyes glued to my pants.

"You want me naked?"

"Um... when do I not want you naked?"

"Your wish is my command."

Flicking open the button on my jeans, I push them and my boxers down my legs and kick them off before climbing on the bed, crawling over Sadie's body. "Fuck, you're beautiful," I breathe, kissing up her chest, her neck until I'm at her jaw.

"Wesley, please," she moans, arching her back and offering herself up to me. "I missed you too much for the teasing."

"Tough. You're all I've thought about for two days. This isn't going to be quick."

Tucking my hand beneath her head, I tilt her exactly

as I want and slam my lips down on hers, claiming her in a bruising kiss.

"But the party," she says between heaving breaths when I finally release her.

"Fuck the party. We can celebrate with the new prez in our own way later."

Ripping the cup of her bra aside, I dip my head to capture her nipple, dragging it through my teeth, making her moan.

"Okay, you convinced me."

"If only you agreed to everything so easily," I say against the soft skin of her breast.

"If you don't make me come soon, I might never agree to anything ever again."

I smile, brushing my lips down her stomach as my hand disappears beneath her so I can unclasp her bra. Dragging it from her body, I throw it across the room, not paying any attention to where it lands.

Cupping her breasts in both my hands, I continue down, kissing over her lace-covered mound and then onto her thighs, which she widens in her need to feel me elsewhere. "Rhett's right, princess. You're a dirty slut."

"Yeah, and you all love it."

"Fucking right we do."

"Oh fuck, yes," she cries when I lick her over her soaked panties.

"You taste like heaven," I say, pressing my tongue against her clit, making her writhe beneath me.

"Wes, please. I don't want anything between us."

Wrapping my fingers around the side of her panties, I murmur, "It's a shame these are so pretty and that the others won't get to see them."

The sound of ripping lace fills the room a beat before another loud moan falls from Sadie's lip.

"I'm pretty sure they'll prefer me wearing none anyway."

"Hell, yeah."

Pressing my palms against the inside of her thighs, I spread her wide, staring at her swollen cunt. "Fuck, yeah. I've missed you, baby."

I lick up the length of her, savoring her taste as she tries to close her legs around my head. "Behave or I'll stop," I warn, although I think we're both aware that I'm lying.

Her fingers thread in my hair, pulling tight and holding me in place. I chuckle against her and she growls my name. Focusing on her clit, I lift two fingers to her entrance and push them inside her.

"Wesley," she screams when I find her G-spot and rub exactly how she likes until she shatters beneath me. "Fuck, you're good at that," she pants once she's come down from her high.

I lean over her, one of my hands planted beside her head, the other wrapped around my cock as I run the head through her folds, coating myself in her juices.

"Yeah?" I ask, a smirk pulling at my lips.

"More. Give me your cock, Pretty. Fuck me like the bad boy biker you are."

I don't correct her, because getting onto a bike was another lesson that Dane and Ray have helped me with the past couple of days. Another little surprise I should have for her in a few weeks.

Fuck, I can't wait to feel her wrapped around me as I gun an engine between my thighs.

"Yes," she screams as I thrust into her, filling her in one quick move.

"Princess, your pussy is... fuck."

My fingers grip onto her hips as I pull almost all the way out before slamming back inside as deep as I can go. Leaning over her, I kiss her until we're both breathless, her nails clawing at my back until she's on the brink of coming again.

Dropping my hand between us, I rub circles around her clit.

"Yes, yes, yes," she cries. "Wesley." Her body arches as she throws her head back, her pussy tightening around me, almost tipping me over the edge with her.

I'm just about to fall when the click of the door catches my attention. I don't need to look over my shoulder to know who it is. I feel it.

"Well, my night just got a whole lot better," Dane slurs, walking over to us.

It's not until his eyes capture mine that I realize just how off his ass he is. He clearly had way more shots than the couple I saw him drink.

"She's so fucking beautiful when she comes."

Sadie comes back to herself as Dane trails his fingers over her breasts. "Dane?" she breathes, her voice rough from her cries.

"Hey, Sadie, girl. You're looking good there with Pretty's cock deep in your cunt."

She reaches out, rubbing at the tent in his pants. Her pussy clamps around me and I can almost hear her thoughts before his eyes shoot up to me, silently asking me for permission.

"Whatever you want, Sadie, girl. I guess I was on borrowed time, getting you to myself anyway."

I keep my pace slow as Sadie rips open Dane's pants, allowing him to push them down over his ass to let his cock spring free.

"Princess," he groans, his eyes closing for a beat as he absorbs the sensation of her tiny hand wrapping around him.

"Pretty's so fucking hard," she tells Dane as she works him.

My cheeks heat, unable to deny that things got a whole lot hotter in here the second I heard the door close.

"Oh yeah. Did he make you come hard, princess?"

Sadie nods, her eyes locked on Dane's cock. "Fuck my mouth, Stray. I want to feel both of you coming."

"Well, when you ask so nicely."

Threading his hand into her hair, he tugs her to where he wants her before brushing the tip of his cock over her lips, painting them with his precum.

She laps it up, heat filling her eyes as her pussy gushes.

"She fucking loves that, bro."

"Yeah? What about this?"

He pushes inside her mouth and all the way to the back of her throat.

"Oh, hell yeah," I grunt as she sucks me deeper into her body.

"Move, Wes. Fucking move," she groans quickly when Dane pulls out.

"You got it, princess."

I fuck her, gripping her hips hard enough to leave bruises as I watch Dane feed her his cock, my balls drawing up way too quickly. But from the way his body locks up, I know he's close too.

"Suck him harder. Make him come."

Pressing my thumb to her clit, I rub her, sensing that she's just as close as we are. She moans around Dane's length, her eyes locked on mine.

Knowing she's watching, I act on instinct, because she'll fucking love it. Reaching out, I twist my fingers in Dane's hair and force his face in my direction, slamming my lips down on his.

It takes all of three seconds, just long enough for our tongues to collide, before all three of us come simultaneously.

21

SADIE

I wake up to a wall of heat pressed up behind me. Rhett's inked hand cups my breast, his leg pushed between mine.

I smile.

He's so possessive, even when he's asleep.

But that isn't the only reason I'm smiling.

"You're not Pretty," I whisper over my shoulder, and he grunts.

"I should fucking hope not." He leans in, nudging his nose along my shoulder and kissing the skin there. "He went to help Stray."

"Help him with what?"

"I dunno, club business. It's early, and my head feels like it's gonna explode. Go back to sleep." He pulls me back against his hot body, but I turn, snuggling close.

Rhett sounds like he's asleep, the gentle rise and fall of his chest suggesting he is. But his fingers move gently over my chest, painting lazy circles.

"Rhett," I whisper, my stomach coiled tight.

It should be impossible to want more after the way they all loved my body last night.

Dane and Wes had been just the beginning, and it wasn't long until Rhett showed up and we started all over again. Eventually, we made it back out to the party, but they barely let me sleep when we finally turned in for the night.

He remains silent, breathing deeply behind me. But his fingers keep exploring my skin, trailing lower until he's brushing the apex of my thighs. A whimper escapes my throat.

"I know you're awake." I slide my hand down his body, grazing his growing erection, and a muted groan rumbles in his chest.

"Keep doing that, princess, and you can ride me all the way to heaven."

Laughter spills from my lips as I palm him harder, slowly dragging my hand up and down his hard length.

"Fuck," he hisses, his eyes snapping to mine. "That feels good."

"I aim to please." I throw my leg over his waist and straddle him. Rhett's eyes flare with hunger as his hands go to my hips.

"Nuh-uh." I swat him away. "My turn."

Sliding down his body, I kneel over him and take him into my mouth eagerly.

"Fuuuuck!" He fists the sheets as he hits the back of my throat.

"Hmm," I purr, closing my fingers around the base of his cock and sucking him again.

"Holy shit, you couldn't have let me wake up first?"

"You're complaining?" My brow lifts as I hold him away from my lips, flicking my tongue over his slit.

"N-no complaints," he chokes out.

I flatten my tongue and drag it down his veiny shaft and back up, twirling it over the metalwork in the tip. "I fucking love this piercing," I murmur, pumping him harder. Faster.

"Get on me then," Rhett starts pulling me up his body, "and I'll remind you how good it feels."

I lose the fight as he manhandles me up the bed until I'm straddling him. "I wanted to make you come." I pout.

"And you will." He smirks. "In your pussy."

"Did anyone ever tell you you're so romantic, Rhett Savage?" I lean down, kissing him while I slowly drag my pussy over his swollen cock. We both shudder when his tip hits my clit.

"Bounce on my dick, princess."

I roll my eyes. "So charming."

His hand shoots out, collaring me as his smile turns wicked. "But you'll do it, won't you? Because you're our filthy little princess."

A smirk plays on my lips as I lift my knees slightly and line him up at my entrance, slowly sinking down. I clench as hard as I can but don't move.

"Fucking tease," Rhett barks, tucking his hands behind his head, clearly happy to let me run the show.

Oh, how things have changed.

"What?" he asks, narrowing his eyes.

"Nothing." I sass, rolling my hips, grinding down on him.

His eyes flare, jaw clenched tight as I keep my movements slow and deep—so fucking deep the line between pleasure and pain blurs.

"Take it," he orders. "Take what you need."

I lean down, brushing my lips over his and whispering, "Oh, I plan on it, Savage."

I plan to take everything.

His heart.

Body.

And his dirty black soul.

"Morning." I find Dane and Wes in the clubhouse, scrubbing what looks like a puddle of blood on the floor. "What the hell happened?"

"Morning, Sadie, girl." Dane's eyes sweep over my body, darkening with memories of the night before. "You look well fucked. Savage have fun with you this morning?"

"Maybe I had fun with him." I smirk, and the guys chuckle.

"Sounds about right." He throws the brush in the bucket of water. "That should do it."

"That's a lot of blood," I remark.

"After we called it a night, things got a little out of hand with a couple of the guys."

"They're okay, right?"

"Yeah. Thought it would be funny to see who could —" Something catches his attention over my shoulder. "Rough night, brother?"

"Rough morning." Rhett slaps my ass before looping his arms around my waist and dropping his chin on my shoulder.

"What the fuck happened out here?"

"Never play with knives, boys and girls. Because people tend to end up bleeding out."

"Who?" Rhett snorts.

"Axe and Bones thought it would be funny to play five finger fillet."

"Fucking idiots."

"Like we haven't all done it."

Me and Wes both raise our hands. "We haven't, because we're not absolute idiots," I say. "Are they both okay?"

"Nothing a few stitches won't fix."

"Men." I scoff. "Always out to prove who's got the biggest dick."

"Oh, I think we all know who's got the biggest dick." Rhett bites my neck, soothing the sting with his tongue.

"I hate to say it, bro, but I reckon Pretty's got at least an inch on you," Dane says nonchalantly. Wes almost chokes on air as he gawks at Dane, while I smother the laughter bubbling in my chest.

"You wanna test that theory?" Rhett grunts.

A shiver runs down my spine and I suck in a sharp breath.

"Oh fuck, she loves it." Dane stalks toward me. "Bet she's thinking of lining us up and—"

"Mornin'." Crank appears, looking a little worse for wear. "What's going— Am I interrupting something?" His eyes flick between the four of us.

"You're good, man." Dane backtracks to greet him. "Listen, thanks for last night. Sorry we disappeared for—"

"No apologies necessary." The VP's gaze finds mine, twinkling with amusement. "Although I'm surprised she can walk this morning."

"I like you, Crank," Rhett says, "but if you talk about our girl like that again, you and I are going to have a problem."

"Relax, brother, I'm just bustin' your balls. Apologies, Sadie Ray."

"No apologies needed." I slip out of Rhett's hold and smirk. "You're right. They obviously didn't fuck me hard enough if I'm still walking this morning."

And with that little remark, I blow my guys a kiss and head back to Dane's room, leaving them all speechless.

The guys stick around the Red Ridge compound to help Dane and Crank, but they're busy with club stuff, so I take up River and Quinn's invite to go shopping.

"So... how did last night go?" I ask River the second we find a seat in the coffee shop.

A dreamy expression washes over her as she glances out of the window, no doubt searching for our chaperone.

"It was... amazing." She leans in close. "He kissed me."

"He did? Good for you, Riv. I'm so happy for you."

"Oh, Sadie Ray, it was perfect. He took me up on the roof and... well, you know."

"And there was just kissing?"

Her cheeks burn. "There might have been some groping, but we didn't..."

I let out a little squeal of approval. "I knew Jax had it in him."

"I like him so much." Her expression drops. "But I know he's worried about Rhett. Which why you can't say anything, not yet. It's new and exciting, and I don't want anything to ruin it."

"I'm not sure hiding it is—"

"Please, Sadie. You can't tell him. You know how he

gets, and Jax looks up to him. If Rhett finds out and kicks off, Jax won't choose me, he'll choose the club." She drops her gaze.

"Riv, look at me." She lifts her head. "Don't underestimate Jax. He's a good guy. He would never hurt you like that."

But as I say the words, I understand her concern. The club comes first, and he's still only a prospect. If Rhett ordered him to leave River alone... I want to believe Jax would make the right choice, but she's right.

Crap. Maybe I shouldn't have pushed this without talking to Rhett first.

"You won't tell him?"

"No, but you're going to have to tell him eventually."

"I will, I promise. We just want some time to explore things before everyone finds out."

Quinn and Kat return with our order, and I take my caramel latte.

"Thanks," I say.

"Thanks for letting me gate-crash," Kat replies, sliding into her seat. "It's nice to have girls to hang out with."

"You don't have friends at school?" Quinn asks.

"Some." She shrugs. "But it's not exactly easy being the sister of a Reaper. Shit, sorry, I mean Sinner. Still getting used to the change."

"It's all good." I offer her a warm smile. "And I know exactly what you mean. It's easier to keep people at arm's length than hope they'll understand club life."

Kat nods, running her thumbs around the rim of her mug. "There's a few other club kids, but I've never really bonded with them."

"Well, now you have us," River says, as if it's the simplest thing in the world.

"Thanks, I'd like that."

The girls launch into a rundown of the party last night, and Kat gets us up to speed on who's who over at Red Ridge. When she mentions Crank, I don't miss the way Quinn stiffens.

"Something you want to tell us?" I ask her.

"Nope." She casts me a dismissive look, and I chuckle.

"You know, in my experience, bikers can be pretty determined when it comes to what they want."

"Leave it, Sadie Ray." She pins me with an amused look. "I am quite capable of fighting off the unwanted attention of a guy like Crank."

"I wouldn't be so sure about that. Killian can be... very single-minded." Kat grins.

"Killian who?" Quinn bats her eyelashes, smiling sweetly. But I see the flicker of fear there. What I can't work out is what she's afraid of. That he wants her...

Or that she wants him back.

I guess only time will tell just how strong her resistance is, because something tells me Crank isn't going to stop until he gets what he wants.

"So what are you getting Dane for his birthday?" River changes the subject, reminding me of the actual reason I decided to come along.

"What you get any guy who already has everything he needs, of course." I grin over my coffee mug. "Sexy lingerie."

22

RHETT

Since waking up Saturday morning at the Red Ridge compound, everything was weirdly... normal.

Grant seemed to fuck off as quickly as he appeared, which sadly meant that none of us got to put a bullet through his brain. Although something tells me he's running out of time.

Wes might be okay with his dad's meddling that got him thrown off a team he didn't really have any interest in being on anymore, but the second Grant steps out of line and does anything to hurt either Wes or Victoria, then he has to know that he's going to have the heat of not one, but now two, clubs on him.

And it is not going to end well for him, no matter what precautions he thinks he's put in place to protect himself.

"Sadie, girl, are you ready yet? I want my first surprise," Dane calls from beside me on the couch where the three of us are anxiously waiting for her to get ready.

Today is Dane's nineteenth birthday, and I don't know everything Sadie has got planned for him other than our night out, but I do know that she and Wes have been scheming up something for the birthday boy that they won't let me in on. I might be curious, but also, I'm more than happy to leave them to it because... well, it could be anything.

"Impatient much?" she calls back, her voice teasing.

"Damn fucking right I am," he calls back, fidgeting on the couch as his anticipation gets too much. "Kat said we're gonna love it."

"Kat?" I ask.

"Diesel's sister."

"Right. Well, let's hope she's right then, huh?"

Wes sits silently on the other couch.

"You're quiet, Pretty," Dane points out. "Everything okay?"

Sitting forward, he rests his elbows on his knees and looks directly at Dane, his fingers twisting around each other nervously. "Of course, man. Things are good."

He's right. They are. The past week has been quiet, peaceful even. And that in itself is unnerving.

We haven't experienced this before. Since the moment this thing between us started, all we've had is drama. This easy, being able to breathe and actually chill the fuck out thing is weird.

"Fuck this," Dane barks after a couple more minutes of silence. He pushes from the couch and storms toward the bedroom. "Princess, we were meant to leave like twenty min— holy fuck," he gasps as he throws the door open.

Silence ripples through the air and Wes and I

exchange a knowing look. She's just knocked him on his ass with whatever she's wearing.

My fists curl as my curiosity almost gets too much.

"Change of plans," Dane calls a few seconds later. "We're not going out."

"Shut up, Stray. We're going, and we're all going to have fun. Before we come back here for some more, I'm sure," Wes says with a wink in my direction.

Oh yeah, he and Sadie definitely have something up their sleeves.

Heels tap against the floor a few moments later as Dane concedes, or at least lets her out of the bedroom.

"Holy fuck," I bark the second she steps out of the room and into my line of sight. The black leather dress she's wearing wraps around her body like a second fucking skin.

"What?" Wes asks, jumping from the couch so he can see as I tug at my pants, trying to make space for my boner. "Jesus," he breathes the second his eyes lock on her.

If I could rip my eyes from our princess, then I know I'd see a similar tent in his pants, too, because fuck me, she's fire.

"Are you even wearing panties?" I ask, my eyes taking in the split that goes all the way up her thigh, damn near to her hip.

"You'll have to find out later when Dane unwraps me." She toys with the zipper between her breasts. It's like the one all those weeks ago that Wes and I stripped her out of down by the lake.

"How long are we going out for?"

"Twenty minutes?" Wes suggests.

"Come on, the others will be waiting."

Thanks to a serious number of fake IDs and some phone calls to the right people, we've managed to secure the VIP section of Poison for tonight.

All our brothers, both Savage Falls and Red Ridge members alike, have been invited, and all of them are more than ready to cause some carnage outside of the compounds.

"We need to go before I fuck her," Dane says from over her shoulder, his hands fixed on her hips and I'm sure her ass crushed back against his dick.

Running my eyes down her body again, I focus on the come-fuck-me black boots that are wrapped around her calves. "She's leaving those on later. I want those heels imprinted in my ass," I mutter, reaching for my cut and shrugging it on.

"They look kinda painful," Wes points out, eyeing the pointed studs on them.

"Yeah. You know how I roll." I smirk. "Let's go before Dane blows in his pants."

"Fuck you, man."

Ignoring him, I march right up to Sadie, collaring her throat with my hand. She gasps at my rough touch, her eyes darkening a few shades. "You look fucking beautiful, princess."

My mouth waters for a taste of her, but I know one of those heels will end up impaled up my ass if I ruin her makeup, so I settle for dipping my head and kissing up her neck instead.

"You gonna tell me your plans yet?" I growl in her ear.

She chuckles darkly. "None of your business, Savage.

And you're probably not going to want anything to do with it."

"Exactly as I feared. Fucking love you, Sadie Ray."

Aside from Sadie and River, Dane is the most important person in my life, and knowing that she's planning something to make his nineteenth the best birthday he's ever had, however wicked her intentions might be, makes me hella happy. Dude deserves it and then some after everything. There's isn't anything I wouldn't do for that motherfucker—almost—but the fact that those two idiots are willing almost melts my dark, fucked-up heart.

"Come on, birthday boy, let's move out."

I shove Dane away from our girl and force him out of our apartment before we all change our minds and have a private party between us instead. Behind us, I hear Wes tell Sadie just how beautiful she is as Dane continues to protest about us leaving.

"She'll make it worth your while later, Stray," I tell him, clapping my hand on his shoulder.

"That dress should be fucking illegal. I almost came, looking at her."

"We heard." I laugh.

"She's aware that the three of us are going to be walking around all night with fucking hard-ons, right?"

"I think that was probably part of her plan, yeah."

"Fucking torture."

"You love it."

"Hell yeah."

There's a car idling in the parking lot, waiting for us with one very pissed-off driver sitting behind the wheel— although his eyes soon light up the second he spots Sadie behind me.

My teeth grind and my fists curl. Dropping down to his open window, I lean right inside. "Fucking look at her again and this will be your last trip."

His mouth drops open in shock, all of the blood draining from his face. "O-okay," he stutters.

"In you go then, princess," I say, my eyes still on the driver as I pull the back door open for her.

The second she bends to climb in, Dane smacks her ass so hard she almost tumbles inside headfirst. "Asshole," she snaps.

"You love it."

"Fucking good thing too," she complains, getting in and allowing Dane to follow.

Pretty goes around to the other side and I drop into the passenger seat, much to the driver's delight if his nervous swallow is anything to go by.

We're halfway across town when Sadie's moan rips through the car, making the driver shift uncomfortably in his seat.

"Dane," I warn. "Get your hands off the princess."

"But—" he whines like a toddler as Pretty bursts out laughing.

"He's like a kid in a candy shop and not allowed to eat anything."

"Fuck. All I can think about is eating. Or one of you doing it. I'm not fussy."

The driver's grip on the wheel tightens as he shoots me a bemused glance.

"Don't knock it until you've tried it."

"We'll fulfill all your dirty fantasies later, Stray," Sadie promises.

"You been reading my dirty diary again, Sadie, girl?" he jokes.

"No need. I know you well enough to know what you want."

"Damn fucking straight."

She moans again before there's a slap of skin and Dane complains.

Shaking my head, I keep my eyes on the road, thankfully as does our driver as Dane continues his antics in the back of the car. I knew the shots and blunt I gave him while Sadie was getting ready were a mistake.

We pull up in front of Poison and climb from the car beside the long-ass line that wraps around the huge building.

"Whoa, how many invites did you send out?" Dane jokes, running his eyes down the line of people.

"Come on, you idiot," I say, wrapping my arm around his shoulder and dragging him toward the security at the front of the line.

"Dane Stray," one of them says, clearly knowing exactly who we are. "Happy birthday, man."

"Thanks. You boys have got one hell of a party waiting for you up there."

I lead the way toward the roped-off stairs leading to the VIP mezzanine that looks down over the rest of the club.

Glancing over my shoulder, I find Dane and Wes flanking Sadie's side, both holding her hands in a death grip. A smile twitches at my lips as I stare at the three of them before another security guy lifts the rope and we all head up.

Whoops and hollers sound out as everyone notices that the birthday boy has finally arrived. Some scantily-clad waitress appears out of nowhere, offering the four of us a glass of champagne. I take it, but fuck if I actually want to drink it.

"Here," I say to Sadie. "I'm going to get a real drink."

"Savage," she calls before I vanish. A wicked smile pulls at her lips when I turn back to her. "Meet me on the dancefloor later, yeah?"

"I don't dance, princess."

"It wasn't a suggestion, Savage."

Shaking my head at her, I slip through the crowd of people to find the bar. Glancing back, I watch as Dane swallows his champagne in one and Wes stares at him with his lips curled in disgust.

With a laugh, I order the three of us decent drinks before finding my way back over.

"I think he's enjoying himself," I whisper in Sadie's ear as we stand and watch Dane dancing with Crank, Diesel, and a couple of the other Red Ridge guys. He's got the widest smile on his face as they all laugh together.

"Yeah. This was a good idea."

"Do you know what an even better idea would be?" I groan in her ear, my hand slipping up her bare thigh.

"Rhett," she warns.

"Aw, come on, princess. The second we get out of here, you're gonna focus all your efforts on the birthday boy. Let me have my moment." I nip her earlobe and a shudder rips through her. "I know you're wet for me."

Her throat vibrates with her moan. "No one is getting in my panties tonight before Dane does. Same rules apply for your birthday, big guy."

"Fucking killing me, princess."

Her laugh is wicked and full of dirty intentions. It goes straight to my aching cock.

"We can dance, though."

"You still want that?" I ask with a groan.

She turns to me, her eyes dark and hungry. "You mean you don't want to run your hands all over me?"

"Yeah, on second thought..."

I push her from the bench we're sitting on and damn near drag her to the edge of the dancefloor.

I fucking hate dancing, but with her pressed up against me, her ass grinding back against my cock and her hand in my hair, I could quickly get used to it.

Or at least I could until my cell starts buzzing in my pocket.

"Ignore it," Sadie shouts when I stop.

"It could be your dad," I bark back.

He and Victoria were invited tonight, along with some of the other older club members, but they all politely declined, more than happy to leave us to our fun.

Pulling it out, I find I'm right. "I need to take it, princess."

"I know," she murmurs, stepping away from me and joining Quinn and Kat where they're dancing a few feet away from us.

With my eyes trained on her, I back away from the crowd and toward the corner of the room. "Savage," I bark down the line.

"We've got a problem." I can barely hear Ray, but the fear in his voice says it all.

"What's wrong?"

"Victoria. She's gone."

"Shit," I hiss. "We're coming. Right fucking now."

Cutting the call, I pocket my cell as I make my way

back across the dancefloor, Sadie in my sights and ready to grab the others.

I fucking hate to ruin Dane's night, but it's Victoria.

He'd want to know.

For Wes.

23

SADIE

I watch Rhett as his entire body goes stiff, his eyes darkening to two black orbs.

"That doesn't look good," Quinn says over the music.

No, it doesn't.

"I'll be back." I make my way through the crowd, reaching Rhett just as he pockets his cell. "What is it?"

"We need to find Dane and Pretty. Now." He grabs my hand, leading me back to where we left them drinking and talking to Crank and the guys earlier.

"Rhett, what's going on?" I ask, but he's a man on a mission, all but dragging me across the bar, anger rippling off him.

We bump into a couple of guys who give us dirty looks, but Rhett doesn't even acknowledge them.

Okay then.

Dane notices us and grins. "Here she is, my birthday treat." The guys all snort as he stalks toward us, plucking me from Rhett and lifting me into the air, spinning me.

"Dane," I murmur.

"I think I want my birthday surprise now," he whispers into my ear, his hands all over my body, not caring that we have an audience.

"Dane," I say again. "Something's wrong."

His entire body goes rigid as he meets my gaze with narrowed eyes. "What happened?"

"Rhett got a call." I flick my head to where Rhett is silently fuming. His eyes dance between us and Wes, who looks clueless and more than a little drunk.

"Hate to do this to you on your birthday, brother, but we need to get back to the compound."

"You need backup?" Crank stands straighter.

Dane claps him on the shoulder. "I'm sure it's nothing, man. Just Savage overreacting, right?" He laughs off the sudden tension rippling around us, but Rhett doesn't return his easy smile.

"I'll text if we need you." Dane and Crank share a silent look, and I'm taken aback by how in sync the new Prez and his VP are.

But I shouldn't be surprised. It's Dane. Everyone loves him, and he makes things easy with his laid-back charm and humor.

"What happened?" Dane asks Rhett the second we all step away from the guys. I take Wes's hand, shooting him a look.

"Are you okay?"

"Those shots were strong." He grimaces.

"Lightweight," I sass, but it's a front. Trepidation snakes through me, making my stomach churn.

Something is wrong, and whatever it is, it's bad enough for Rhett to interrupt Dane's big night.

"Guess this means I won't be getting my birthday surprise?" Dane glances at me and Wes, hunger flashing in his eyes, when we finally reach a quieter corner of the club.

"Ray called."

Those two little words douse any heat between us.

"I don't know how to say this, man." Rhett fixes his eyes on Wes, who immediately stiffens.

"Say what? What the fuck is going on, Savage? He begins to tremble, and I press closer, letting him know I'm right here.

"It's your mom. She's... fuck, she's gone."

"G-gone?" The blood drains from his face.

The word echoes through my skull.

Victoria can't have— Not unless—

"What do you mean, she's gone?" Wes's voice doesn't sound like his own.

"One minute she was at the compound, and the next she had vanished. Ray thinks—"

"Fuck." Wes rips out of my hold and punches the nearby wall, the sickening crunch of bone making me flinch.

"Easy, Pretty." Dane pulls him into a guy hug, whispering something in his ear. Wes shakes his head and Dane holds his face as he talks him down.

"We should get back," I say, reeling at this new development. Just when things were finally looking up. I should have known it was too good to be true. "My dad will be going out of his mind."

Rhett pulls out his cell phone and starts texting someone. "Precautions," he says, when I ask who. When he glances at Dane and Wes, who are still talking in hushed, intimate tones, he adds, "You should go to him."

With a soft nod, I make my way over to them, slipping

between them. Wes instantly wraps his arms around me and buries his face in my shoulder.

"We'll find her," I whisper, tightening my hold on him. "We'll find her."

"Come on, Pretty. Let's get out of here." Dane squeezes his shoulder and Wes tucks me into his side.

"Stay close," Rhett barks, moving ahead of us with purpose. He's worried, and although the situation is dire, it makes my heart soar that he considers Wes one of us now.

Wes's arm tightens around me as we head for the exit. Dane stands on his other side. It shouldn't be like this. We should be leaving with the anticipation of things to come. Wesley and I had something special planned for the birthday boy.

We're almost at the door when a guy barrels into Rhett. "What the fuck?" he growls, shoving the drunken idiot away.

Dane is at my other side in an instant, shielding me from the guy's glassy gaze.

"Where'd you get the whore?" he slurs. "I need to get me one of—"

"What the fuck did you just say?" Rhett gets in the guy's face, his fists clenched at his sides.

"Rhett, leave it," I snap.

"Yeah, sweetheart, leave him. Come have a little fun with a real man." Asshole cups his junk, fixing his eyes right on me.

"Motherfucker has a death—"

All hell breaks loose as the guy gets in Rhett's face and Rhett takes a swing, sending him flying back into his group of friends.

"Rhett!" I cry, watching as they begin to fight, fists

slamming into soft tissue, their grunts and groans of pain drowning out the music.

"Do something," I hiss at Dane, who shakes his head. "Watch her, Pretty." He levels me with a stern look. "Don't leave his side, princess."

"Just go and help him already." Although from the way Rhett has the guy pinned against the wall, it looks like he's gotten things under—

Another guy comes at Dane, barreling into him, and the two of them crash into a shaker table, glasses and drinks smashing everywhere.

"Holy shit." Wes pulls me aside, keeping his arm around my waist. Soon the rest of our guys wade in, Crank and Diesel tag teaming some meathead. It's chaos, people screaming and furniture flying everywhere.

"We need to get out of here," I breathe when security finally starts pushing through the crowd.

I'm just about to tug Wes toward the exit when someone shoves me from behind. "Watch it, asshole." I whirl on the guy, losing Wes's hand as he gets swallowed up by the brawl.

Quinn finds me, screaming over the chaos. "Thank God, this is crazy."

"I know, but security's here."

"The cops, too." She points to the door, where police officers stream inside the building.

"Crap, we need to get to the guys." They can't get arrested again.

But as we try to fight our way through the crowd, strong arms go around my waist and haul me backwards.

"Let me go." I thrash against the officer's grip. "I haven't done anything wrong, asshole."

He chuckles darkly, dragging me to the back exit. "That's what they all say."

More cops rush in, paying us no attention as I'm manhandled out of the club.

"Got a live one there, Duke," another officer says, passing us.

"Help me get in her cuffs. Fucking bitch tried to bite me."

"He's lying," I shriek. "I didn't—"

The snap of cuffs startles me, and I look down to see my hands cuffed together. "What the fuck—"

"You'd better get in there, it's carnage. I'll deal with this live wire."

"You can't do this, I did nothing wrong. I didn't—"

Yanking open the back door of his cruiser, he throws me inside.

"You can't do this," I seethe, trying to grab my across-the-body purse to retrieve my cell phone—only to find my purse is gone. Which means my phone is gone.

Fuck.

"Sadie Ray Dalton," the officer says with a tsk as he climbs into the driver's seat. "Why am I not surprised?"

"Do I know you?" I eye him in the rearview mirror.

He doesn't answer.

"Hey, asshole." I kick the back of his seat. "I'm talking to you."

The car rumbles to life and panic sets in. "Where are you taking me?"

He whistles a tune as if he doesn't have a care in the world, focusing on the road ahead of us.

"Am I under arrest? Because I know my rights, asshole, and I didn't do anything wrong."

The pit in my stomach grows.

Think, Sadie Ray. Think.

But it's useless. My hands are restrained, and the car door is locked. There's no escaping. No calling for help.

My head drops back against the headrest as I try to think. It's obviously personal, the way the guy greeted me when he got in the car. Maybe he's bringing me in for questioning about my dad and the club.

Maybe he's—

I glance out of the window, and I realize we aren't heading downtown to the station.

We're heading out of town.

"Where are we going?" Fear snakes through me. Police officers don't just apprehend and kidnap people in plain sight. "Where the hell are you taking me?"

The guys will be going out of their minds... assuming they aren't all in cuffs too.

God, tonight was supposed to be a celebration. But now everything has gone to shit, and I don't even know what's happening.

Unless...

No.

No!

Officer Duke pulls his cruiser off the main road, taking a dirt road to nowhere. My stomach churns with every passing minute.

"Please!" I try appealing to his badge of honor. "You don't want to do this."

He ignores me.

"They'll find out I'm missing. They'll find out and they'll—"

"Not my problem," he drawls, catching my eye in the mirror. Something dark passes over his expression, making me shudder.

Headlights flash up ahead, and my breath catches as I spot a dark van. "What is..."

"Your chariot awaits, princess." There's a knowing lilt in his voice, full of disgust.

"N-no. I won't go. You can't make me."

Two hooded figures appear, moving toward the cruiser. The door is yanked open and one of them leans in and grabs my arm, wrenching me from the car. Pain explodes through my shoulder, and I cry out.

"You don't have to do this." I thrash and buck, trying to kick out at the two guys who wrestle me between them.

"Please, you don't have to—"

A fist flies toward me so fast I don't see it coming in time and my head snaps back, agony washing over me. "W-wh..." Stars fill my vision as the *clunk* of a door sliding open sounds somewhere in the distance.

"Get her inside," someone barks, and I'm being lifted, up, up, up, until my body collides with something hard.

And darkness swallows me.

24

WES

A fist collides with my temple, and I stumble back into an overturned table, crashing to the ground, my vision blurring.

Motherfucker.

But I don't stay down. I can't.

Officers are streaming through the door, beginning to drag people from the chaos. I have to get Sadie out. I need to get the guys out before they're both locked up in Savage Falls PD again.

"Sadie?" I call when I get to my feet, realizing for the first time that she's no longer right beside me. "SADIE?" I scream into the mayhem.

Panic begins to claw at me, its icy fingers closing around my throat, making every breath hard work as I scan the thinning crowd before me.

"Sadie?" This time my voice is more of a whimper as reality dawns on me.

"Pretty, what's wrong?" a deep voice booms before Rhett and Dane flank my sides, both of them looking less than perfect. Blood covers their faces, Dane's shirt is

233

damn near red, and their knuckles are busted and swollen.

"I-I—"

"Where's Sadie?" Dane asks, his eyes wide, his face probably pale if it weren't for the blood covering him.

"I don't know. She was right there and then some guys ran into us and... fuck... I don't know."

"Jesus fucking Christ," Rhett barks, scrubbing his hands over his short hair as he looks around. "She's got to be here somewhere."

"Let's split up. Pretty, you stay here. We'll bring her back."

My heart thunders in my chest, fear that I don't want to acknowledge poisoning my veins. I don't know how I know, but they're not going to find her. She's not here.

She's gone.

My knees buckle as reality hits me.

He's got them both.

My cunt of a fucking father has both my mom and my girl.

My stomach twists painfully, and there's nothing I can do but lean over the table behind me and puke. As I lift a trembling hand to wipe my mouth, images of all the things he could possibly do to them to punish me—us—for our disobedience play out in my mind.

My stomach rolls once more, but I manage to hold it this time.

Dane approaches, a grim expression on his face. Our eyes meet, but no words are needed. He feels it too, the arctic chill of fear racing down his spine that something is going to happen to her.

"Anything?" Rhett barks, joining us only seconds later.

Neither of us says anything. We don't need to.

"Fuck." A hopeless expression passes across his face, and it does little to make me feel better about any of this. He's the strong one, the one who always finds a way out of this shit, who gives me the strength to see things in a slightly more positive light. The fact that he's panicking is not a good sign.

"Check her cell," Dane says in a rush. "You've still got the tracker on her, right?"

"Yeah." Rhett digs into his pocket, pulling his cell out, and taps on the screen.

Dane and I stand there, waiting with bated breath to find out if she's got out and to safety or if this is worse. If the dread that's sitting heavy in my stomach is there for a very good reason.

"It says she's still here," he says, looking up at us.

"Bathroom?" Dane asks.

"Go check. Pretty, let's sweep every fucking inch of this place for our girl." He hits call on her number and lifts his cell to his ear, but he quickly shakes his head.

I take off in the opposite direction to Dane as the three of us push aside the fact that this place is now teeming with cops and focus on our girl.

Sadie is smart—smarter than us, most of the time. She'll have got herself out of the way, to safety.

Wouldn't *she?*

Turning my back on the chaos, I search each booth, behind the bar, even an unlocked storage closet I find, but I don't find any sign that she's still here. I'm making my way back to where I left the guys when something amongst a pile of broken chairs and upturned tables catches my eye.

"Fuck," I bark, recognizing the studded, black leather purse.

Shoving all the remnants of furniture away, I grab it, finding the strap broken. I rush to pull it open, and inside I find exactly what I was expecting. Her cell and wallet. The screen lights up, and in a panic, I swipe it.

"Sadie?" Rhett barks, the emotion and fear in his voice more than evident, and only feeds my own.

"No. It's Pretty. I just found her purse."

"Fuck," he breathes, making my heart plummet into my feet. "I'll get Stray. Meet you out back. Don't get fucking arrested, Pretty," he warns. "We're gonna fucking need you."

His words should make me happy, but I feel nothing but bone-chilling fear.

"O-okay."

Making my way back past the bar, I slip out of a back door, and after a couple of minutes, I stumble out into the parking lot. Blue flashing lights fill the air, and more sirens in the distance tell me that this situation isn't going to get any better anytime soon.

Not two seconds later, the door at my back flies opens and Savage and Stray race from the building, blood still covering them.

"Pacman is picking us up down the street. Come on," Rhett shouts, immediately taking off through the lot toward a dark alley at the back.

Pacman is sitting with the engine running when we get to him and all pile into the truck.

"Go," Stray barks, his voice cold, empty.

"What do we know?" Savage demands.

"Statham came with a couple of guys for a meeting with Ray. Everything was fine. A couple of his boys stayed out in the clubhouse with us, but there was nothing unusual about it until Rosi noticed that Victoria went to the bathroom and never came back."

"Fuck," I hiss. "She wouldn't have left. She just fucking wouldn't," I say.

"We know, Pretty," Dane assures me, his hand clamping down on my thigh in support.

"This was him. He's got enough of Savage Falls PD in his pocket to be able to pull something like this off."

"Yeah, but so have we. Statham would never allow—"

"He didn't know." Dane says what I'm thinking. "Some motherfucker has double-crossed us."

"Then he's going to fucking pay," Pacman growls, sharing our anger.

He doesn't ask about Sadie, so I can only assume that Savage has already explained just how fucked up Dane's birthday is turning out.

And to think, I was nervous as fuck about our plans for tonight. Don't get me wrong, I was totally on board with Sadie's wicked plans for Dane. I was just... yeah. Safe to say that this thing between me and Dane is new, and I can't deny that it makes me a little anxious. He deserved the best fucking night, and I wanted to be a part of that. I certainly didn't want anything like this.

I'd give anything right now to be back at the apartment with Sadie right beside me as we—hopefully—rocked his fucking world.

Lifting my hand, I push my hair back from my brow, pulling until it stings. Tipping my head back, I stare up at the roof, praying that this is all some fucked-up nightmare and that I'm going to wake up any moment and find I'm actually in bed with Sadie safe in my arms.

Warm fingers wrap around my wrist, prying my hand from my hair before they twist with mine and hold tight.

"We'll find them. And then we'll kill that motherfucker. I fucking promise you, bro," Dane says, his voice deadly. When I drag my head down and look at him, I find his eyes dark and murderous, as if he's already planning a million and one ways to make that killing as painful as fucking possible.

The second we pull through the compound gates, the three of us jump from the truck before it's even come to a stop. Some of our brothers have already made it back safe and are inside the clubhouse, but most we left behind still fighting or in cuffs.

None of us have time to think about them, though. The only two people who matter right now are Sadie and my mom.

"Down here," Ray barks as we make our way through the room toward his office—only he doesn't lead us in there. Instead, he pushes open the door to Church.

Ray, Micky, Pike, Crank, and Diesel are already seated. I don't even question how the latter two beat us here.

"What do we know?" Ray asks, his voice calm but dangerous as he casts an eye over Savage and Stray's beaten faces.

"Pretty found her purse. It's got her cell inside. We have no way of tracking her."

"Fuck," Prez barks.

"Victoria?" Dane asks.

"Same."

"Motherfucker," Savage grunts.

"So what the fuck are we meant to do now? We can't

just sit here and wait for that cunt to give us a breadcrumb or two."

"What did Statham say?" Dane asks

"He knew nothing. Thought his boys were loyal," Prez assures us.

"And we trust him?" Savage asks, his brow quirked. It's no secret that he's never been Statham's biggest fan, but he's always trusted Ray's judgment when it comes to Savage Falls' police chief.

Silence ripples through the room, the reality of the situation making it hard to even suck in a fucking breath, let alone attempt to figure this shit out.

"The second the guys start coming back, we send them out searching. This fuck isn't going to win this thing. He... h-he can't," Ray says, his voice cracking, which only makes the ball of emotion currently lodged in my throat grow.

"You two go and get cleaned up. I don't need you coating all my floors in blood."

"No, Prez. We need—"

"What you need, Savage, is to do as you're fucking told," Ray barks, his patience quickly running out. "I need to make some calls. It's time to call in some favors and put this motherfucker in the ground for good."

Ray's eyes meet mine. There's an apology within them, but I don't need it.

"I take the final shot," I say, my voice hard and colder than I was expecting.

"You got it, son."

"I'll call my boys," Crank says, pushing back from the table and pulling his cell out. "We'll get this motherfucker and get your girls back." He squeezes Dane's shoulder in support as he slips out of the room with Diesel hot on his tail.

"We should have fucking killed him the first time he laid a hand on your mother, Pretty."

"Agreed."

The three of us stand, our shoulders dropped in defeat as we make our way out of the room.

"Rhett, oh my God," River screams, running at him at full speed. "Are you okay? Where's Sadie?"

"We don't know," Dane says, dragging River's attention from her brother.

Her eyes widen in horror right as Quinn and Kat join us.

"We think my dad has her. My mom, too."

"Shit. Can you track her? Can you—"

"No. Neither of them has their cell."

Quinn slams her hands down on her hips, anger and disbelief washing across her face. "And you didn't think to fucking inject her with a chip or something?" she asks, shocking the fuck out of me. "You're meant to be fucking protecting her, you assholes," she squeals, beginning to lose her shit as she starts slapping Rhett as if it's going to fucking help.

"Someone restrain her," he grunts. "I'm going to clean up. Then we need to get out there."

River and Kat pull Quinn back, allowing both Dane and Savage to escape.

"It's going to be okay," I assure Quinn, pulling her into my arms and holding her tight.

Thank fuck she returns my embrace, because hell if I don't need it right now.

y eyelids flutter open as pain ricochets through my skull, and I sit up.

What the—

Ouch.

The room spins as I reach blindly for something to steady me. But my body crumples against the hard, unforgiving floor.

"Sadie Ray," a voice calls from somewhere inside the darkness. "Sadie, sweetheart."

"V-Victoria?" I choke out, trying again to get my bearings, but a brass band beats in my head.

Bang. Bang. Bang.

Inhaling a ragged breath, I try pushing up again, only to find my arms are like jelly. "W-what... I... can't..."

"I think they drugged us," she says, her voice clearer this time.

"W-who?" Darkness edges into my poor vision, my head rolling on my shoulders. I'm losing the fight to stay conscious, fear and pain pulling me under. But I hear her. Like a whisper in the wind, I hear the name she spits.

"Grant."

The next time I wake up, everything is a little clearer and the pain has reduced to a dull throb. Gingerly, I push up onto my hands and manage to shuffle back to the wall.

"Victoria?" I scan the small space. "Vic—"

"Over here, sweetheart."

My eyes snap to the far corner of the room, bile rushing up my throat when I find her in the shadows. "Oh my God," I breathe. "What did he do to you?"

She cracks a sad, exhausted smile. "Nothing he hasn't done a hundred times before."

Her face is a patchwork of bruises, cuts and scratches. It barely looks like Wes's mom.

"W-why is he doing this?"

"My husband, ex-husband, is a very sick man." She inhales a shuddering breath, and I feel it all the way down to my soul.

"My dad—"

"Will find us, I know he will," she says, as if there's no other option here.

But I don't feel her confidence as memories of the club slowly come back to me.

"I lost my purse," I whisper. Which means I have no cell phone, which means Rhett won't be able to track me.

Which means...

No, Sadie. Don't go there.

We'll make it out of this in one piece. We have to.

Grant Noble is a well-respected member of society. He has friends in high places. Friends on the—

"A cop took me."

"Officer Duke," Victoria says.

"How do you—"

"Dan Duke is one of Grant's oldest friends. The two of them went to college together. There's nothing they wouldn't do for each other."

There's something in her words that make me sit straighter.

"What do you mean?"

"Dan knew, sweetheart. He knew what Grant was capable of, what he was doing to me and Wes all these years, and he... he never once intervened."

Heavy footsteps sound beyond the door and fear races down my spine. Although I'm lucid now, I still feel the lingering effects of whatever drug they gave me. And I know I won't be able to fight my way out of this, not yet. Not while I can barely lift my limbs.

A lock jangles on the other side of the door before it swings open, black suit pants and polished shoes stepping out of the abyss.

"Ahh, I see the club princess is awake." Grant Noble looms down over me like a monster in the dark. "Nice of you to finally join us. Although my Victoria kept me company while you were out cold."

A shudder runs through me at his empty tone, at the way his eyes eat up my bare skin. I felt sexy and confident wearing this dress for my guys, but now I feel dirty, tainted by his sleazy gaze as he leers at me.

"My daddy will rip you limb from limb for doing this," I snarl.

His hand shoots out, grabbing me by the throat. He yanks me forward so hard, my head feels disconnected from my shoulders.

"Your daddy is the reason we're all here in the first

place. Touching what's mine. Taking things that belong to me. If I had my way, he and that vile club would have been burned to the ground a long time ago."

My vision begins to blur around the edges as his fingers tighten around my windpipe.

"Grant," Victoria says calmly. "Grant, don't do this. Look at me."

His body begins to tremble.

"Sweetheart, look at me."

That works, and his grip loosens as he slowly glances in her direction.

"It's me you want, Grant. I'm right here. I won't fight, I promise. But you have to let Sadie Ray go... you have to—"

He drops me like a sack of bricks, and I whimper as my elbow smashes against the hard floor.

Tears stream down my face as I watch him move toward her. It's like he's in a trance, solely focused on the beaten bruised woman crouched on the floor.

Grant scoops Victoria up, holding her like she's something precious. "I need you, Vic." He presses his head to hers, breathing her in. "Don't leave me again. Don't ever fucking leave me."

"I won't, darling." She touches his face, smiling up at him. For a second, the whole scene has me confused, but then her eyes slide to mine and she gives me an imperceptible nod. In that split second, I know... I know she's trying to save me.

"N-no," I cry out as Grant walks out of the room with her and the door slams shut behind them.

Silence echoes around me, my heart hollow as I hear another door close by open and shut. Bed springs creak and groan. Grant's muffled voice and Victoria's soft purr.

It doesn't take a genius to work out what's happening.

What she's sacrificing to save me from the same fate.

Tears stream down my cheeks as I jump to my feet, desperately searching for something—anything—to help us out of here.

But the room is empty, stripped of any potential weapon or tool.

I do find a bottle of water, and I'm so thirsty I tear off the cap and gulp it down. Sliding down the wall, I drop my head back against the cool surface. My dad and the guys will be going out of their minds, especially with no way to trace us. I just hope they don't do anything reckless before they fall into the trap Grant has set for them.

Because I don't doubt that's what this is—a trap.

Grant Noble hates the club. He hates my father. In his eyes, he lost everything to the Sinners. And there is nothing more dangerous than a man with nothing left to lose.

I don't know how long I sit there, trying to ignore the gentle creaks of the mattress, the muted grunts and groans. Burying my face in my hands, I try to block it all out and ignore the reality of what's happening down the hall somewhere.

But it isn't long before the screams start.

And those...

Those I can't ignore.

When the door finally bursts open and Grant shoves a barely conscious Victoria inside, I'm not sure how much time has passed.

When you're listening to something so vile, so cruel and heart-wrenching, time has a funny way of suspending itself.

He glares down at her, a strange mix of regret and anger etched into his features. Then with a murmured "Fuck," he retreats out of the room and locks the door.

"Victoria." I crawl over to her and pull her limp body into my arms. "Victoria?"

She's a mess with fresh cuts and bruises, her thighs and neck littered with finger marks and vicious red welts.

"I... I'm okay." She inhales a sharp, pained breath. "W-water."

"Of course." I gently lay Victoria down and hurry to retrieve another bottle. "Here." I cradle her head in my lap and bring the bottle to her lips.

"I'm so sorry. I'm so—"

"Shh, sweetheart." She pats my hand, and I'm awed by this woman's inner strength.

Here she is, broken and beaten... raped by that... that monster, and she's reassuring me.

"I'm going to get us out of this." I promise as I stroke her hair.

It doesn't take long for Victoria to drift off, leaving me alone once more.

I lean back against the wall, careful not to move her, and I close my eyes, making a silent vow to myself and her. We'll make it out of this.

We have to.

Because we both have too much to live for.

And that...

That's worth fighting for.

Time is meaningless.

The next time I wake up, Victoria's gone. But there are no screams, no grunts of pleasure or creaks of a mattress.

When she returns, the blood has been washed off her face and she looks brighter. Grant hasn't come for her again, not yet. But we both know he will. He fills the spaces between us, blotting out what little light we have from the crack under the door.

"Do you want to talk about it?" I ask, wondering how much time has passed.

It feels like forever, when in reality, I know it's probably no more than a day or two.

"Oh, sweetheart." She sucks in a thin breath. "I don't even know where I'd start."

"The beginning?" I suggest.

"It was always him, you know. Always your dad." She gives me a small, sad smile. "I loved that man, something fierce. I see a lot of myself in you, you know. Swept up in those intense first love feelings."

"I... I don't know what to say."

"You don't have to say anything. I see the way you look at your boys. It's the same way I used to look at your daddy."

"I can't imagine you both back then."

Victoria lets out a soft sigh. "We were young and in love. We thought we had our whole lives..." She trails off, staring out at nothing. "But it wasn't our time."

"Has... has Grant always been this... violent?"

"Sadie Ray." She looks at me with those kind, knowing eyes of hers. "It wasn't always like this... but as the years went by, he became... obsessed."

"With the club?"

She nods. "I didn't think he'd actually ever do anything besides lobby the mayor about the club's presence in Savage Falls. But then you met Wes and..."

"And the rest is history." Guilt floods me.

Is this all my fault?

Am I responsible for everything?

"No, sweetheart. Don't even think it. Even if you hadn't met my son, and I'm so happy the two of you found each other, Grant would have found another reason."

But she's said the words now, and she can't take them back. They fester inside me, growing roots and snaking around my heart.

"I'm so sorry," I whimper, my heart breaking clean in two. "For everything."

"Wesley loves you, sweetheart. And I love your father," she says, tears filling her dull eyes. "I always have."

26

DANE

I t's been four days since we last saw Sadie, since Wes last spoke to his mom.

And despite the time that's passed, we're no closer to finding either of them.

We can only assume that they're together. Or at least we hope they are, because the thought of them being alone and terrified is too much to take.

I grab the two mugs of coffee I just made and walk over to where Wes is currently sitting at our usual table at the back of the clubhouse. Only, he's no longer really sitting. He's slumped over the table with his head on his arms, his back steadily lifting and falling with his exhaustion.

"I brought you a coffee," I say softly to see if he's actually asleep or not.

His body tenses as I sit down beside him, giving me my answer. "I can't do this anymore," he mutters quietly into his arms.

Reaching out, I squeeze his shoulder in support. "We'll find them."

They're three words I've said countless times over the past few days, yet the promise within them has never felt emptier than it does right now.

There's a huge gray cloud over the entire compound. I swear I haven't seen a single fucker smile for four whole days. And as much as I don't want to fucking smile, I could really use someone else's joy right now. Anything that will help distract me from this reality.

Lifting his head, Wes looks over at me, his dark, exhausted eyes locking onto mine. My breath catches in my throat.

I want to do something. I want to make it better, even just a little bit.

But what can I do that's going to have any effect other than find them and bring them home safely?

He's drowning in his own despair right in front of me. I've never felt more useless in my entire life. He's my brother, and right now, I'm failing him. I'm failing everyone. Rhett, Sadie, Victoria, Ray, even myself.

"Bro," I breathe, not knowing what else to say.

He just shakes his head, slumping back this time and staring at the ceiling, forcing my hand from his shoulder.

The sight of him wrecks me.

"I brought you coffee," I say again.

Silence falls between us as I fight for something to say, but there are no words. The longer this goes on, the more unlikely it is that there will be a good outcome here. But I can hardly say that to him. It's bad enough that he's probably already thinking it.

Just when I think he's not going to do anything, he surprises me by grabbing my hand.

His grip is brutal, like he needs my support just to keep him afloat. "I need to do something," he whispers. "I can't sit here any longer, looking at all these miserable faces."

"You and me both, man."

Rhett, Ray, Pacman, and a few others are out searching. But all our efforts have been pointless this far.

"Drink that, then we'll get out of here."

He nods, not even asking what my plans are, just trusting whatever I'm thinking.

We drink our coffees in silence, the weight of everything pressing down on us.

"Come on," I say, grabbing his empty mug once he's finished and taking them both back to the bar for someone else to wash up.

Wes follows me down toward my room. Ray's given him his own room now, but he seems to prefer hanging out in mine. Fine by me. I don't particularly want to be alone either.

If it weren't for him and Rhett, I'd be a fucking mess. But without even knowing it, both of them are keeping me going.

"Here," I say, throwing a pair of sweats at him. "We're gonna go work out."

He catches the fabric when it hits his chest and watches me as I shrug out of my cut and drop my own jeans in favor of some shorts.

He follows my moves, and in only a couple of minutes we're heading back down the hallway toward our gym. It's old and most of the equipment needs replacing after years of abuse by us, but it still does its job. Although, it's not the equipment I've actually come down here for.

It's empty, much like I was expecting it to be.

Plugging my cell into the speakers, I hit play on one of

my workout playlists and grab the tape from the shelf, where I leave my cell.

"Hands," I demand, walking over to Wes.

"What are you doing?" he asks, barely sounding like he's got the energy to hold them up, let alone to spar with me.

"You're channeling your energy wrong," I tell him.

"I don't have any fucking energy."

"I know. You're drowning. You need to find your fight. When we find them, they're going to need you, Pretty."

"When?" he mutters, watching my every move as I tape his hands.

"Yes. When. Anything else isn't an option."

The second I release him, his arms drop to his sides as I set to work on my own. With my hand wrapped around his upper arm, I drag him into our makeshift ring. "Come on then," I say, shoving him in the chest.

"I don't want to fight you, Dane," he says, but there's no strength behind his words, and as I stare into his eyes, I see darkness wash through them.

"See, I think you do. I think you're desperate to do something, to take some control back. Hit me."

"No."

"You want to feel useful right now? Then get in fucking shape. You're a mess, Noble," I say, taking a risk using that name. "You're unfocused. You've dropped the ball. We need to be able to rely on you. But right now, we can't."

His lips purse, a sure sign that my words hit their mark. They're total bullshit. I'm only baiting him, but I know him better than he thinks I do, and I know exactly which buttons to press to get him riled up.

"You're everything he's accused you of being, Noble. Useless. A failure."

A growl rumbles deep in his throat.

"A disappointment."

"Argh." His low roar filters through the air as he surges forward, taking a swing at me.

I block it, only for him to come at me from the other side, his taped fists jabbing me in the ribs, making my breath catch.

"No," he booms.

"Then fucking prove it, Noble. Show me who you really fucking are. Prove that you're a man Sadie can be proud of, someone she can depend on."

He flies at me like a man possessed, and I smile at him like a fucking lunatic when his fist races toward my jaw.

"Yes, Pretty," I bark as pain shoots down my neck. "Give me some fire. Some fucking fight."

We dance around each other, taking hits where we can.

"Fuck, yes," I pant, pausing for a beat to grab a bottle of water, throwing another at him, and dragging my sweat-soaked shirt off. "Again," I demand.

He throws a punch that collides with my eyebrow, instantly splitting it open.

"More. Give me everything you've got." And he does.

The music gets drowned out by our heaving breaths and grunts and groans each time we collide, putting our desperation to good use.

"Harder. Fuck. Come on, Pretty. You're a fucking Sinner now. Show me how we do it."

My muscles burn, my body aches, but at no point do either of us give in. I always knew he was as sadistic as me. He just needed a push in the right direction to show him how much he needed the pain.

"Holy shit," I bark when my bloodied, taped-up fist connects with Pretty's mouth, his lip splitting open, blood spraying everywhere as he stumbles back.

He bends over at the waist, sucking in a huge lungful of breath as I stand watching him. My own chest heaves from the exertion, but fuck do I feel better.

We might be no further forward, but I needed that. I needed the outlet for some of this fucking fury that's poisoning my veins from not being able to fix this fucked-up mess.

"More?" I ask when he stands, his eyes meeting mine, a deadly expression on his face. "Pretty, are you—"

He collides with me. This time, it's not his fist but his entire body. We only come to a stop when he presses me into the ropes around the ring.

"Fuck," I breathe, still holding his eyes as his fingers thread into my hair.

His lips collide with mine in a brutal, desperate, hungry kiss. His tongue licks into my mouth, searching for mine, which eagerly joins in as he presses harder against me.

"I need—" he starts, only to be cut off when he keeps kissing me. It's wet and dirty, the perfect exorcism for the despair we're both drowning in. "I need to feel something, Dane. Something other than the pain," he confesses into our kiss.

"I've got you," I promise him, turning the tables and taking charge, pushing him until his back hits the wall.

My fingers wrap around his shirt, dragging the damp fabric from his body. I'm just about to shove my hand into his sweats to take things further when a throat clears behind us, like a fucking ice-cold bucket of water.

I jump back, putting some space between us. I'm not ashamed. Far fucking from it. But we've got e-fucking-nough going on right now. We don't need any more fucking drama.

Looking at the door, I find a furious looking Rhett standing there with his arms crossed over his chest. "Are you two for fucking real?"

"What?" I bark, wiping my sweaty brow with my forearm. "We were sparring."

"Yeah, it fucking looked like it."

His eyes drop below my waist. I don't need to follow his gaze. I'm more than aware of the fact that my cock is trying to bust out of my shorts.

"We need you both in Church. Statham's here with news."

"What's happened?" Pretty asks, seemingly coming back to life and stepping up beside me.

"I don't know. I came to get you two fucking pricks."

Swiping my shirt from the floor, I use it to clean my face and wipe my chest, following Rhett out of the room without looking back.

I know Pretty is behind me. I can feel him.

Grim faces stare back at us from the table, and my heart sinks into my feet.

"What's happened?" I demand, trying not to jump to conclusions from their expressions.

"We've found the officer who took Sadie."

Relief floods me. "That's good news, right?" I ask, my brows pulling together in confusion.

"He'd had his throat slit. We're no further forward."

"Motherfucker," I mutter, dropping into an empty chair.

"Tell us you've got something positive," Rhett demands, drilling Statham with a deadly look.

The chief swallows nervously, and any hope I had withers and dies right along with it.

27

SADIE

"You can't keep doing this," I say to Victoria after Grant shoves her into our room again.

She's dirty and unkempt—we both are, thanks to the endless days of little food or water or chance to clean ourselves.

Grant and his goons—I've seen at least two of them come and go—keep us locked up in this dank room, only letting us out for a toilet break. Or when Grant wants to take his anger out on Victoria.

Her body is littered with bruises, bite marks and scratches. At first, I cried. I cried so much over how much he's hurting her. But now I'm just angry. It doesn't matter, though. I've scoured every corner of our sparse room and there's nothing.

Nothing that will help us escape this mess.

"I'm fine." Victoria waves me off, wincing with the sharp movement.

"He's not going to stop..."

"No, he isn't." She sniffles, trying her hardest to put

on a brave face. "But I know my ex-husband, sweetheart, and this is all part of his game."

Yeah, his game to drive my dad and Wes out of their minds.

"It's been days." My voice cracks, defeat weighing heavily on my chest.

Wherever Grant is holding us, Dad and the guys haven't been able to find us. Which means he holds our fate in his hands.

But looking at the state of Victoria, I'm not sure how much longer her body can take this.

"There must be something," I mutter to myself, pacing back and forth. At least when I'm moving, I feel a little more in control.

"We just have to wait it out," Victoria says weakly.

"For how long?" I let out a weary sigh, coming to a stop in front of the door. There's no use in trying to open it; it's locked.

It's always locked.

Like we're caged animals. Prisoners.

...Or prey.

The thought makes me shudder. It's hard to believe that the monster beyond the door is Wes's dad, the man who raised him.

Wes is so full of love and warmth and goodness... He's everything Grant Noble will never be. But my heart still breaks for the boy with the weight of the world on his shoulders.

Footsteps sound outside and Victoria urges me away. I drop down beside her, gently tucking her into my side, bracing myself for Grant to appear.

The door swings open and he steps inside, taking the

air with him. He sneers down at us, disgust etched into every line of his face as he studies me.

"What do you want?" I ask the question I've asked numerous times before.

"Victoria." He snaps his fingers. "Let's go."

"No." I lurch forward, shielding her with my body. "She's had enough."

"Listen here, you little bitch." He grabs a fistful of my hair and yanks me up. Victoria screams, trying to keep me rooted to the floor, but it's useless. Grant is too strong and we're both weak from being locked away in here.

I press my lips together, swallowing the yelp of pain crawling up my throat.

"Scream, bitch. Scream like you do for that useless son of mine and your biker boyfriends." He winds his hand tighter, ripping the roots from my skull. Silent tears roll down my cheeks, my body shaking with rage and pain, but still, I trap the screams behind my lips.

He lifts a brow at my defiance. "I can think of a hundred other ways to make you scream. Maybe I should—"

"N-no!" Victoria rushes out. "You don't want her. She's nothing more than a club whore. You're better than that, Grant. So much better."

I know she's trying to distract him, but her words still sting.

Grant hesitates, his eyes flitting between me and his ex-wife. "Grant, baby, don't do this, please." Victoria manages to push up into a sitting position, reaching for his hand. "This isn't you. It's not—"

The blare of his cell phone cuts through the room. At first, he ignores it, his wrath fixed on me. But when it doesn't quit, he finally releases me with a jerky shove and steps back to check his cell.

"Fuck," he barks, swiping a hand through his hair. "I'll be right back. Don't go anywhere." He smirks darkly and marches from the room.

"Thank God." Victoria lets out a shaky breath, reaching for me. But I gently grasp her wrists.

"That's it," I blurt out.

"W-what is?"

"I know how we can get out of here."

Confusion crinkles her eyes, and I get it, I do. But this could work.

We can make it work.

We have to.

"Are you sure?" I ask Victoria for the tenth time since Grant left us abruptly.

"It's our only shot."

"But if he hurts you..."

"Sadie Ray, look at me." She takes my hand in hers. "We can do this. I'm stronger than I look, okay? Just be ready."

I nod, hardly able to look her in the eye.

Her face is a patchwork of ugly bruises, the split in her bottom lip swollen and sore.

If this works and we make it out of here alive, it will kill Wes and my dad to see Victoria like this.

"We can't tell them," she says, as if she can hear my thoughts.

"Excuse me?" I gawk at her.

"Your dad and Wesley. We can't ever tell them what

really happened here. I don't want them to have to carry that. The guilt... the agony."

"Victoria, you can't ask that of me. They need to—"

"They need to know we're okay and come out of this thing alive. That's all they need to know. Promise me, sweetheart." She clutches my hand tighter. "Promise me you won't ever tell them."

"I..."

"Please."

"Fine, okay. I won't tell them. But they're going to know something bad happened. You're a mess."

"We'll deal with that later, okay?" Her weak smile does little to ease the giant knot in my stomach. "No matter what happens, you need to stick to the plan."

It was my plan, and yet Victoria is the calm one right now.

"Sadie," she snaps when I don't answer.

"Uh, yeah?"

"Tell me you can do this."

I nod, my mouth dry and stomach empty. It's probably a good thing we've hardly been fed anything because my stomach contents would be all over the floor just thinking about this.

But it's this...or nothing. And we can't stay here much longer, not with the way Grant is abusing Victoria's body. Maybe that's his plan all along. To break us slowly. One at a time. Return us in little pieces to my dad.

With a shuddering breath, I nod again. "I can do it. Just... just be careful."

"Come here, sweetheart." Victoria pulls me into her arms, holding me tightly. "Whatever happens, Sadie Ray, I want you to know I'm so happy I got to know you. And if something happens to me but you get the chance to run, I want you to take it, okay?"

"What?" I jerk back as if she's slapped me. "I'm not... I can't—"

My heart is racing so fast, I don't hear the footsteps outside the hall or the door freaking open. I don't feel Grant until it's too late. Until he's got a fistful of hair and he's yanking me backward. Pain ricochets through me, and this time there's no holding back the yelp.

"Grant, don't, please..." Victoria cries, crawling toward us.

"It's time I taught the Sinners' princess a lesson," he grits out.

This isn't the plan.

It isn't how it's supposed to go down. But a strange sense of calm washes over me.

I can do this.

I can take whatever punishment he's so determined to dish out. I manage to twist around, locking eyes with Victoria. "It's okay," I mouth. "You do it."

But she shakes her head, tears rolling down her cheeks.

"Take me instead," Victoria cries. "It isn't Sadie you want to hurt, it's me. I betrayed you. All these years, I pretended, I—"

Grant stills, a ripple going through the air.

No.

No. No. No.

It isn't supposed to happen like this.

Grant shoves me hard, and I crumple to the cold, unforgiving floor. He walks right past me, picking Victoria up with a hand wrapped around her throat.

"No," I cry, reaching for his pant leg. "Don't, you

bastard. Don't touch her."

He brings his foot down hard on my hand and I almost puke, pain splintering me apart.

Fuck. That hurts.

But I steel myself, shutting off my emotions as I try to get to them. He has Victoria pinned against the wall, glowering at her.

"I always knew you regretted leaving him. That you'd rather spread your legs for that piece of biker trash than the likes of me." His hand goes to his belt, snapping it open. "But he never came for you. All those years you were right under his nose, and he never came for you. Why do you think that was, my love?" Dragging a finger down Victoria's cheek, Grant leans in and brushes his mouth over hers, shoving one hand roughly up her torn skirt.

"No," I yell again. "Don't."

"Shit the fuck up, you little bitch." He pins me with a wild look. "Or you're next."

Yanking Victoria away from the wall, he throws her down onto the floor and drops to his knees behind her. "Fuck the wrong right out of you," he mutters, pushing her skirt up around her waist. I try not to look, forcing the urge to fight back. To charge at him and kick and scream and scratch and bite until he stops. But that isn't the plan... and Victoria made me promise. She made me promise not to intervene, no matter what happened.

So I sit there, breathing heavily as I watch Grant rape his ex-wife, my eyes not on his jerky, rage-filled movements, but his pants loose around his hips.

Victoria moans, feeding his ego, the sick, twisted part of him that needs to dominate her. "Why do you feel good... shouldn't feel so good," he murmurs.

Victoria catches my eye, silent tears streaming down her cheeks, giving me an imperceptible nod. It's now or never. But I'm not sure I can move... not while he's—

"Now," she mouths.

And I can't breathe.

I can't do anything.

Except, I'm moving, dragging my sore and aching body across the floor inch by inch, careful not to distract Grant. His groans fill the room as he punishes Victoria's body, making my stomach lurch.

"Is that all you've got?" Victoria taunts him, and he backhands her so hard, a sickening crunch goes through the air. I still, holding my breath.

But then Victoria laughs. A wild strangled laugh that sends Grant into a rage.

"I'll fucking show you," he seethes, but I block it all out, reaching for his pant's pocket.

I clamp my lips together, fighting the urge to gag as I manage to retrieve his cell phone. Panic sets in for a second when I realize he could have it PIN protected, but to my relief, it unlocks with ease.

Quickly, I type out a message and hit send, delete it from the sent folder, and stuff it back in his pocket, inching away again.

Lying motionless, I wait for Grant to finish. Wait for him to clamber off Victoria, pull up his pants, fasten his belt, and stalk out of the room as if he didn't almost kill his ex-wife.

And when I see the state of Victoria, barely conscious with fresh bruises littering her body, stark realization hits me.

If this doesn't work...

Neither of us will make it out of this alive.

28

RHETT

I'm lying awake, staring at the shadows moving across my ceiling, when my cell dings with an incoming text.

I know the chances are slim, but still, my heart jumps into my throat that it might be something, anything that could give us a fucking clue as to where we might find our girl.

I'm fucking dying without her, and with each day that passes, the agony of knowing I let her slip through my fingers in that club, the guilt, gets that little bit more unbearable.

This is my fault.

I should have seen the threat coming.

I never should have let her out of my sight.

Reaching for my cell, I lift it in front of my face, squinting against the bright light that makes my eyes water instantly. "FUCK OFF," I boom, damn near launching the thing across the room when I find some bullshit ad for a new half-price tablet.

Putting it back to sleep, I let it drop to my chest with a

thud as I go back to chasing shadows and allowing my grief to consume me.

My exhaustion must eventually win out, because the next thing I know, the ping of my cell fills my ears once more, scaring the ever-loving shit out of me.

My heart races as I scramble to find it.

Something is different this time. I have no idea how I know, but I do, and it makes my hands tremble as I wake my cell up.

Unknown: Track this number DO NOT RESPOND

"Fuck. Fuck. Shit."

I fly out of bed so fast that I don't even realize my foot is twisted in the sheets. Well, not until my entire body weight sends me crashing to the floor, my cheek colliding with the hardwood.

"Fuck," I grunt as pain explodes from the side of my face, but I don't have time to be a pussy about it.

I'm on my feet and pulling on yesterday's clothes in a second before ripping my door open and running down the hallway.

Thankfully, Dane's door is unlocked when I twist the handle and I go flying through, barely stopping before I hit the bed with... both of them in it.

My teeth grind for a beat that while I'm here, barely keeping my shit together about Sadie, they're getting their fucking rocks off.

Pushing that aside, I focus on the issue at hand. "Wake the fuck up," I bark, startling both of them.

I drag the sheets back, somewhat relieved that they're

wearing clothes and not fucking cuddling like nothing is adrift.

"Wha— Sadie?" Dane says in a rush as he wakes.

"Yes, now get fucking dressed."

"Where is she? Is she okay? Mom?" Wes stutters, taking a little longer to come around.

"I don't have details. Meet us in Church."

Turning my back on them, I run from the room, pounding my fists on every single door I pass. "Prez, get up. It's Sadie and Victoria."

By the time I march toward the door to Church, Ray, Pacman, Dane, and Wes are hot on my heels.

"What do we know?" Ray asks, taking his seat at the end of the table, looking more awake than he should for this hour. But then, I guess news about your missing daughter and the love of your life will do that to a man.

"I just got this..." I slide my cell across the table with the message open.

"Yes," he hisses, determination etching into the lines of his face. "Pac, trace this number. Now."

Pacman takes my cell and rushes from the room, leaving me feeling a little deflated. Now we've had contact, I want action, not to have to sit here and wait even longer.

"We're going to get them back," Ray says to no one in particular. I can't help wondering if the words are more for him than any of us. He needs the reassurance just as badly.

I swear to God that it's the longest ten minutes of my fucking life before Pacman comes back with the answers we need.

"It's in the middle of nowhere, right on the other side of Red Ridge, on the Colton border."

"Get the men ready. This fucking ends today. Grant Noble's life ends to-fucking-day." His chair legs scrape across the wooden floor as he harshly pushes it back.

Following his stare, I look across at Pretty, who's as white as a fucking ghost, wringing his hands in his lap and his eyes wide.

"Your time to shine, son."

Pretty's chin drops, and for the briefest of seconds, I expect him to refuse, to not want to be a part of ending his own father's life.

But then determination like I've never seen on him before covers his face, and he stands. "You got it, Prez. That motherfucker is dead."

With a nod, he marches from the room—I assume to go and get his newly-issued pistol and switchblade, but it could quite easily be to go and puke, based on the panic in his eyes.

"We ride in ten," Ray says, his hand clamping down on my shoulder. "We're gonna get our girls back."

"Fuck yeah, we are."

"Stray."

"Prez." He nods.

"Call your boys. We need everyone on this. That cunt isn't getting a fucking chance to weasel out this time."

"Crank is already on the case."

Ray marches out of the room before us.

"You sure about this?" Dane asks, concern in his tone.

"Yes. Aren't you?"

"What if it's a trap?"

"And what if it's not?" I understand his words. They make a hell of a lot of sense. But for some reason, I know that this isn't a trap. Sadie was behind that message.

I just know it.

"It's not. That was Sadie."

"But how—" My lips purse in frustration and Dane just nods at me. "I trust you, brother."

"Let's go get our girl."

When we get back out to the clubhouse, we're just in time to see Ray knock back a shot of whiskey. Dane shoots me a concerned glance, but I wave it off.

"Go and check on your boyfriend. He looked like he was gonna puke his—"

"He's not my fucking boyfriend," Dane snaps. "We just— Do you know what? Fuck you, Rhett."

He storms off with his fists curled at his sides.

"You want one?" Ray asks.

"No. I'll be outside. This needs to end."

In only ten minutes, the silence around us is ruined when every bike in the lot rumbles to life.

Adrenaline shoots through my veins as Dane and I ride out right behind Ray.

We're coming, princess. We're fucking coming.

The ride to the Red Ridge compound seems to take forever, but when Crank and their guys emerge through the gates, falling into formation with us, I'm even more convinced that this is the right thing to do.

After Pacman got all the intel he could about the location in just a few minutes, we made a quick plan—but really, we're going in blind. We could be about to walk into anything.

It's not stopping any of the guys who are following us, their need for revenge burning almost as brightly as mine.

The sun is just starting to come up when we approach the abandoned house that sits on top of the hill where we believe Sadie and Victoria are being held. But the morning fog stops us from getting a good visual as we approach.

The Red Ridge guys overtake us, heading around the back of the land in the hope of catching the motherfucker if he decides to try to run.

My fingers tighten around my handlebars and we begin to slow as I narrow my eyes at the house.

That's not fucking fog.

It's smoke.

"Prez," I shout, hoping like fuck he can hear me as I pull up beside him. "It's on fire."

His eyes widen as he looks at the house. "Motherfucker."

Revving our engines, we get closer before abandoning our bikes and running the final distance.

As we approach, the flames we couldn't see from the bottom of the hill begin to flicker behind the windows.

"Ready for this?" Ray asks me as I run beside him, Dane, Wes, and the others right on our tail.

"Always."

But right before we can get to the door, something inside explodes, blowing out all the windows and forcing us all backward.

The flames that were previously restrained now lick up the outside of the house.

"Sadie," Dane screams, his voice full of unrestrained fear as he runs for the front door. The second he has it open, flames billow out of it, stopping him from even trying to get inside.

"Around the back," Wes shouts, following a couple of other guys already heading in that direction.

The scent of devastation fills my nose as I fight to drag

in each breath through the smoke, the house crackling and crumbling beside us.

Frantically, I look around, hoping like hell she's already got out, that both of them are safe somewhere, but there's too much smoke to see anything.

Ray is the first one to the back door, and he pulls it open a beat before a loud bang sounds out.

"Ray," I scream, knowing what's about to happen.

I grab his arm and pull him back just as an explosion in the house sends all of us flying back. "Fuck. FUCK," I bellow as I watch the house consume with flames before us all.

"SADIE."

29

SADIE

"Victoria, you've got to try to stay awake." I brush the hair off her face, taking in her battered and bruised skin.

Images of Grant raping her are imprinted on my mind, but I try to focus on the fact that she's alive, and I managed to get a message out to Rhett.

At least, I hope I did.

It's been at least thirty minutes since Grant left, and so far, nothing. Just the sound of Victoria's pained breaths and the blood roaring in my ears.

"Y-you did good, sweetheart." Victoria manages to smile up at me and it breaks my heart. She's so strong. A survivor in every sense of the word. But if help doesn't come soon...

No, I refuse to believe this is how it ends. That everything we've gone through is for nothing.

"Shh," I soothe. "Save your breath." She might need it before the night is out.

I drop my head back against the wall and inhale a sharp breath.

"They'll come," I whisper. "They have to."

———

I wake up suddenly, startled by the yelling beyond the door.

Victoria is asleep, her face scrunched up in agony as she lies beside me, curled up on the cold, dank floor.

"Fuck, fuck," Grant bellows, his voice drowned out by the loud crash that follows.

Gently lifting Victoria's head off my lap, I creep over to the door and press my ear against it.

"Plan, boss?"

"Get ready to roll," Grant barks.

"And the women?"

"I'll deal with them. You're gonna want to get far away from here before they arrive."

Their voices become muffled, but I heard enough to know help is coming.

Rhett got my message.

It worked.

It really worked.

"Victoria?" I rush over to her and crouch down, trying to wake her.

"S-Sadie," she moans, her eyes fluttering open.

"They're coming, the guys are coming."

"I-it worked?"

I nod, tears springing from my eyes. "We need to be ready, okay?" Carefully, I help her sit up, letting her lean against the wall. When Dad and Wes get a look at her, Grant better be long gone, because no one will protect him from their wrath.

Not that he deserves to walk away.

Not this time.

"Sadie." She clutches my arm. "He won't let us... Grant won't let us—"

"Shh, it's okay. It's going to be okay." I lean in, gently hugging her. "Just sit tight, and when it's time, we'll—"

The lock clunks and the door swings open. Grant's eyes immediately go to Victoria, flashing anger and something else. Something that looks a lot like regret. But it's too late for that, after what he's done.

"What's happening?" I ask innocently.

"Change of plans. Get her up," he demands.

"She's hurt, she can't—"

Grant whips out a gun and aims it right at me. "Get her up and follow me. Make one wrong move and I'll blow her fucking brains out."

He wouldn't, would he?

Think, Sadie. Think.

"Where are you taking us?"

"Taking you?" He lets out a bitter laugh. "Oh, sweetheart, I'm not taking you anywhere. You and that fucking club deserve each other. You can all burn in hell for all I care." Contempt coats his words as he motions for me to get Victoria.

She manages to clamber to her feet, but I have to take her weight, sliding my arm around her waist. "Okay?" I ask, and she nods.

She doesn't look good.

She doesn't look good at all, but I have no choice but to lead her from the room and follow Grant down the hall.

"In there." He tips his head to a doorway with no door hanging on the hinges. My eyes drink in every detail, just in case. It's an old, abandoned house by the looks of it, the paintwork chipped and dirty, the carpet underfoot sticky and well-trodden.

"Sit her down on there and tie her up."

"Grant, no," Victoria cries, but he jabs the pistol in my face.

"Tie. Her. Up."

"Victoria, look at me. It's okay." She practically falls into the chair, wincing in pain. I try my best not to hurt her as I take the cable ties and bind her wrists together behind her back. "I'm so sorry," I whisper, aware of Grant watching my every move.

"Now you," he barks once Victoria is secured to the chair. "Over there."

I spot the second chair and take a seat. He's going to leave us here. Leave us here and try to escape.

But there's something about the unhinged glint in his eye that makes my stomach sink.

"What are you doing, Grant? They're coming, aren't they? My daddy and Wes and the rest of the club are on their way here, right now."

"Shut up, you fucking little bitch." He waves the gun around and I inch backward with my hands up, hoping I haven't made the wrong call here.

"I'm right, aren't I? They're coming." I pause, cocking my head. "I think I hear them. Listen."

Fear flashes in Grant's eyes as he moves to the boarded-up window and peers through a crack in the wooden slats. "I don't see anything," he mumbles, but his words barely register as I dive for the tatty lamp stand on the table. When he turns to see what the commotion is, I'm already there, swinging it high and wide, sending it flying toward his face.

A sickening crunch fills the room, and he roars,

"FUCKING BITCH," staggering backward, clutching his bleeding face.

"I'll fucking gut you for that. I should—"

"Boss," someone yells from inside the house, "we need to leave. Now."

Grant glances to the door and back to me, indecision warring in his eyes. "It'll be sweeter this way." A dark smirk tips his mouth as he backs up toward the doorway, keeping his gun trained on me. "Send Ray my love." He spits the words and then he's gone, slipping into the hall, running from the house.

"Damn coward," I breathe, inhaling deep, as deep as I can.

"Sadie Ray, you're okay... my God..." Victoria sways on the chair, barely lucid.

The rumble of bikes rises in the distance, and relief like I've never known slams into me. "They're here, they're here," I cry, adrenaline surging through me as I scan the room for something to cut the cable ties wrapped around Victoria's wrists.

I'm searching the room, overturning the abandoned pieces of furniture and trash when I stop.

"What is that?" I sniff the air, confusion crinkling my brows. "Do you smell that?" I ask Victoria, but she's too out of it to hear me.

"Fuck," I hiss, hurrying to the doorway and peeking around the corner. Wisps of smoke billow through the cracks, turning the air acrid.

"Oh my God, Victoria," I yell, backtracking into the room.

But she's slumped over, unconscious.

"Shit." I rush over to her, trying to wake her. "There's a fire, we need to get out of here. Wake up, please wake up." Grasping her shoulders, I gently shake her. She moans, barely coming to.

"Crap, okay. Think, Sadie, think." I scan the room again, searching for—

Bingo.

I spot a mirror propped against the far wall. Rushing over to it, I lay it flat on the floor and stomp on it. It shatters into jagged pieces, and I carefully grab the biggest one. It slices into my skin, but there isn't time to worry—not with how quickly smoke is filling the room.

"Okay, here goes nothing." I move around Victoria and start sawing the glass across the cable tie. At first, it doesn't do anything, but then the plastic thins enough for me to snap it in half.

"Yes." I make the fatal mistake of sucking in a breath, almost choking on the smoke.

"Come on, we need to go. Now." Hoisting Victoria's limp body against mine, I all but drag her from the room, my eyes stinging against the now dense air.

The fire is coming from what I assume is the front of the house, so I turn right out of the room, back toward where Grant was keeping us. My lungs smart with every breath, fear racing up and down my spine. But I don't quit.

I can't.

The guys are almost here... I have to do this.

I have to find a way out.

Everything hurts. My muscles threaten to give way under Victoria's dead weight, but we're almost there, at the back of the house. There must be an exit, another way out—or at least a window we can escape through. But I can barely see, barely breathe as the fire rages behind us.

Heat licks against my back, singeing the fine hair on my skin.

"Just a little further," I grit out, my sight growing thin.

There.

I spot it.

A door.

Thank God.

But my relief quickly dies when it won't open.

"No. No, no, no." I slam my palm against it, banging as hard as I can. It rattles on its hinges as if something is blocking it from the other side.

Fuck.

Sitting Victoria down against the wall, I draw back and rush at the door, throwing my entire body weight behind it. It gives a little more, but I'm not sure I can go again. I'm so lightheaded and everything hurts.

Everything.

I will not die here, though.

I can't.

I have too much to live for... too much to fight for.

Fight, Sadie Ray. You have to fight.

With an almighty roar, I rush the door again, slamming my shoulder against the wood. It splinters open and I'm falling. Down, down, down.

I land with a crack, my head spinning.

"What the—" I try to clamber to my knees, glancing back at the door. At Victoria. But something explodes, knocking me backwards, and I lie there, my vision blurring at the edges.

"Victoria?" I yell, but the word doesn't come, my throat raw. "No, no."

Crawling onto my stomach, I take in the house, the

fallen beam blocking the door. The flames licking into the night sky.

The whole house is about to go up, and Victoria is still inside.

She's still inside.

Unconscious.

"No," I cry, clutching at thin air as I try to get to her. "No, please... no."

But I can't. I can't do anything except succumb to the pain radiating in every part of my body.

Forgive me, Wes.

Forgive me.

30

DANE

"Holy fuck," I groan, rolling onto my back as the pain begins to subside from being thrown from the— "Sadie," I scream, the agony from a few seconds ago long forgotten as I scramble to my feet and race toward the almost destroyed house.

Flames still lick up high into the air, smoke billowing from the crumbled remains of what was the old house. There are bodies scattered on the ground from the blast, our men groaning and trying to clamber to their feet. But I don't focus on anyone in my search for her dark hair.

"Sadie, please. Fuck. Please be okay."

"Stray." I spin around, that familiar strangled cry sending a bolt of icy fear straight down my spine.

"Oh fuck." I run at Rhett and drop down to my knees beside him, my eyes filling with tears and making the sight of a broken and battered Sadie in his arms blur.

Blinking them away, I reach for her, cupping her cheek in my dirty hand. "I-is she—"

"Breathing, yeah. But we need to get help. We need—"

A body looms over us, casting us in a dark shadow, and for just a split second, I think it's him. But then reality hits. That cunt isn't stupid enough to hang around here to witness the fallout.

With any hope, he's already dead.

"Have you seen Victoria?" Ray asks in a rush, focusing my mind back on the here and now.

"No," we both answer in unison.

"I'm going in to find her," he states, his voice cold, void of anything other than bone-chilling fear.

Movement behind him catches my eye and I spot Wes drag himself up. But much like when I came back to, it only takes him a second to remember what we're in the middle of.

"Sadie," he cries, his eye fixing on where we're sitting only a few feet away. "Sadie."

He scrambles over, his face twisted in pain. I can't see any obvious injuries on him, but there clearly are some based on the way he fights to join us.

"Is she...?"

"Yes, she's breathing."

A sob erupts from him as he reaches for her. "Mom?"

"I'm going to find her." Ray looks over at the three of us, clearly realizing that Pretty is in no shape to move. "Savage, Stray, with me."

"Shit. Y-yeah. You got her, Pretty?" Rhett doesn't give him a chance to say no, just carefully lowers her body into his arms before the three of us take off toward what's left of the house while Ray calls for her.

"You can't go in there," Rhett states when we get to the twisted remains of what used to be a door.

"I need to find her. You'd do the same for Sadie." It's not a question, it's a fact. One we all know is true.

If Rhett hadn't already found her, we'd tear this place apart until we did.

Sirens blare in the distance, but they're too far away to help, to possibly save Victoria should she still be inside. So after pulling our hoodies over the lower halves of our faces, we follow Ray into the burning remains.

The heat from the fire is unbearable, but we push on, moving aside broken furniture by the door in the hope that she was almost out when the house went up.

Sadie was, and something tells me that she would never have left Victoria.

Ray and Rhett push a dresser aside, and a pair of feet emerge. They're bare, bloodied, bruised, but it's her, I know it is.

"Here," I scream, reaching out to move some of the other rubble that's fallen around her, my hands burning the second I touch any of it.

My breath catches in my throat when my eyes land on her face. Anger was already bubbling inside of me, knowing that motherfucker had them both locked in here, doing fucking knows what to them the past few days... but looking down at her right now, it's all I can do to keep a lid on it.

Thankfully, Ray is able to keep his cool a little more. Fuck knows how.

"Baby," he breathes in the softest voice I've ever heard from him as he reaches down and scoops her up from the floor.

Her body is limp, her arms and legs hanging down as if she's nothing more than a rag doll.

"Pacman and Jax are tailing him," he states as we fight to get out of the house.

My head is spinning, my lungs burning from the

smoke inhalation, but I put it all aside for my concern for both Sadie and Victoria.

What we're dealing with right now is nothing compared to what they've been through.

"Mom," Wes cries, tears already cascading down his blackened face from the blast. "Mom."

"We need to get to the truck. Now," Ray spits. "We can't wait for an ambulance, they won't make it in time."

I look down at Sadie just in time to see her lips move.

"Victoria?" she croaks.

"We've got her, princess," Rhett says before I have a chance, tucking his arms under her body and taking her weight from Wes. "We've got her, and you're both going to be okay. We've got you now."

His soft, encouraging words mixed with Wes's quiet sobs cause a giant lump to form in my throat.

"Let's go," Ray barks, already making his way to our bikes and the truck.

"Come on," I say to Wes, dropping down to help him.

With my arm around his waist and his thrown over my shoulder, we get him to his feet.

"I-I'm okay. Just look after them."

"I'm not fucking leaving you here, bro. Come on. They need you."

I help him into the passenger seat before diving for the driver's side and wheelspin away from the devastation behind us.

Softly spoken words of encouragement come from the back of the truck, Ray and Rhett's voices mingling into one as they speak to Sadie and Victoria.

Every now and then, I hear my girl's voice. But as reassuring as that might be, the pain within it damn near kills me.

So does the sight of Wes slumped in the seat beside me with his head in his hands.

Reaching over, I drag one away and twist my fingers with his. "They're going to be okay, Wes. We found them. We—"

"He blew up the fucking house with them inside, Dane. My father. My own fucking father."

"I know, man. I'm so fucking sorry."

The sound that rips from his throat wrecks me as I catch sight of more tears falling onto his cheeks. I want to comfort him, hold him, fucking anything in an attempt to make this better. But I can't.

We've got to get to the hospital. And then we've got to find his cunt of a father and make him pay for this.

Time for healing can come later.

I abandon the truck in the middle of the ambulance bays outside Red Ridge General ED and jump from the car. Someone must have seen my less than calm arrival, because a couple of nurses come running out of the main entrance.

"We need help," I shout. "Two women from a house explosion."

I pull the doors open to allow Ray and Rhett out and stand back.

Everything starts to blur around me as I watch nurses and doctors surround the vehicle. Gurneys are wheeled from inside, and I can't do anything but watch as both Sadie and Victoria are lowered onto them, people fussing around as they're pushed through the doors to be treated.

I know it's where they need to be, but fuck, watching them push Sadie away from me damn near rips out my heart.

"They're going to be okay," Ray says, but his voice is

anything but firm. He's cracking just like the rest of us, the uncertainty of Victoria's condition weighing down on him.

My eyes find Wes as he leans against the side of the truck. He looks wrecked. Utterly fucking wrecked.

"Bro," I breathe, walking up to him and pulling him into my body, wrapping my arms around him and holding him tight. "It's going to be okay. Anything else isn't an option."

His body trembles in my hold, loud sobs erupting from him that almost make me lose my shit right alongside him.

What happens next doesn't fucking help either, because a heavy arm wraps around my back, and when I drag my face from Wes's neck, I find Rhett beside us, his arms around both of us, his face showing everything he usually hides. His fear, his love, his unfiltered desperation that all of us are going to walk away from this.

"We need to get inside," he says after a few moments as he drags his mask back down into place.

When he releases us and I look over my shoulder, I find Ray already stalking toward the door, his shoulders slumped in defeat.

"Ray needs you," I tell Rhett. "I've got Pretty. He needs checking out."

He hesitates, not wanting to leave us, but he knows I'm right. "Go. The big guy has a fucking heart too, and it's shattered right now."

"Y-yeah." At my words, Rhett turns his back on us and runs to catch up with Ray.

Abandoning the truck where it is, I pull Wes into my side and help get him into the hospital. Ignoring the chairs where both Ray and Rhett are sitting when we get inside, I take him straight to the desk.

"My friend needs attention," I tell the nurse.

"No, I'm fine," Pretty states, although his voice is laced with pain. "Just look after them."

"Check him in, yeah?" I tell the nurse, ignoring his pleas.

"They've already got your mom and Sadie. Checking you over won't stop them helping them."

We take a seat beside Ray and Rhett, the four of us sitting in silence. The world continues to turn around us, but our lives are entirely on pause until someone comes and gives us some information.

I still have no idea if Victoria was breathing or not. I can only hope the fact that Ray was talking to her was a good sign.

I have no idea how long we sit there. How long Wes uses me as a prop to keep him upright with his head on my shoulder and his hand clamped in mine... but by the time a young doctor emerges from the double doors we've all been staring at and locks eyes on Ray, a ripple of dread flows through the air at what he's about to tell us.

"I don't think I can hear this," Wes whispers so quietly, I'm not sure if I'm meant to hear it.

"Whatever happens, we've got you, okay? And we're not going to let go."

Holding him a little tighter, I look up and wait for the news I'm fucking praying for.

31

SADIE

My eyes flutter open, pain rolling through me. "Wh-what?" I push the word past my lips, but it comes out a mere croak.

My throat is raw, dry and tender. I feel like I swallowed glass.

Holy shit, that hurts.

Craning my neck, I scan the room, smiling when my eyes fall on my three guys. Dane and Wes are asleep on one end of the couch underneath the window, while Rhett dozes in the chair beside my bed.

They're here.

They made it.

We made it.

But then memories of what happened rush me, like a floodgate opening. One after another, images of Grant raping Victoria fill my mind, him standing with a gun pointed at me, the smoke, the fire chasing us as we tried to escape.

Oh God, Victoria. My stomach churns and I dry heave.

"Sadie?" Rhett bolts upright. "Fuck, princess, you're awake. You're— shit." He leaps up and grabs a plastic bowl, shoving it under my nose. I retch again, my stomach contracting in violent waves. But nothing comes up.

When the nausea passes, I push the bowl away and sink back against the pillows. "Hey," I whisper.

"Hey." He swallows hard. "Shit, Sadie, I thought... I—"

"Shh." I reach for his hand. "I knew you'd come. I knew you'd find us. Victoria, is she..."

"It's bad, real fucking bad. What happened back there?" His eyes search mine, and I don't doubt for a second that Rhett has put two and two together. But I shake my head, my eyes flicking to where Dane is beginning to stir.

"Princess?" Dane cracks an eye open. "Thank fuck." He's up and out of his seat in less than a second. Rhett steps back, letting Dane get close.

He drops his head to mine carefully and inhales deeply. "Never letting you out of my sight again, Sadie, girl."

"How is he?"

His eyes shutter as he pulls away slightly. "He'll be okay."

Something lurks in Dane's eyes, something that sends a shudder through me. But I don't have a chance to ask what's going through his mind because Wes wakes up, yawning as he stands up and makes his way over.

He looks the worst out of the three of them. Dark circles ring his eyes, and I'm pretty sure he has some bruising on his face that he didn't have the last time I saw him.

"Please tell me that isn't what I think it is." I glance

between Rhett and Dane.

"Don't look at me." Rhett shrugs. "That was all Stray."

"Dane!" I gasp, reaching for Wes. He comes closer, letting me trace the fading bruise along his cheekbone. "You let Dane hit you."

"Don't worry, princess. I got in a few good hits of my own." A faint smile traces his lips, but it doesn't reach his eyes.

"I'm sorry." Tears burn my throat. "I'm so sorry."

"She'll get through this," he says robotically. "She has to get through it."

My eyes flick to Dane and he discreetly shakes his head. I read the message loud and clear.

Don't push him.

"Of course she will," I say, willing every ounce of confidence into my voice that I can muster. "Your mom is so strong, Wes. She'll be bossing my dad around again before you know it."

Speaking of my dad...

"He's with her," Wes confirms. "Hasn't left her side since we got here."

"You should go be with her, too. I'm okay." And it's not like I'm going anywhere.

"You're sure?" Pure torment glitters in his eyes.

"Go." I nod. "Tell my dad I'm awake."

"Yeah, okay." Wes turns to walk away, but I grab his arm.

"Thank you." His eyes collide with mine. "For saving me. All of you."

Wes looks stunned, disbelief swirling in his depths. But I need him to know that he saved us.

I need him to absolve himself of the guilt.

"I should go," he says, hurrying for the door as if he can't get out of here quick enough.

The second he slips into the hall, Dane lets out a low whistle. "He's running on empty."

"What do you expect?" Rhett says.

"I'm gonna go keep an eye on him. You two going to survive without me?"

"I think we'll manage." I chuckle, but it hurts so bad, both of them scramble around to get me a glass of water.

"Doc said it might hurt for a while due to the smoke inhalation."

"How long have I been out?"

"A few hours." His eyes darken as he leans in and gently brushes the hair from my face. "You had us so fucking worried, princess. When Pretty got to us in the club and you were... gone..." Rhett swallows.

"It's okay. I'm okay."

They found me. I'm safe.

"Nothing about this is okay, not a damn thing." He lets out a long breath, scrubbing his jaw. He looks like crap. They all do.

"I thought you were—"

"Rhett, don't do this." I reach for him, twisting my hand into his t-shirt. "Don't dwell on what might have happened."

"Did he... hurt you?" He visibly trembles, anger rolling off him in angry waves.

"Not in the way you're thinking, no."

"And Victoria?"

I inhale a sharp breath. "That's... that's not my story to tell."

"Fuck. Your Dad and Wes—"

"Need to focus on her, nothing else." I blink away the

tears threatening to fall. "Did Grant escape?"

Just saying his name sends a lick of fear down my spine. But he isn't here, if he was, he'd be dead.

"Pacman and Jax caught up to him. They're holding him somewhere off the grid."

"W-what are you going to do?"

"What do you think?"

"Good." My lips flatten. "He deserves it."

"Do you want to be there?"

"No." I shake my head. I never want to see Grant Noble again, not as long as I live. But I love Rhett for asking, for giving me the choice. For not trying to wrap me up in cotton and keep me away.

"What?" He snorts as if reading my thoughts.

"You," I smile. "You're so different now."

"Yeah, well, almost losing you will do that to a guy." He moves in closer, until the warmth of his breath hits my face. "You're the sun, princess, and we just move in your orbit. If we lose you, everything will go dark."

"Holy shit, that was hot." I smirk and he rolls his eyes.

"I'm trying to be serious and you're—"

"Shh, don't ruin the moment." My lips trace his. I'm weak and dirty and feel like I could sleep for days, but this... this is what I need.

"You know, I walked in on Dane and Pretty fighting..."

"And?"

"And they weren't only fighting."

"Really?" I pull back slightly, eyes wide with surprise. "Tell me more." Soft laughter spills from my lips.

"I don't want to talk about that shit."

"You weren't happy about it?" My brow lifts.

"I don't want anything to change between us, all

of us."

"It won't. But if they want to explore whatever is between them, I won't stand in the way, Rhett."

I've always sensed the bond between Dane and Wes, and it doesn't make me jealous one bit.

"I guess if they're off doing whatever they do, it gives me more time with you." He nuzzles my neck, but I wince, pain rippling through me.

"Shit, Sadie, are you—"

"Fine." I smile, half-amused, half-swooning at the panic in his eyes. "I'm fine, I promise."

He presses a tender kiss to my forehead, cupping my face in his big, inked hand. "I love you, princess. I love you so fucking much."

"I love you too." My voice cracks as I cling to him, the reality of what happened washing over me.

How close I came to losing them.

Losing everything.

"I'm here, princess. I'm right here." His voice is thick, pained, as if he's also imagining everything he could have lost.

"Don't ever let go," I whisper, a fresh wave of tears breaking free.

"No fucking chance, babe. No fucking chance."

After arguing with the nurses for almost thirty minutes, they finally relented and let me get out of bed to go see Victoria.

Rhett wheels me to her room, but the second I see her through the small window, lying in bed and hooked up to numerous machines, I'm overcome with emotion.

"You good?" Rhett asks me.

"I just need a second."

My dad and Wes are sitting on either side of her, staring at her, willing her to wake up while Dane stands over at the window, his eyes glued to Wes.

I swallow the giant lump in my throat. "She's going to make it, right?"

Because if she doesn't...

I can't even imagine what it will do to Wes and my dad.

"She has to," Rhett says, as if there's no other option.

And he's right. There isn't.

If we lose Victoria, we'll lose a part of them too.

My heart breaks all over again as I wipe the tears from my eyes. "Okay, I'm ready." Inhaling a deep breath, I force my lips into a smile as we enter the room.

Dane immediately looks up, relief etched into every line on his face. "Princess," he breathes.

"Sadie Ray." Dad stands, his larger-than-life presence eating up the room. "Thank fuck, sweetheart."

"Hi, Daddy." Silent tears stream down my cheeks. "How is she?"

"Doc says we have to give her time. The fire and the trauma..."

"The machine is breathing for her?"

He nods, his eyes glistening. "I came to see you, but you were sleeping."

"It's okay, Dad. You should be with her." *She needs you.*

"Wesley," I whisper, and he finally lifts his eyes to mine. But what I see there guts me.

"Hey, princess."

Rhett wheels me closer so I can sit beside Wes. I lay my hand on his arm. "We're all here for you. Both of you."

He barely nods, lost in whatever demons haunt his thoughts.

"Any news on—"

An alarm goes off on one of the machines. My heart jumps into my throat as I stare at Victoria lying motionless on the bed. Wes reaches for my hand, squeezing tightly in his panic.

"Mom?" he asks, his voice cracking with emotion. "Mom, no. Please. You've got to fight this. Please. Don't... don't let him win."

Tears cascade down my cheeks as I cling to him, wishing I could do something to take his pain away, to make all of this better.

Two nurses flood the room behind us, their faces set with determination. "Okay, everyone out. Code blue," one of them yells, hitting a button on the wall.

"We need you to get out, now."

"Mom," Wes cries. "No, Mom." He grips her hand, refusing to leave.

"Come on, man. Let them help her." Dane wrestles him away as the nurses start working on Victoria's lifeless body.

"No," I whimper. "No, no, no."

This can't be happening.

It can't, not after everything we've been through.

My heart splinters apart, and I know we'll never be the same after this.

But nothing hits me harder than watching my father, the man who has always protected me, sink to his knees, a stricken expression on his face as the woman he loves teeters on the edge of death.

306

32

WES

I feel nothing.

Absolutely nothing as I sit staring at the cream wall of Sadie's hospital room.

Her hand is locked around mine in an attempt to support me. Dane's is on the other side.

But it's like I'm empty.

Hollow.

Nothing.

There's a distant beeping from somewhere down the corridor, and every now and then I hope it might be a sign that everything is okay.

That she's still with us.

But no one comes to give us anything. And while Sadie might keep trying to convince me that no news is good news, how can it be? The longer we sit here clueless, the less chance she has.

They should have recovered her by now.

She should be healing.

She doesn't deserve to go out like this. Because of him.

My entire body tenses in anger. My need to go to him, to rip him fucking limb from limb for doing this to her, burns through me like poison.

Sadie's hand tightens and I sense her glance over at me, but I don't look back.

I can't.

Seeing any kind of hope in her eyes—or worse, desperation and grief—will shatter me.

I want to be here for her. She's just been through hell.

But I can't.

All of this is my fault. All of this is because I allowed her into my life.

If I never kissed her that night at the Arches. If I never—

"Stop it," she hisses as if she can hear exactly what I'm thinking.

"All of this is my fau—"

"No," she snaps, anger laced through her tone. But she doesn't immediately continue. Instead, she relaxes a little. "Could you guys go and get me a decent coffee?" she asks Dane and Rhett.

"Uh..."

"I just need a few moments with Wes."

After a few seconds, they both push to their feet, Dane's hand releasing mine, immediately chilling the right side of my body. I almost reach for him once more, refuse to let him leave, but I know Sadie is right. We need a moment.

Reluctantly, they slip out of the room just like Ray did only a seconds after following us in here. He paced back and forth a few times before blowing out of the enclosed space like a tornado.

We have no clue where he went, although I have a good idea.

"Wes," Sadie sighs the second the door closes behind the guys. "None of this is your fault." She shifts so that she's facing me, but still, I don't look at her. I can't.

"I was the one who brought him into your life. If it weren't for me then—"

"I want you in my life, Wes. Don't you get that? I want you. I love you."

"But—"

"There are no buts here. All of this..." Out of the corner of my eye, I see her gesture to her body, her injuries. "All totally worth it."

"But he hurt you."

"Because he's sick." I wince at her description. Sick doesn't even begin to cover what a fucking monster my father is. "But he won't win. He hasn't won."

"But Mom..."

"Wes," she says, a humorless laugh falling from her lips. "Your mom, fuck. She's..." Her pause as she considers her words forces me to finally look over at her. Despite knowing exactly how she looks from the hours I spent staring at her while she slept, my breath still catches in my throat at the sight of her. Cuts, bruises and burns mar her beautiful skin, and it reignites my anger once more. I'm so lost in my own head that when she continues speaking, her soft voice startles me. "She's so fucking strong, Wes. I'm in awe of her."

I nod, aware of all the things she must have been through to protect me over the years. The final few beatings were just the tip of the iceberg, I'm sure.

"She's going to get through this because she's not going to allow him to get the better of her."

"I hope you're right, princess. I really fucking do."

"Come up here."

She taps the small space on the bed beside her, and I waste no time in doing what she asks of me. I have a hard time ever saying no to her anyway, but with her looking so vulnerable and broken, I'm a total lost cause.

"Tell me if I hurt you," I say, laying on my side so I'm facing her.

"I'm good," she breathes when I wrap my hand around her hip, hoping it's a safe, non-bruised place to touch as I press my brow against hers.

"I'm sorry you're having to go through all this."

"Me too," I mutter, unable to keep the sadness out of my voice. "Those few days without you were the worst of my life."

"Dane looked after you though, right?"

A small smile twitches at my lips. "You're insufferable, Sadie Ray."

"What? It was a serious question. I was so worried about you."

"Yeah, princess. He helped me vent some anger. Hence the bruises. He's got a solid punch on him."

She shakes her head. "I can't believe you were fighting."

"We weren't. Not like that. Although Rhett looked a little more serious about the whole situation when he interrupted us," I confess.

Sadie laughs. "He doesn't understand."

"Princess, I'm not sure I understand it."

She chuckles lightly. "Just do what makes you happy, Wes. Life's too short to hold back and live with regrets."

"Fuck, Sadie. You're incredible, you know that?"

I brush my lips gently over hers, careful not to cause

her any pain but needing to feel her, needing her to feel just how much she wrecks me in all the best ways.

"So you kissed, right? Tell me you kissed."

"You're wicked, Sadie, girl. I love it."

Leaning forward, she deepens the kiss, pushing her tongue past my lips, and I happily let her sweep me away. It's a hell of a lot easier than drowning in grief, that's for sure.

I hold her tighter, unable to stop myself, but we're interrupted after only a minute or two when the door slams back against the wall.

"She's okay," Ray booms, standing at the end of the bed with his chest heaving. "She's going to be okay."

"Yeah?" I ask, releasing his daughter and sitting upright.

"Well, she's still got a long way to go. But we haven't lost her."

"Fuck," I breathe, dropping my head into my hands. "Fuck."

My body trembles as I try to keep a hold of myself.

"It's okay, Wes," Sadie whispers, her warm hand rubbing up and down my back. "It's okay."

Twisting around, I drag her into my arms and tuck my face into the crook of her neck as I break. Not once does she move despite the fact that I know I must be hurting her. She holds me back just as tight and helps put me back together all over again.

"I love you, Sadie Ray," I whisper in her ear, my voice rough with emotion. "I love you so fucking much."

"I love you too, Wesley."

She finally releases me, and I drag my head up from her, finding her hospital gown soaked from my tears.

I've never cried so fucking much in my entire life.

Seeing my shame, she cups my cheeks, holding me firm and forcing me to look into her exhausted eyes. "You're allowed to cry, Wes. You can scream, punch things, anything. Just... don't do it alone, yeah?"

I nod—well, as much as her hold on me allows me to.

"We're here. All of us. Let us help in whatever way we can."

"You already are."

I rest my brow against hers, soaking up all the strength she gives me by just being here. By just being her.

"Come on, let's go and see your mom."

It's not until she releases me that I realize Ray has already left.

"Y-yeah."

I help her out of bed and into the wheelchair in the corner of the room, despite the fact that she argues like hell about it.

We find Ray exactly where we were expecting to, right beside Mom and holding her hand as if she's his lifeline. Although, if the past few days have taught me anything, it's that she is.

How the two of them survived without each other all these years, I'll never know.

I can't imagine anything that would force me to walk away from Sadie right now and live a life with someone else. Have a child with someone else. It just goes to prove how much control my father had, even back then, because it's clear who Mom's heart always belonged to. And it wasn't him.

"She's stable," he says when we join him. "Stats are a lot better. They sound more hopeful."

"Thank fuck for that. Hey, Mom," I say, taking her

other hand and lowering myself to the chair on the other side of the bed from Ray, Sadie right at my side.

"Sadie Ray," Ray whispers, looking at his daughter through dark and dangerous eyes. His relief from earlier seems to be long gone, the need for blood in its place. My father's, to be exact.

"I read some of Victoria's notes."

"Dad," she sighs. "You shouldn't—"

"I know. But... I need to know what we're dealing with here."

"Does it matter? You're going to kill him regardless."

"Ultimately. But I need to know how long to make him suffer for."

Sadie shakes her head, biting down on her bottom lip. "He needs to suffer for a long time," she states, the venom in her voice making my blood run cold.

"He will. He doesn't get to hurt anything that belongs to me and get away with it." Ray's fist curls, his knuckles cracking with the move and piercing the air around us.

Silence falls around us as we lose ourselves in our own thoughts. I hate to even consider the things that Mom and Sadie have been forced to endure. Sadie doesn't seem keen to talk about it, and I understand why. But I think she needs to, no matter how much it's going to hurt me—us—to listen to. She can't bottle it all up, keep the horrifying things that must have happened inside that house to herself.

Movement at the window catches my attention, and when I look up, I find Rhett and Dane staring in at us.

"She's okay," I mouth, although they've probably figured that much.

Dane points down the hallway, indicating they'll be in Sadie's room before they both disappear.

"This is it now," Ray says after long, silent minutes. "Once we get you two home and put that rat down, we're all restarting our lives."

"Sounds like a plan, Dad," Sadie says, squeezing my hand tightly. "I'm ready for a new normal."

"Me too, sweetheart. Me too."

33

SADIE

"Hi, you're awake." I give Victoria a smile. Much to everyone's disapproval, I've ditched the wheelchair in favor of walking.

I feel okay. My lungs still smart a little and my body feels sore in places but I'm alive, and compared to Victoria, my injuries are superficial.

"Hey, sweetheart." She reaches for me, her words a little broken still thanks to all the smoke inhalation. "It's so good to see you're okay."

"How are you feeling?" I drop down in the chair beside her bed.

"I'm okay." Her eyes glaze a little, but she fights back the tears.

"You had all of us scared."

"I hate that you all went through that. I—"

"No, Victoria, don't do that. This isn't on you, none of it. Grant—"

She sucks in a sharp breath, wincing with pain. "Please, don't..."

"I'm sorry. I wasn't thinking."

"It's okay, sweetie." Her fingers tighten around mine. "We made it out, that's all that matters."

"You know my dad and Wes... they know... about what he did."

"I don't want to talk about it, Sadie Ray. Not to you or my son or Ray. What happened is between me and Grant, and I will not give him another second of power over me."

"You need to talk to someone," I whisper. Because that kind of trauma changes you. The memories don't just go away. And I'm worried that if Victoria bottles it up, it will only lead to more problems down the line.

"Sadie, I—"

"There's my two girls." Dad strolls into the room and comes over, bending to kiss my head. "How are you feeling?"

"I napped for like three hours, Dad. I'm good." I smile as he walks around the other side of Victoria's bed and leans in to kiss her. "Need anything?"

"I have all I need right here."

"Did you manage to get some rest?"

"I did, thank you. Now stop fussing and sit down and tell me where that son of mine has disappeared to."

Dad's eyes flick to mine, and I say, "Rhett and Dane took him for a ride to clear his head."

After visiting Victoria once Dad burst into my room and announced she was out of the woods, Wes had retreated into himself again.

"He's okay though, right?" Victoria glances between the two of us.

"Wes will be fine." I smile as best I can because the truth is, I'm worried. They've been gone for hours, and although Dane has texted to say they're okay, I'll feel better once they get back here.

"The guys will take good care of him," Dad adds, "but I'm going to need them with me tomorrow."

Silence falls over the three of us, the air growing thin.

"Y-you have him?" Victoria's voice trembles.

"Yeah. Jax and Pacman got him holed up in a place just outside of town." Dad scrubs his jaw. "There's a lot about this life that I never want you to have to know about, darlin', but this ain't one of them. That motherfucker hurt you. He—"

"Ray, please..."

"He's done hurting you. Both of you." Protectiveness glitters in his eyes. "When someone comes after someone I love, he comes after the club. I let him walk away once. He won't get the chance again."

"I don't disagree." Her eyes flutter as if the conversation is too much to bear, but in true Victoria style, she opens her eyes and pins my dad with a knowing look. "You have my blessing, Ray. But I need you to promise me something."

He gives her a small nod, but I don't miss the way his throat bobs.

"Once he's... gone, we leave all this in the past. I want to look forward to the future... with you and Wesley and the club. That's all I want."

"Maybe I should go," I say, feeling all kinds of awkward. This is a conversation they need to have without me.

"You sure, sweetheart?" Victoria gives me an apologetic smile. Her face is even worse since the house explosion, but her resolve is still right there. This woman is so strong, I don't think I'll ever get over what she did to give us a shot at escaping.

"Yeah." I shuffle to my feet. "I'm sure the guys will be here soon, anyway."

"Straight back to your room," Dad says. "I'll come check on you in a while."

"Got it, Daddy." I chuckle softly, making my way to the door. But I pause, glancing back at them. "You know, I'm really glad you found each other again after all these years."

Victoria's face lights up as she gazes at my dad and she says, "It was just a matter of time."

I'm watching some mindless TV show when the door bursts open and Dane saunters in, his arms full.

"What's all that?"

"Supplies." He grins.

"Supplies… you do know I'm in the hospital, right?"

"Yep." He drops down on the edge of my bed and tips out the contents of the bag. "I got snacks, candy, a pack of playing cards, some magazines, and—"

"A stuffed toy." I snatch up the little fluffy bear and smile. "He's cute."

"Rhett's idea."

"Rhett?" My brows crinkle. "There's no way Rhett—"

"No way Rhett what?" The guy in question strolls into the room and drops down in the chair beside me. "You good?"

"Yeah, I'm okay."

He gives me an imperceptible nod, his eyes full of fire. "Love you," he mouths, and I swear my heart melts.

"If I would've known getting kidnapped would turn you into a sap, I would have done it sooner."

322

"Not funny, princess," Dane remarks, tearing into the candy. "Not fucking funny."

"Where's Wes?" I ask, grabbing a packet of Twizzlers.

"Went to see his mom."

"Is he... okay?"

"He will be," Rhett says cryptically.

"What does that mean?"

"Turns out, Pretty has a pretty poor sense of coordination."

"What did you do?" I narrow my eyes.

"Thought we could pick up his bike lessons."

"Dane! He's barely holding on and you thought... unbelievable."

"Relax, princess, he'll live." Rhett shrugs, kicking off his boots and throwing his legs up on the edge of my bed.

"Make yourself at home, why don't you," I grumble, tearing the end off a stick of candy.

"Fuck, that's hot." Dane stares at my mouth. "Do it again."

"You're a horndog."

"Never claimed to be anything else."

"She's supposed to be resting," Rhett growls.

"Like you aren't desperate for a taste, bro."

"I have something called self-restraint, asshole. You should try it sometime."

"Nah." Dane lies back over the end of the bed. "Where's the fun in that? Besides, all that bloodlust makes me hungry, if you catch my drift." Heat swirls in his eyes.

"No seducing the patient," I playfully scold him. "Nurse Janine is already concerned about the number of guys coming through here."

"Nurse Janine needs to get laid."

Rhett and Dane start bickering about hospital etiquette when the door swings open and Wes appears. "Hey." He looks a little sheepish, but I pat the bed beside me.

My eyes immediately go to the nasty cut under his jaw. "Tell me that isn't from your lessons." I shoot Dane a hard look.

"Don't look at me, princess. I told him to hold on."

"Boys and their toys," I mutter, grabbing Wes's hand and pulling him down next to me. His arm goes around my shoulder, and I snuggle into his side. "How's your mom?"

"She's okay. Your dad is guarding her like a pitbull."

"You know, he talked to her... about your dad."

"I figured he would." Wes drags a hand down his face, letting out a shuddering breath.

"You don't have to do anything you don't want to, Wes. My dad and the guys can handle it..."

"I know," he breathes, "but I need to be there." His eyes flick to Dane, something passing between them. "I need to be the one to... fuck."

"Relax, man." Dane sits up and slides off the bed, going over to the couch. "We've got your back. Always. Just say the word and I'll do it."

"Stray's right," Rhett adds. "Don't think you're alone in this because you're not. You're a Sinner now, Pretty, and we stick together. You want the kill shot, it's yours. You don't... well, that's okay too."

"Thank you," I mouth at Rhett over Wes's shoulder. I can see the torment in his eyes. We all can. This decision is weighing heavily on him.

"Just promise me that whatever you decide, you'll come back to me."

Wes leans down, brushing his lips over mine. "Didn't you know, princess... you're stuck with me now." He kisses me softly, afraid to get too close. And maybe I should push him, demand more. But I won't. Not tonight.

Not while he's trying to process everything that's happened.

Because the time for healing will come.

Once Grant Noble is no longer a problem.

"You getting on or what?" Dane asks, throwing his leg over his bike while the others all get ready to ride out.

I had said that I'd take my truck. My riding skills might be improving—albeit slowly—but I'm nowhere near ready to join them yet—not that I even have a bike.

I'm also not feeling entirely stable right now.

I'm trying to put a brave face on it, but the thought of having to look my dad in the eyes after everything he's done makes me want to vomit.

I want him dead, sure. I want to be the one to pull the trigger, of that I'm certain. But I kinda just wish it could be over already.

Screw torturing him, I feel like I'm the one suffering right now. Right along with Sadie and Mom, because something tells me he's enjoying this. All of this.

He can't have seriously thought that coming up with a plan to abduct both Sadie and Mom would ever mean that he'd walk away alive. He might be smart, but he is only one man. We're an entire club with the majority of Savage Falls PD, and now Red Ridge PD, on our payroll.

He was never going to win.

Does he want to die?

Is this what he wants? Are we just feeding into his sick plans? Should we fuck them all up and just keep him alive and locked up? Just let him whittle away, wondering if we're ever going to come for him?

No.

I crack my knuckles, a bolt of adrenaline shooting through me, warming my body from the inside out. I need this. I need to see it. I need to see him suffer for hurting everyone I love.

"Y-yeah." Placing my foot on the small step, I throw my leg over and settle behind him, immediately feeling better.

I shouldn't find this much comfort in someone else, but his and Rhett's presence the last few days, along with being with Sadie at the hospital of course, has kept me going. I've no idea how I would have handled all this without both of them.

"Hold on tight," Dane demands, kicking the starter and bringing the bike to life beneath us.

It might be early days in my bike riding career, but hell, I can already feel the addiction to this seeping through my veins.

I get it. I really fucking get it.

Bikes rumble to life around the compound and Rhett rolls to a stop beside us.

"Ready for this, Pretty?"

I lock my mask firmly in place and give him a quick nod.

"We meant what we said yesterday. We're in this together."

Gratitude for their support swamps me.

I have no idea how the fuck I was lucky enough to end up with not just Sadie by my side, but these two as well. Yeah, I must have done something good in a previous life, or the beginning of this one has just been so fucked up that karma sent some good shit my way.

Ray barks something up ahead, and Dane's spine stiffens.

"You got this, Pretty," he shouts over the engines, reaching back and squeezing my leg. "We all start over after this. All of us. Together."

I nod again, unable to speak through the lump that's clogging my throat.

Fuck, I can't wait to walk back through Dane's apartment door with Sadie by my side and just spend a normal night eating takeout and shooting the shit with the guys. Hell, I can't even wait to get back to school once more and deal with the douchebags I used to call friends. I just... I need this done.

All too soon, Dane's bike lurches forward and we fall into formation with the others again, Savage Falls and Red Ridge together as one.

We weren't the only ones to have guys injured in the blast. Dane and Crank have guys in the hospital with varying injuries too, so they want their pound of flesh from my father, although nowhere near as much as me.

The place they're holding him is a derelict house right on the edge of Savage Falls. I know it's not a coincidence that they brought him back here. Statham is well aware of the situation and has already assured us that the 'accident' that is about to occur will stay that way.

All too soon, the dark shadow of the house comes into view and my stomach turns over. It's been five days since they captured him. I can't imagine Pacman and Jax have been treating him like fucking royalty, so I can only imagine the state of him.

Good.

The rumble of engines begins to cut out and a smile pulls at my lips as I wonder if he's scared. If he knows we're here and his time is up.

It's far overdue, if you ask me.

We should have done this the night he ran. I should have let Ray and Rhett go there that night and blow his fucking brains out.

If I had, none of this would have happened and Mom and Sadie wouldn't have had to endure what they have.

Sadie is going to be fine. I have every confidence that once the cuts and bruises have faded and a little time has passed, she'll rediscover the incredible person that she is, but Mom...

I let out a heavy sigh.

There's a darkness in her eyes that never used to be there. And it terrifies me.

What could he have done that's worse than all the years of abuse she suffered to put that look there? Just how fucking deranged is my father?

Something tells me that I might never find out the real depths of his abuse. Sadie will probably give me the CliffsNotes of their time as his prisoners, but I doubt Mom will ever let it all out.

I hate it, but also, I get it.

I understand her need to protect me, even now, as he's breathing his last breaths. I'm pretty sure I'd do the same for my own kid, if I ever have any one day.

My thoughts shift to the future, to how things might be, and I find myself breathing a little easier.

I always do whenever I think of her.

Of them.

Of us.

Our family.

Okay, so it's unconventional as fuck, and we have a lot of obstacles in our way. With not one but two MCs, college, and life, it's going to be complicated. But I'm confident. I believe that we're going to make it work.

"Ready?" Dane asks, killing his engine and once again squeezing my thigh.

"Yeah. Let's get this done."

I climb from the bike with my heart in my throat, but there's a strong determination running through my veins that I'm not sure I've felt before. I might be nervous about this. I'm pretty sure that's fucking normal, but I know it's what has to happen.

With Dane and Rhett flanking my sides, we walk toward the old house, right behind Ray. Everyone else stays behind us. Their supportive stares give me the strength I need to do this.

To face the monster who's tried time and time again to single-handedly ruin both mine and my mother's lives.

The scent that hits me the second we walk inside makes my stomach roll. "Holy fuck, what is that?"

I mean, I don't really need to the question to be answered—I've got a pretty good clue, seeing as he's been locked up here for days, but still, the words fall from my lips.

"Death. Welcome to the dark side, my friend," Rhett growls, his own bloodlust clear in his voice.

Ray continues down a short hallway before turning

toward a dirty door and kicking it open. Immediately, the smell gets worse, and I almost vomit right there on the floor.

"Breathe through your mouth," Dane instructs, and I take a couple of seconds to get myself together before we follow Ray.

"Grant Noble, we meet again," Ray booms, his voice terrifying and deadly. I know for a fact that if it was aimed toward me, I'd probably shit myself.

A weak whimper sounds out, and as I round the door, I discover why it's so pathetic. They've got my father tied to a chair in the middle of the room.

His clothing is ripped, dirty and soaked through with his blood.

His face... fuck.

If I didn't know it was him, I'm not sure I'd believe it. He looks nothing like the man I've been forced to live with all these years. His nose is shattered, his eyes dark and swollen to the point he can hardly open them. Blood slowly drips from his chin, although I have no idea if it's coming from his nose or mouth.

"Dad," I announce happily, forcing down my nerves.

I'm not here to look weak. I'm here to prove that despite everything he's done to try to hurt me, he's only made me stronger. Because I'm the only one who's going to walk away from this.

"W-Wesley," he breathes, his voice rattling in his throat.

"You've sure looked better," I say, taking a step forward from my protectors and bending down so I can look him right in the eyes.

He just stares back at me, yet I swear I see something like relief flicking through his dark depths.

"You fucked up, old man," I tell him.

His chest heaves as the blood continues to pour from his face.

"You signed your death certificate the first moment you ever laid a finger on my mother, you worthless piece of shit. This," I say, lifting my arms to indicate the room we're in, looking around at all the torture equipment that's dirty and covered in blood from the past few days, "has been a long fucking time coming."

"Please," he whispers, but I don't let his pleading affect me.

"You never deserved her. All these years she fucking protected you from this. From the man she should have always been with."

A pained groan comes from my father's throat.

Did he ever love her? I'd like to think that maybe things didn't start out quite so twisted, but it's hard to know, and I'm not going to sit and have a conversation about it now.

Taking a step away from him, I run my eyes over all of the instruments laid out on a side table. But I settle on a little hammer.

Wrapping my fingers around the blood-stained handle, I lift it, bouncing it in my hand a little, feeling it's weight.

"I don't think there's enough pain in the world for true revenge for everything you've done. It seems to me that Pacman and Jax have already attempted it.

"I'm not sure whether I'm disappointed or relieved that they've saved me a job." As I say this, though, I know it's the latter that's true. I might want to have my say, make it known to him before he takes his final breath that

I dealt the lethal blow, but I'm not really into all this torture shit.

I glance back at Rhett, however, and notice that he's almost fucking drooling to get involved. Dane, though... despite knowing just how much violence turns him on, his concerned gaze is locked on me.

I nod at him once, needing him to know that I've got this. That I'm in control.

Turning back to my father, I don't allow myself a chance to think as I lift the hammer and bring it down on one of his fingers that's loosely gripping the chair. His entire body jolts at the pain, a strangled cry getting stuck in his throat.

Without missing a beat, I go for the next one, then the next and the next, unexpectedly yet quickly getting addicted to the sound of the bone shattering and my father's broken cries filling my ears.

I notice as I switch to his other hand that his nails are all gone, the flesh red and raw from them being ripped clean from his fingers.

"ARGH," I cry, taking out his second hand as my heart thunders in my chest.

By the time I'm done, he's barely conscious, the pain of the breaks adding to the beating the guys have already given him leaving his broken body right on the brink.

"Don't you fucking pass out on me now, motherfucker." I stare into his barely open eyes. "I'm one of them now, Dad," I tell him proudly. "You think it suits me?" I ask, showing him the prospect patch on my cut.

No sound leaves his mouth, but his body jolts. On the brink of death, he still wants to fight.

"Give it up, old man. You lost. And the big, bad bikers

won." Reaching behind me, I wrap my fingers around the pistol tucked into my waistband.

Ray gifted it to me specially for the occasion. He thought my first, and probably most important kill meant I deserved it.

Couldn't really argue with him, even if holding my own gun felt weird as fuck.

But this is my life, now. I guess I need to get used to this kind of shit. Although, I hope to fuck that this is the one and only time I have to kill a member of my own family. That I have to visit Sadie and Mom in the hospital and see them broken and weak because of a man who should be on our side.

As I pull the gun in front of me, Dad's eyes flick down to it.

It's hard to read his reaction with his face as fucked up as it is, but something tells me he'd be laughing at me. That despite his broken fingers, he doesn't think I've got this in me.

He's wrong, though. So fucking wrong.

The hate I feel coursing through my veins is stronger than he could ever imagine.

"Son?" he questions when I raise the pistol and point it at his head.

"I'm not your son, Grant. You lost the right to be a father and a husband the second you laid a hand on my mother and began controlling my life. You're nothing. Fucking nothing."

My hand trembles with the weight of the gun, and I hope to fuck that he can't see it. "You hurt the two women I love more than anything. You deserve all of this and more. If I thought it wouldn't be a waste of good oxygen, I'd leave you here until you rotted in your own filth." My eyes flick to his dirty clothes, the source of most of the stench in here.

Just do it, a little voice demands in my head as my hand begins to tremble more violently.

The eyes of everyone in the room are drilling into my back, willing me to do it, probably wondering if I've got it in me.

My finger flexes on the trigger as I pull the safety down, just like Rhett and Dane showed me.

But still, I hesitate.

I have no idea why. I want this. I want him gone. But...

A warm hand lands on my shoulder. I don't need to look back to know who it is.

He squeezes, his support surging through me. "You don't have to—"

Pop.

The bullet hits exactly as I intended, right between the brows.

I stand there for a couple of seconds, watching as the life drains out of the cunt who tried taking my girl and my mom from me, before spinning around and coming face to face with Dane.

"Let's go get our girl."

SADIE

"Guys, seriously, I can manage a few stairs." I wiggle out of Dane's hold as he attempts to carry me up to his apartment.

If I thought they were bad before, fussing over me in the hospital, it's nothing compared to how they've been since I was discharged earlier today.

"The doctor said you need to rest," Rhett says.

"Rest, Savage. Not let the three of you manhandle me up to the apartment. I'm fine."

"Brat," he grumbles.

"Asshole." I poke my tongue out at him.

"I'm surprised Ray agreed to let you stay here," Dane adds.

"He has his hands full with Victoria," Wes replies.

While she's set to make a full recovery—in the physical sense, at least—the doctor wants to keep her in the hospital a little longer.

Ever since the four of them returned the other day with solemn looks in their eyes, he hasn't left her side. It's kinda sweet. But if he's anything like these three when she's finally released... God help her.

Rhett unlocks the door and pushes it open and disappears. Wes keeps one arm wrapped around my waist as he guides me inside.

"Seriously, I can—"

"Just let me have this." He pouts, and it's so adorable, I can't help but relent.

Dane pulls me back into his chest the second we enter the apartment, and my mouth falls open.

"What—"

"Welcome home, princess." A huge bouquet of flowers adorns the counter, and there's a balloon and another stuffed toy.

"Well, aren't you three just the cutest." I twist around to kiss him.

"We even left your pink girl shit everywhere." Rhett smirks, and I flip him off.

"Okay, it's bed rest for you." Dane scoops me up in his arms and stalks off toward the bedroom.

"Seriously, Stray, what did I say?"

"Yeah, yeah. Rhett's right. You're a pain in my ass."

"He didn't say that."

"No, but he probably thought it."

I smack Dane's chest but can't stop the tugging at my mouth. It feels good to be home.

Once inside the bedroom, Dane lowers me gently to the bed. Hovering over me, his eyes sparkle with concern.

"Dane, I'm fine. I prom—"

"I know." He leans down, brushing his nose against mine. "It was just really fucking scary thinking we'd lost you, princess."

"I'm right here." I palm his cheek, kissing him softly.

"Hands off the patient," Rhett growls from the door, and Dane chuckles. "We're clearly thinking very different things, brother. Because I'm thinking since she's confined to the bed, we could take advantage of that little fact and—"

"The doctor said she needs to rest, so back the fuck up and let her."

"Sorry, princess. Mr. Grumpy Pants has spoken." Dropping a kiss on the end of my nose, Dane pulls away. "If you need anything, call for Rhett, since he's so concerned with your health." With an amused wink, Dane saunters out of the room, leaving me alone with Rhett.

He comes over and sits on the edge of the bed. "How are you feeling, really?"

"Really, I'm fine." A little tired, but that's to be expected. My cuts and scrapes are almost healed, and my lungs don't smart as much now when I inhale.

But he still gives me a skeptical look.

"I'm a little tired," I concede.

"And what happened with Noble... what we did..." He glances away, running a hand down his face.

"Rhett," I take his hand, "look at me."

His stormy eyes lift to mine. "Grant Noble deserved to die for what he did. What you did doesn't scare me, and it doesn't make me think any less of you."

"You're sure? This life, princess... it's messy and raw, and a lot of fucked-up things can happen."

"I choose this life, Rhett. I choose you, all of you."

Something akin to relief flashes across his face.

"How is he doing? Really?" I ask, my eyes flicking to the door.

When Wes returned with the guys from putting an

end to Grant Noble, he was quiet. But he'd climbed up on the hospital bed with me, pulled me into his arms and held me.

We haven't talked about it yet, and I don't want to push. But I also don't want Wes to carry around guilt with him, not when he did what needed to be done.

He set himself and his mom free. And no one close to us will ever blame him for that.

"He'll be okay."

"I'm glad he has the two of you."

"And you, Sadie Ray. You're the glue that holds us together."

"The glue, huh?" My lips twist. "I guess it's better than the pain in your ass."

"That motherfucker, he told you—"

"So you did call me that?" I fight a grin, unable to take the opportunity to bust his balls.

Rhett rolls his eyes, and I chuckle.

"I'll let you get some rest." He stands. "If you need anything—"

"I need to not be treated like an invalid."

"Tough shit, princess. You need to rest, doctor's orders."

"Stay with me?" I pouted.

"You need—"

"Rest, yeah, yeah, I got the memo. But I'm not that tired, and we haven't snuggled in a while."

"You want to... *snuggle*?" His brow lifted.

"Get in here, Savage. Before I change my mind."

Rhett kicks off his boots and slips in next to me, sliding his arm around my shoulder and tucking me into his side. My hand goes to his stomach, brushing back and forth, and he stills.

"Behave."

Soft laughter spills from my lips, only growing when Dane and Wes burst into the room. "What's— Hey, no fair." Dane frowns. "What happened to 'she needs to rest?'"

"We are resting." I smirk.

"Well, we're getting in on that action. Move over." Dane slides in behind me, nuzzling my neck. "Good to have you home, Sadie, girl."

"He's right," Wes says, slipping his arm around Dane to get to me. I thread our fingers together, my heart so full.

"You know, technically, this could be considered a group snuggle."

Rhett grunts at that, mumbling his disapproval.

"You know what I think?" I grin up at him. "That secretly you love it."

"I love you." He drops a kiss on my head.

"Love you too, brother," Dane adds.

"Love you three, Savage." Wes barely contains his laughter.

"I'm only doing this for the patient," Rhett says.

"Sure, you are, big guy. Sure, you are."

When I wake up, Rhett and Wes are gone, but Dane is curled around me like a spider monkey.

"Can't breathe," I gasp, fighting a smile when his eyes fly open, and he practically scrambles off the bed, a look of sheer panic in his eyes.

"Joke. I'm joking."

"Not funny, princess," he glowers, climbing back on the bed and pulling me into his arms.

343

"We didn't get to celebrate your birthday." I slide my arms up his chest, thinking of the plans Wes and I had for him.

"You being here, being safe and okay, is more than enough for me." He kisses my forehead.

"Where are the others?" I ask, pulling back to look at him.

"Pretty got restless."

"How long was I asleep?"

"Four hours."

"Four hours?" My eyes widen. "Sorry, I didn't—"

"Stop. It was nice, lying here with you all. I think even Rhett enjoyed it." A smirk plays on his lips. "He took Wes out on his bike."

"He did?"

"Yeah, the two of them have bonded over you. I'm starting to feel a lick of jealousy." His smirk grows and I swat his chest.

"You're such a dork."

"Yeah, but I'm your dork, princess." He gazes at me with so much love the weariness inside me melts away, replaced by lust.

"Yeah." I lean up, dusting my lips over his. "You are."

"Rhett will kill me if I take advantage of you right now."

"Rhett isn't here." I kiss him harder, dipping my tongue into his mouth and coaxing him to join me.

"Sadie, girl." My name reverberates on his throat. "You're testing a man's resolve."

I pepper tiny little kisses over his mouth, the corner of his lips, and down his jaw.

"You're not playing fair, Sadie, girl."

"So, you don't want me?" Hooking my leg over his, I

fit my curves against him, sucking on the skin beneath his jaw, teasing him with my tongue.

"Shit, princess..."

He grows hard at my stomach, and I can't resist rolling my hips against him.

"Fuck," he rasps, collaring my throat with his hand and pinning me in place while he kisses me. "You're killing me."

"So don't fight—"

Male laughter fills the apartment and Dane groans. "Fucking cockblocks." He drops his head to my shoulder, inhaling deeply.

"Sadie? Stray?" Rhett booms, the bedroom door flying open.

"I fucking knew it. You owe me twenty bucks, Pretty."

"Hey, we're not fucking."

"Doesn't like look it." Rhett's brow lifts.

"If I was inside her, you'd all fucking know about it."

"Excuse me, I am lying right here," I huff, pretending to be annoyed. But I'm not.

I'm so happy, I feel like my heart could explode.

"How did the lesson go?" Dane asks Wes.

"Better."

Rhett snorts. "Let's just say he won't be riding out with the club anytime soon."

"Asshole," Wes mumbles, but I see the amusement in his eyes.

"Has anyone checked in with my dad?" I ask.

"Yeah. He called me." Wes approaches the bed and sits down. "Mom is busting his balls, so she must be feeling better."

"Atta girl." I grin.

"Spoke to Crank, too," Rhett says. "He and the guys over in Red Ridge want to throw Dane a party."

"Ugh, I'm not sure I'm ready to go to any more parties."

"This would be at the compound. It's safe." Rhett locks his eyes on me. "I think it would be good for morale."

I arch a brow, flicking my gaze to Dane, and Rhett adds, "If their Prez agrees."

"Fuck off with that shit. I'm still your brother."

"Damn straight."

"I think we can organize something, but I want to wait until Victoria is out of the hospital so she and Ray can be there." Dane glances at Wes, who gives him an appreciative nod.

"Thanks, man."

"You're family now, Pretty. You, your mom, Ray. You know if they get married, Sadie will basically be fucking both her stepbrothers."

"Asshole." I grab a pillow and hit him with it.

"Yeah, but you love me, princess."

He has me there.

Because I do.

I love him and Rhett and Wes more than I ever thought possible. And now Grant is dead, we can finally look to the future.

Together.

As per the doctor's orders, we forced Sadie to stay on bed rest for two days after she came home from the hospital, much to her annoyance. But none of us really gave a shit, because after coming so close to losing her, we all just wanted her healthy and back to herself again.

I wasn't naïve. I know that what she and Victoria went through will probably take a while to deal with. They've both got a long road ahead of them to come to terms with what happened inside that house.

Neither of them has told us in so many words yet what they endured, but the three of us are in agreement as to what we think it might be.

Wes, understandably, didn't want to talk about it when I bought it up the other night when Sadie was sleeping. But something told me that he needed to get it off his chest, even if what he fears might have happened never actually did. It's eating away at him, and I could see it claiming more of him with every day that passes. Well, that and the feelings that come from killing your own father.

I guess Pretty and I now have something more in common than just our addiction to our girl, because we've both got family members on our death tally.

As much as I hated Darren for everything he did to me as a child—hell, as an adult too—it still affected me, knowing I put that bullet through his head. Wes is currently going through something similar. Worse actually, because he didn't just kill his father. He killed his first. That's enough to fuck up most people, let alone when it's someone you're meant to love unconditionally. But if I've learned anything over my nineteen years, it's that family doesn't have to be blood. The family you choose can be stronger, more important, and love as unconditionally as a blood family should.

I should know. All my family chose me. And I would literally kill for them. For every single member of the Sinners, Savage Falls and Red Ridge alike. They were all there for me when I needed them the most, and I wouldn't blink at doing the same for any of them.

"Go anywhere nice there?" Crank asks me with a smirk as he passes a fresh beer toward me.

"Sorry, just daydreaming."

"Your birthday do-over going that well?" he asks with a knowing twinkle in his eye.

"No," I mutter. "I've barely even seen her to get any special treats," I say, wiggling my eyebrows.

In fact, I haven't had any fucking action in... too long to remember. Well, aside from my own hand when things have become too... hard... to handle.

Watching her flaunt everything she's got around the apartment and then at school these past few days but not allowing any of us to get what we want has been fucking torture.

It's our fault, I guess. We—Rhett—imposed the sex ban when she first got discharged. A rule that I've almost broken more than a handful of times in the past few days, but it's like the motherfucker has a sixth sense or something, because every time I managed to get her alone for some potential action, he fucking gate-crashed.

He is the ultimate cockblock, and I'm one more solo hand job away from putting him out of his own misery. Grumpy fuck.

"Well, maybe tonight is your lucky night. Where is she, anyway?"

"I'm not sure. Rhett was meant to be bringing her over."

"He's here. I've seen him out in the shop."

So where the fuck is my girl?

I swear to God, if he's got inside her before—

"Stray, how's it hanging?" the guy in question booms, clamping his hand on my shoulder and squeezing tightly.

"Fucking aching," I mutter, much to Crank's amusement before he lifts his beer in an attempt to hide his joy at my expense.

"Where is she?" I ask, quickly losing patience.

"Can't a girl have any secrets?" He winks. Actually fucking winks. Fucker. "Can't you just enjoy your party?"

"While I don't know where she is? No. No, I fucking can't."

"She's safe, Stray. That's all you need to know."

"So, she's with Pretty?"

"Nope. Pretty is over there, talking to Jax and some blonde chick."

Marissa," Crank adds, following Rhett's nod in their

direction. "He needs to be careful with that one. Or, maybe not, you know." He winks, taking another pull on his beer.

"Pitbull isn't like that," I say confidently. "Plus, he's totally hung up on River." A growl rips up Rhett's throat at the mention of his sister and a guy, even if it is a guy like Jax. If she were my sister, I'd just be happy she wasn't drooling after someone like us—or the us we used to be, prior to finding Sadie. "Where is River? She coming tonight?"

"She's getting ready with Quinn and Kat."

"Getting all dressed up for Pitbull again. I saw her flaunting it about at our last party."

"You need to fucking stop, or I'll tell Sadie to..." His voice trails off into nothing when my cell buzzes on the bar and Sadie's name lights up the screen.

Can you come down to your room?

"Excuse me," I say, cutting off Rhett, who's still ranting about something. "I've had a better offer."

Rhett shoots me a knowing smirk before taking my stool the second I'm off it and gesturing for a new beer.

Turning my back on them and the party that's starting to get going behind me, I make my way down toward my room.

It's the best room in the compound. I didn't want it. I was happy for Crank to take it, seeing as he'll be here more than me, but he wouldn't hear of it. I couldn't really argue when he pointed out that the four of us needed more space than he did and the fact that the room was big enough for an extra wide bed. The second he mentioned that, I stopped trying to be the bigger man. The temptation was too much.

Stepping up to my door, I don't rush straight inside like I usually would. I know she's waiting on me, I really fucking hope that it's not just to help her zip up her dress, because fuck... Reaching down, I rearrange myself, already hard and ready to go just from the thought of her waiting for me.

Jesus, I'm so fucking whipped and desperate.

Shaking the thought from my head, because quite frankly, I don't care, I lift my hand and knock, hopefully teasing her as much as she is me.

"Y-yeah?" she calls, sounding a little confused, but I remain quiet, waiting for her to come to the door.

The second she cracks it open and spots me through the crack, she narrows her eyes. "What the hell are you doing?"

"I was wondering the same thing. What are you up to, princess?"

She backs away. "Come in and find out."

Pushing the door wide, I step inside, my eyes locking on her and my chin damn near hitting the floor. "Fuck me, Sadie girl. You look..." I scrub my hand over my mouth just to catch any drool that might have spilled over. "Fuck."

"You approve, huh?"

She's got her hair piled up on top of her head, her makeup dark, her lips a sinful red. I can't help but imagine what they'll look like wrapped around my cock. She's wearing this strapless leather and lace bodysuit thing that shows way too much skin to go out in public, but for right now, it's fucking perfect. Her legs are encased in the tightest of black skinny jeans with a pair of high fuck-me heels that I can already imagine digging into my ass as I rail her.

"Too fucking right, I approve. You look fucking insane, if you didn't already know." Reaching down, I rub my aching cock through my pants.

"You want your first birthday present?" she asks, sauntering toward me, her hips swaying seductively.

"Hell yeah, I do."

Although I must admit, if she pulls out an actual fucking present right now, I'm going to lose my damn mind.

Reaching up, she wraps her hand around the back of my neck, bringing her lips almost to mine.

"Sadie, girl, you're being a tease."

"I know. You love it."

"Do you know what I'd love more?"

She chuckles. "Dane Stray, I know exactly what you'd love right now."

I gasp as she grasps me through my pants. "Princess," I grit out through clenched teeth.

Grabbing my chin, she twists my head to the side and places a hard kiss on the underside of my jaw.

Brushing her thumb beneath where her lips damn near burned me, she murmurs, "Cute." But she doesn't give me a chance to respond, because she drops to her knees before me and my breath catches in my throat as she reaches for my waistband and rips my fly open.

"Fuck, Sadie, girl," I groan, my eyes locked on her hand as she wraps her fingers around my length and begins stroking me slowly. "I need you so fucking bad, babe."

She doesn't respond. Instead, she just leans forward and licks the bead of precum that's pooling at my tip.

My entire body jerks at her delicate contact, my balls aching for more. "Sadie, girl." I sound damn near desperate, but I don't give a shit. I want her to know much I want her, need her. "Wrap those pretty lips around me, princess. Let me see how that lipstick looks on my cock."

She hums in agreement before parting her full lips and slowly sinking down on me, taking inch after inch at a torturous pace.

It takes every ounce of willpower I possess not to thrust forward and just fill her mouth and throat in one quick move.

Her hand wraps around my hip, her nails digging into my ass. The bite of pain adds to the mind-blowing pleasure as I bottom out in her throat, her lips meeting her other hand that's wrapped around the base of my shaft.

"Yesss," I hiss, when she pulls back just as slowly. "Fuck, I need to fuck your mouth so badly right now, princess."

"It's a good thing you're not in charge tonight then, isn't it, Prez?"

"Fuuuuck."

She places a kiss to the side of my cock. "Tonight." Kiss. "All you need to do." Kiss. "Is enjoy." Kiss. "We've got you covered." Kiss.

"We?" I ask as she licks all the way back up.

"If you're a good boy, we'll reward you."

"Anything. I'll do fucking anything you want to get more of this. Argh," I shout when she takes me in her throat once more, working me faster all of a sudden. Her mouth, tongue, and hand work in perfect harmony, and in only a few more minutes, I'm shooting my load right down her throat, my fingers twisted tightly in her hair, holding her in place.

She sucks until I'm spent, and then she pulls back and licks the tip of me clean.

She looks like a fucking goddess on her knees for me with her lips swollen from my cock and her lipstick obliterated.

"Right, time to party," she says, hopping up and throwing me for a loop. I was already gearing up for the next round, but it seems she has other ideas.

"Y-you want to go out there and—"

"Party? Yeah. We're celebrating. I'm not missing that. Plus, I've got an outfit to show off. Do you think Rhett and Wes will like it?" she asks, giving me a twirl and letting me see me just how much skin she's got on show.

"They'll fucking love it. Your dad, on the other hand..."

"What's he going to do? Send me to my room for being a naughty girl?" She winks, a wicked smirk playing on her lips. "You three could come with me to keep me company."

"You're going to put him into an early grave, princess."

"I'm willing to take the chance, knowing that you're going to look at me like that all night."

I'm powerless but to watch as she fixes her makeup and reapplies her lipstick before taking my hand and leading me back to the door.

"Come on, birthday boy. Let's go show them how it's done."

37

SADIE

M usic thrums through my body as I shake my hips and weave mine and River's hands through the air.

"He's watching you," I grin.

"Don't be so obvious." River frowns.

"You're not going to seduce him if you don't go talk to him."

"I don't know." Her eyes dip. "He was talking to that woman earlier, and ever since we kissed, he's been... distant."

"Hey." I drape my arms over her shoulder and pull her closer to me. "Jax doesn't want some club whore, Riv, not when he could have you."

"But Rhett—"

I roll my eyes. "How many times do I have to tell you? Let me worry about Rhett."

"Speak of the devil, he's glaring at us." River flicks her head over to where Rhett stands with Kat's brother, Diesel. I can't help but snicker at the two of them, scowling at the sight of their sisters enjoying themselves.

359

"I'll distract Rhett, but you have to go talk to Jax, okay?" I give her a pointed look and she nods.

"Fine. But you can't let Rhett come over to us, promise me."

"I promise." I can think of a hundred ways to keep my grumpy biker distracted.

River melts into the crowd as I make a beeline for him.

"Where's River—"

"Let's dance." I wrap my arms around him and press my boobs up against his chest.

"Shit, man. Good luck with that." Diesel grips his shoulder and chuckles. "Catch you two later."

"Come on." Refusing to take no for an answer, I grab Rhett's hand and lead him to the makeshift dancefloor. Quinn and Kat chuckle at Rhett's stiff body movements as I spin around and start moving my body against his.

But it only takes a couple rolls of my hips and his hands slide around my waist, pulling me flush against his body.

"Do you want me to fuck you right here in front of everyone?" His voice is a low growl in my ear, sending shivers down my spine.

"I think my daddy would have something to say about that," I sass.

"Nah, princess." One of his hands skids up my stomach and grips my jaw, tilting my head over to where my dad is standing over Victoria like her big brooding protector.

He hadn't wanted her to come to the party, but Victoria insisted.

"They're so cute." I swoon.

"And you look like fucking sin in this outfit."

"That's the idea." I manage to twist my face to kiss the underside of his jaw.

Rhett turns me in his arms and touches his head to mine while his hands find their way to my ass. "Fucking love you, princess."

"I hope you're not going soft on me. I had plans for you later. And they didn't include you whispering sweet nothings in my ear." I flash him a saccharine smile.

"Tease." He snorts.

"You love it."

We dance slowly, even though the music is something more upbeat, our bodies pressed impossibly close.

"This is nice," I say.

"It's not so bad."

"Asshole." I poke him in the chest, but he snags my hand, bringing it to his mouth and biting the end of my finger.

"Maybe we should—"

"Group hug." Dane appears out of nowhere, pressing in behind me and looping his arms around us so I'm sandwiched in the middle. "Fuck, I love you guys."

"Oh my God, just now drunk are you?" I glance back, getting a strong whiff of liquor. "Jesus, what did you drink?"

"The guys made me do shots of tequila. Would have preferred licking the salt off your tits though, Sadie, girl."

"Keep it up, Stray, and I'll have to claim your birthday present," Rhett jokes.

Laughter spills out of me, and Rhett immediately stiffens. "Fuck, I didn't mean... I'm not... I mean, I like Pretty and all, but I'm not—"

"Relax, Savage." I lean up and kiss the corner of his

mouth. "No one is asking you to do anything you don't want..." I smirk, and he glowers.

"Relax, big guy," Dane drawls. "Pretty is more my type."

"What the fuck is that supposed to mean?"

"Now now, boys." I pat Rhett's chest while wiggling my ass against Dane's crotch. "Less talking, more dancing."

"You drive a hard bargain, princess," Rhett grumbles, and Dane snickers.

"I know something she makes hard." He rocks into me, letting me know exactly how hard he is.

"Behave, Prez," I quip.

"Fuck, Sadie, girl. Don't think I'll ever get tired of hearing that. Especially when you're on your knees with your pretty lips wrapped around my—"

"Stray, stop fucking dry humping my daughter and get over here."

"Fuck," Dane breathes, jerking away from me as if he's been burned.

"Duty calls, Prez," Rhett teases, and we watch Dane stalk off like a kid caught with his hand in the cookie jar.

I guess he kind of was.

"Alone at last." Rhett's eyes bore into mine.

"You're good with this thing between Dane and Wes, right?"

"Do you think I'd be standing here if I wasn't? Whatever's between them is just that. So long as it doesn't change anything between the four of us, I can deal."

"It won't." I lock my hands behind his neck.

"Good, because I have no plans to lose you, Sadie Ray. This, us... the future... I want it."

"Good." I grin." Because I want it too."

All of it.

"Maybe someone should try to stop them," Quinn says as we watch the guys line up a row of flaming shots. It's late, the party raging on into the early hours. My dad and Victoria left a while ago with Aunt Dee and Uncle Micky, leaving the younger members to their fun.

"It'll be their own damn fault if one of them loses an eyebrow," Kat mumbles.

"Idiots, the lot of them."

"You okay?" I ask River. She's been quiet ever since I sent her off to talk to Jax.

"Yeah, I'm fine." She smiles, but it doesn't reach her eyes.

"Hey," I grab her hand, "do you want to talk?"

"No, I'm fine, I promise."

My brows furrow. She doesn't seem fine, but I don't want to push. And Jax seems happy enough, laughing and joking with the guys as they prepare to do their shots.

Maybe I'm reading too much into it, wanting everyone to be as happy as I am.

Because I am.

Surrounded by my friends and family and my guys, I feel whole. I feel like we've finally reached a place where we can enjoy life.

And I fully intend on doing just that.

Life is too short to worry about what people think about our unconventional relationship, too fragile to worry about what might happen tomorrow or the day after that. I want to live in the moment and soak up every second with them.

If the last few weeks have taught me anything, it's that everything can change in the blink of an eye, so you have to treasure every day and make the most of it.

"You've got that lovesick expression again," Quinn says.

"No, I don't."

Her lips twist with amusement. "Yeah, you do. And I get it. You're a lucky girl, Sadie Ray."

"Whoa, are you feeling okay?" I touch my hand to her forehead.

"Get off." She bats me away. "I'm trying to be nice, and you're being an ass."

"You know I love you, Quinn." I lean my head on her shoulder. "And I just want you to be happy.

"Sadie," she warns.

"What? I didn't even say anything."

"No, but you're thinking it."

"But Crank is so hot. You'd be a fool not to at least take him for a test drive."

"You're such a ho."

"So, I like sex." I shrug. "What's the big deal?"

"You're basically my idol," Kat chimes. "Three guys ready and waiting to fulfill my every need... sign me the hell up."

"I'm not sure I could handle it," River says meekly as the chanting starts.

"Yeah, it's a no from me." Quinn chuckles.

"You don't know what you're missing." I watch as Dane and Rhett knock back their shots, encouraging Wes to do the same. A fire ignites inside me, heat licking down my spine.

Wes catches my eye, his eyes dropping down my body. When they settle on me again, they're dark with hunger. But it's when he glances back at Dane with the same expression that my pussy throbs.

God, I don't think I'll ever tire of this. Them.

Wes whispers something to Rhett, and they both look over at me.

"Seriously, could they be any more obvious?"

"I guess that's my ride." I smirk, and Kat explodes with laughter.

"Fuck, I love you." She grins.

"You'll all look out for each other?" I say, lingering on River.

"Don't worry, my brother and Crank will make sure we have no fun."

"I'll call you tomorrow." I hug Quinn, then River, and head for the back of the clubhouse toward the hall leading to the apartments.

I've barely made it inside Dane's room when the door bursts open and Rhett and Wes carry a very drunk Dane inside.

"Princess," he slurs. "I hope this is the part where I get to fuck your delicious ass."

"Patience, Prez." I flick my head to the chair and Rhett drags him over to it, shoving him down.

"Pretty, get me something to secure him with."

"Ooh, kinky, Savage," Dane chuckles.

"Consider it your belated birthday present." I walk toward him and run my fingers over his jaw.

"Love you, Sadie, girl." He gives me a goofy smile, but his eyes radiate lust.

"Want to watch them touch me?" I ask.

"Fuck yeah."

"No touching, though." I flick my eyes to Wes as he

approaches with one of Dane's belts, snapping it between his hands.

Rhett yanks Dane's arms behind the chair, and between them, they restrain him. "Holy shit, you're evil." Dane shakes his head.

"The best is yet to come," I say, walking backward toward the bed, slipping my hand to my jeans and pushing them down my hips.

"Fuck, yeah," he hisses as I let them pool at my feet.

"When they're done with me, you can have whatever you want."

"Whatever..." He gulps, eyes as dark as the night. "Best. Birthday. Ever."

I smirk, licking my lips. "That's the plan."

38

DANE

A growl of approval rips up my throat as Rhett and Wes close in on Sadie where she stands in front of the bed in just her sexy leather and lace lingerie thing.

Rhett collars her throat, tilting her face exactly as he wants her and slamming his lips down on hers, allowing me to see as his tongue slips into her mouth. My hips lift in the chair, my cock aching against my pants as I watch them—her.

Wes steps right up behind her, his hands sliding up and down her sides as he kisses her neck and across her bare shoulder. Her arm lifts, her fingers twisting in his hair. Her chest heaves as they tease her.

"Fuck, I love watching them drive you crazy, princess."

Tucking her hand under Rhett's shirt, she pulls it up, encouraging him to strip and move things on.

"Getting desperate, Sadie, girl?"

"Just making your day, Stray," she murmurs, her voice deep and sexy as she shoots a look of pure lust at me.

"Too damn right you are."

My eyes don't leave her as both of them shed their clothes until Sadie is the only one of the three of them dressed in anything. Although I'm not entirely sure what she's wearing can be described as clothes.

"Get on the bed, Sadie, girl. I want to watch you blow Rhett while Wes eats you."

"Kinda demanding, seeing as you're just meant to be watching, Stray," Rhett barks.

"I think you'll find this is my party. What the birthday boy wants, the birthday boy gets."

"I'll remember that for my big day," Rhett grunts.

Wes tugs at the back of Sadie's bodysuit, dropping to his knees behind her as he drags it down her body and bites her ass cheek hard enough to make her squeal.

Stepping from the fabric bunched around her ankles, she shoots me a wicked look as she arches her back, thrusting her tits in my direction.

Before she can tease me any more, Rhett lifts Sadie onto the bed, settling her on her hands and knees before him. "Open up, princess. Let's show the birthday boy just how good you are at sucking my cock."

He holds himself for her and she licks him like a fucking popsicle. My cock aches to get in on the action, and I move my arm to reach for it, only it doesn't fucking move.

"Fuck," I bark, remembering what they did to me when we first got in here.

Both Rhett and Wes shoot me a knowing look.

"It'll be worth your while, Dane," Sadie damn near purrs around Rhett's cock as Wes grabs her ass and pushes his face into her pussy.

Her back arches as she moans his name like a whore.

I. Fucking. Love. It.

"That's it, Sadie, girl," I moan when she rolls her hips against him, taking Rhett to the back of her throat.

Fuck. This is the sweetest fucking torture as their three moans of pleasure filter through the room.

"Make her come, Wes. I want to taste her on you later."

"Oh shit," he hisses against her, making her moan as the image I'm painting plays out in her mind.

"Make her come, then switch. I want Rhett's cock stretching her pussy while she deep throats you. I wanna watch your cock sliding past her swollen lips."

At my words, he wraps his hand around his cock, working himself.

I could come just watching them.

But I won't.

I want more.

I want them.

Fuck.

My chest heaves as I stare at them, my entire body burning up with desire and need as my head spins with a mix of alcohol and lust.

Sadie's moans and movements get more and more erratic as her release builds.

"Pretty," I grunt, "make her fucking shatter."

Reaching up, he pushes two fingers inside her and she finally falls, coming all over his face like the beautiful slut she is.

Wes pulls back and locks eyes with Rhett, who nods in understanding. No words are said. They're not needed now. The four of us so in sync we know what the other is thinking at times like this. Even if I didn't bark my orders, I have no doubt they'd give me the same show.

Ripping his cock from Sadie's throat, Rhett moves to the end of the bed, grabs her hips, and drags her exactly where he wants her while Wes settles on his knees in front of her.

"Hey, princess," he breathes, staring at her as if she's the single most important person in the world. Which, of course, she is.

"You gonna come down my throat for Stray?" she asks, not bothering with pleasantries.

"Hell yeah."

She eagerly sucks on him, making his head fall back in pleasure as his fingers twist in her hair. The second Rhett slams inside her, she's jolted forward, forced to take more of Pretty's cock, but she doesn't complain, she doesn't even gag, but she fucking takes it like a pro.

Pride for our girl washes through me.

As usual, Rhett is anything but gentle, and he fucks her like a man on a mission while I watch Pretty lose his fight over his approaching orgasm. He's clearly just as fucking worked up as me, because he blows his load in only a few minutes inside her hot mouth.

I guess it helps that she took the edge off for me a few hours ago. Those two blue-balled motherfuckers have been waiting fucking days for it.

Reaching out, Pretty wipes across her bottom lip once he's slipped from her mouth.

"You gonna come for Rhett, princess?" he growls.

She nods eagerly as Rhett's thrusts become almost violent. "Yes. Yes," she chants, spurring him on.

Seeing as he was the one most concerned about treating her like glass, he certainly isn't handling her like she might break.

I guess his willpower is only so strong.

"Rhett. Yes. More," she cries before she screams out his name, falling straight into the mattress as her arms give out.

Rhett's roar rips through the room only a beat later as he fills her.

For long seconds, the only sound that can be heard is that of our heavy breathing before Rhett lifts Sadie from the bed and crushes her against his chest.

"Love you, princess," he breathes before kissing her until she's squirming for more again.

The second he releases her, Pretty takes over, pulling her onto his lap and tucking his face into the crook of her neck.

"What are you doing?" I ask when Rhett immediately reaches for his clothes and starts dragging them on.

My pulse spikes at the thought that this might be it. That it's all over and no fucker has so much as touched me.

"I'm needed elsewhere," he mutters cryptically before ripping the door open and slamming it behind him.

"Uh... was it something we said?" I ask, confused.

I thought we were going to... Well, I guess it doesn't matter now.

Sadie stands from Wes's lap and looks back at him before locking her eyes on mine.

"Do not tell me that you're about to get dressed and leave too."

"I could, but I'm not sure leaving you alone would make this your best birthday ever." She saunters over, her hips swaying.

She looks fucking sinful with her makeup smeared under her eyes and tear tracks down her cheeks from where she's had both Rhett and Wes's cocks in her throat, and her lips are swollen.

"N-no. It wouldn't," I stutter, my mouth watering for a taste of her.

I thrash against the chair I'm bound to, desperate to free my hands to touch her.

"Stop fighting, Prez. You need to trust us."

"Us?" I ask, my eyes shooting over her shoulder as Wes makes his way over.

"You trust us?" he asks.

"Y-yeah, of course I do."

"Then quit fucking fighting it and let us take control."

Damn, that's hot.

I nod eagerly as they both step closer.

Sadie reaches for me, running her finger from my lips all the way down my stomach, over my waistband until she's teasing my aching length. "You hard for us, Prez?"

"You fucking know it, princess."

Wes pulls his hand from behind his back, something I hadn't even noticed, and holds a knife out in front of me.

"W-wha—"

I don't get a chance to ask what's happening, because he pulls my shirt away from my skin and splits it straight down the middle.

"Holy fuck," I breathe, my eyes holding his as they flash with desire. "Want me naked, Pretty?"

"For what we've got planned? Hell yes," Sadie answers for him, although from the desire in his eyes I know she's only saying what he's thinking.

My body jolts with desire when her knuckles brush my bare stomach as she reaches for my waistband. She pops the button with ease, and after lifting my hips to help out, she drags my pants down, finally releasing my aching cock. It springs back against my stomach, the head angry and purple, desperate for some attention.

"Sadie, girl, I need you."

"I know," she states with a smirk.

She leans forward and I do the same, the magnetic pull that I always feel for her stronger than ever. But right at the last minute, she turns her face away from mine and drags Wes's mouth to hers instead, forcing me to watch them kiss right in front of me.

"I'm starting to dislike this plan," I grumble, watching their tongues twist together.

"Oh yeah?" Sadie asks into their kiss. "What about this?"

Her fingers thread into my hair and she pulls me into them.

"Fuck," I grunt, desire making my head spin as I join their kiss.

As if they've fucking timed it, both of them move from my lips and kiss across my jaw and down my neck.

"Oh fuck. W-what are you two..."

My body goes into overdrive, my cock jerking against my stomach as they move down my neck in perfect sync, kissing, nipping, biting.

"Fuck. I need—" A hand clamps over my mouth. Pretty's, if the smell of Sadie's cunt is anything to go by.

A groan rumbles up my throat as they move lower, down my chest and to my stomach.

"Ready for your birthday present, Prez?" Sadie growls, looking up at me through her lashes.

My mouth moves to say something, but when I look at Wes, a mirror image of Sadie hovering over my cock, all words leave my head.

"I think he's ready," Wes says with a small laugh, his

hot palm skimming up my thigh.

Oh God. Shit. Fuck. Are they gonna...

They look at each other for the briefest second before they both lean forward and lick up the length of my cock.

I damn near come all over my stomach just watching them.

"Fucking shit. Fuck... *Fuck*," I bark, my hips jerking, my entire body burning up.

Wrapping her hand around the base of my cock, Sadie sucks me into her mouth, swirling her tongue around me before offering me up to Wes as if I'm nothing more than a fucking sucker to share.

Fucking fine by me.

They can share all fucking night.

The second his hot mouth wraps around me, I almost lose every bit of my restraint. His eyes find mine, and despite being off my fucking head after the shots, I see his hesitation despite the fact that I'm quite clearly loving this right now.

"Keep going," I groan, desperate to be able to touch him, to show him just how badly I need this.

"Jesus, I could come just watching this," Sadie murmurs, her eyes darker than I'm sure I've ever seen as she looks between the two of us.

"Fuck, I love you. Both of you. Fuck."

Grasping my chin, Sadie crashes her lips down on mine before they switch once more.

"Hey, Pretty," I say when his lips are a breath from mine.

"You make me fucking crazy, Prez."

I grunt into his kiss, my cock jerking, my control snapping as I come down Sadie's throat.

Best. Birthday. Ever.

39

SADIE

Wiping my mouth with the back of my hand, I grin up at Dane and Wes. "That was fun."

"Damn right. Now untie me so I can fuck that sweet ass of yours."

His dirty words make me gush and I nod at Wes, giving him the order to cut Dane free.

Seductively climbing to my feet, I start backing up toward the bed again.

"How do you want her?" Wes asks, his voice thick with desire.

"Both of you, Pretty. How do I want *both* of you?" Dane corrects him. "Get on the bed with me, Sadie, girl."

Suddenly, he seems perfectly sober as he stalks toward me and climbs up, lying so his head is near the end and his feet are near the headboard. "Get up here."

I crawl onto the bed, and he grabs my hips, lifting me in reverse cowgirl style over him. Except, he pulls me all the way back until I'm right over his face and then yanks my hands down so I'm on all fours.

"Pretty, feed her pussy your dick."

Oh God. My womb clenches with anticipation.

"Fuck," Wes breathes. I glance over my shoulder, watching through hooded eyes as he fists his cock and slides one hand down my spine while Dane's face is right there.

"Make her scream," Dane orders, and Wes slams into me, filling me to the hilt. He pounds into me a couple more times, and I'm so lost to the sensations rolling through me that I almost forget Dane is there, underneath me, with a front-row view of Wes fucking me.

Until his tongue joins the party, lapping at me.

At both of us.

"Fucking hell," Wes groans, and although I can't see what's happening, I have a good idea. Dane is touching him, probably cupping his balls or fisting the base of his shaft as he thrusts into me.

Dane's tongue sweeps over my clit, and my eyes roll with the intensity. It feels so fucking good. So illicit and dirty and oh-so right.

I lean back into Wes, smothering Dane's face, but he doesn't seem to care as he licks and sucks and bites.

"In fucking heaven," he murmurs. But I know something that'll really make him soar.

Steadying myself with one hand, I curl my fingers around his rock-hard dick and suck him into my mouth again.

A groan rumbles in his chest, vibrating against my pussy, and I cry out.

"Shit, man. Keep that up and I'm gonna blow." Wes grips my hips harder, fucking me like a man possessed.

"Hold that thought, Pretty. I got an idea."

Wes pulls out of me, and Dane bites my ass before slapping it. "Up you go, princess."

We switch places—only he lies back against the bed and twirls his finger. "Back that ass up on me."

"So bossy."

"You did say whatever I wanted." He smirks.

"Fine. But make it good."

"Sadie, girl, I'm about to blow your fucking mind.

Wes throws Dane a bottle of lube, and he uses it to get me ready, my stomach knotting with excitement. "Nice and slow, princess." He guides me over his cock, working into me an inch at a time. It's a tight fit, and to start with, all I feel is the painful stretch of my skin around him, but that soon changes. Once he's all the way in, he wraps his arm around me and pulls me back against his chest. My body trembles with need as I wait for them to do something.

"She's all yours, Pretty." His voice is teasing.

Wes crawls up on the bed, positioning himself at my front. He pushes my legs wide and lowers himself on me, trapping me between their bodies. The second he fills me, we all moan, the position so intense and full.

"Fuck, man," Wes hisses. "I can feel you."

"So fucking good." Dane thrusts in all the way.

I can't breathe, can't think as they completely consume me.

"It's intense," I murmur, pressing my lips together as I trap another moan. My skin feels too tight and my heart crashes against my chest as they fuck me, fill me, and ruin me.

"Kiss her," Dane demands, and Wes crashes his mouth to mine, plunging his tongue past my lips as they rock into me, over and over.

When I said Dane could have anything, I didn't imagine this.

"You both feel so fucking good." Dane latches his mouth onto my neck, sucking the skin there. "One day, we're going to fuck your pussy together. At the same time."

"Yes, yes," I moan, delirious. At this precise moment, they could do whatever they wanted to me, and I'd let them. Because nothing feels better than this.

Nothing.

"Holy shit, she wants it. She's choking my dick," Wes rasps.

"Of course she does. She's our dirty little whore." Dane slides one hand around my throat, turning my head so he can kiss me, except the angle is all wrong, so he ends up licking my jaw.

"Harder," I cry, waves of pleasure crashing over me. "I'm almost there."

They up the ante, going harder, faster, until there's nothing but the sound of skin on skin and our moans filling the room.

"God, yes." I'm barely holding on as something inside me shatters.

"Gonna fill you up, princess."

And they do.

So good. Until I'm a boneless, breathless mess.

Wes crushes me against Dane as he comes hard, burying his face in my neck. "Fuck," he groans. "Fuck."

"Told you I'd blow your mind," Dane says, and I can feel the smirk in his words.

Wes rolls off us and I draw in a deep breath. "That was..."

"Just the beginning." Dane squeezes one of my boobs. "I want you both every way I can get you."

"Fuck," Wes hisses.

"Don't worry, Pretty." Dane's voice is teasing. "I won't take your ass unless you beg."

My eyes go wide, heat zipping down my spine at the idea of the two of them together like that.

"That get you hot, Sadie, girl? Imagining me fucking him?"

I nod, too spent to reply.

Dane's chuckle washes over me. "You're fucking perfect." He kisses me. "Now get on your hands and knees. I'm not done with you yet."

I wake up cocooned in a wall of heat. But it isn't Wes or Dane curled around me, it's Rhett. I'd recognize his inked hands anywhere.

"Hmm, morning," I say.

"Good morning indeed." He gently thrusts his morning wood against my ass, and I chuckle.

"Someone's happy to see me."

"How are you feeling?" Rhett brushes his lips over the nape of my neck.

"Good. A little sore."

"Were they too rough with you?" It's a question, not a judgement. And I love him for it. I love that he trusts them enough to treat me right.

Our dynamic wouldn't work if he didn't.

"No, it was perfect. Dane was just... a machine."

Rhett chuckles at that, kissing my neck. "Is that a challenge, princess?"

"God, no. I need at least a day to recover. Where are they, anyway? Is Wes—"

"He's fine. Got a call this morning and slipped out. Dane followed like a lost puppy."

Glancing back, I narrow my eyes. "You've got to stop giving them shit about—"

"Relax, they know I'm only busting their balls. I'm good... with everything."

I roll over, nudging my nose along his. "I love you, so much."

"Love you too, princess." Rhett sweeps his tongue into my mouth and kisses me deeply. Passionately. Pouring every ounce of his love into every stroke.

"Hmm. I could get used to this." I wrap my arms around him and bury my face into the crook of his shoulder.

"Gonna spend my life making you happy," he whispers. "You, Stray, and Pretty."

"Yeah?" I peek up at him.

"Yeah."

The door bursts open and we both glance over.

"I knew you loved snuggles." Dane swaggers in looking as fresh as a daisy, as if he didn't drink his body weight in shots and keep me and Wes up half the night.

"Don't you dare, Stray," Rhett mutters as Dane makes a beeline for his side of the bed. But Dane doesn't listen, throwing himself down behind Rhett and wrapping his arms around both of us.

"Pretty has news."

"You do?" I glance at Wes, and he nods.

"Well, get over here and tell us all about it." I smile, and he kicks off his sneakers and climbs into bed behind me.

"Coach called."

"What did he want?" I spit, still pissed that he kicked Wes off the team.

"He spoke to Colton U. They want me to go up there and take a look around, meet with the coach."

"That sounds like a big deal," Rhett says. "You think they're still going to offer you a football scholarship?"

"I don't know. Maybe."

"What is it?" I ask, sensing his hesitation.

"Honestly, after everything, I don't want it anymore. I want this, us... the club."

"So, you don't want football... but it would be nice to go look around and see how we feel about it."

"We?" He drops a kiss on my shoulder.

"Well, yeah. This is kind of a two-for-one offer."

"Three-for-one," Dane adds, and I smother my laughter.

"So you think I should accept?"

"The visit, yeah. We can all go, check it out, get a feel for the place."

"I'm in," Rhett says.

"Me too." Dane adds.

"That's settled then," I say, twisting back to look at Wes. "You don't have to make any decisions about the football thing yet. We have time." Because although part of me knows he's all in with this—me, the guys, the club—the other part isn't ready to let him give up everything for us without considering every option available to him.

"Yeah." Wes kisses the end of my nose, tightening his arm around me.

"Guess this would be a good time to say I have news, too," Rhett says, rubbing the back of his neck.

"You're not planning on abandoning me for college as well, are you?" Dane snorts.

"Fuck off, asshole. Ray called me yesterday. Said he wanted to give me this." Standing, he digs out his wallet and pulls out a small material patch.

"Is that what I think it is?" Dane scoots closer, ripping it from Rhett's fingers. "Holy shit, he did it. That old bastard actually did it. Congratulations, brother." He leaps up and pulls Rhett into a bear hug.

"He made you VP," I breathe, pride filling my chest that my daddy trusts Rhett enough to stand at his side.

"Not quite. He told me to think about it. He knows that this," Rhett glances between the four of us, "is serious. Said he understands we have a lot of decisions to make over the coming months, but it's mine if I want it."

"And do you?" I ask.

Rhett's eyes shutter as he inhales a steady breath. When they open again, I see so much acceptance and hope glittering in them that my heart almost bursts.

"I want it," he murmurs. "I really fucking want it. But it means figuring some shit out." He and Dane share a look.

"It's okay." I get up and go to him. "We have time."

We have all the time in the world.

Because nothing is going to come between us.

Ever again.

EPILOGUE

Sadie

"What do you mean, you're not coming to school?" I snap down the phone at Dane.

"Relax, princess," he chuckles. "We have some business to take care of. We'll see you later."

"What business?"

Quinn mouths, "What's up?" at me and I shrug.

These guys will be the death of me. We're supposed to be attending school. Playing nice for Principal Winston after our recent disappearing act. Dad smoothed things over with him—*again*—but it doesn't look good when the guys are already playing hooky.

"Put Wes on the phone," I demand.

"Now now Sadie, girl. Don't go getting your panties in a... actually, that doesn't sound like a bad idea. You could sneak into the girls' bathroom and send me a photo."

"Dane, stop getting distracted."

"I can't help it, babe. Your pussy is the perfect distraction."

Oh my God.

I roll my eyes. "You are—"

"Good looking. Charming. The best you've ever had."

"Un-fucking-likely," I hear Rhett grumble in the background.

"Hand the phone over to Wes, now."

"No can do, princess. But we'll see you later. Have a good day at school."

The line goes dead, and I gawk at my cell, hardly able to believe it.

"He hung up on me."

"What are they up to?" Quinn asks.

"Beats me." But whatever it is, I don't like it. We agreed no more keeping me out of the loop.

Pulling up our group chat, I text them a piece of my mind and hit send.

"Better?" My cousin smirks.

"A little. But I'll figure out a way to make them pay for keeping me in the dark."

"I'm sure you will." She chuckles. "Did you manage to talk to River yet?"

"No. Every time I ask her what's up, she changes the subject."

It was Halloween last weekend, and the Red Ridge Sinners threw a party out at an abandoned cabin in the woods near their compound. We'd surprised everyone and turned up early, back from our trip to Colton.

"She's hiding something." Quinn muses.

"I still can't believe Jax screwed her over like that." Anger boils inside me.

At Dane's do-over birthday party, the one where I encouraged her to seduce Jax, he only went and got wasted and fucked some club whore.

When I found out, I wanted to rip him a new one, but Rhett said it was for the best, that it was better that River realize his true colors now instead of down the line when it was too late.

Part of me hated that he was so smug about it, but the other part knew he had a point.

I just hadn't expected it. Not from Jax. He always seemed so into River.

I really thought he was one of the good ones.

"It's the biker way, babe," Quinn murmurs, barely meeting my eyes.

"Says you, Mrs. I'll-never-fuck-a-biker."

"Crank is..."

"Different?" I smirk. "Yeah, tell me something I don't know."

I knew there was something brewing between Crank and my cousin, but I hadn't expected them to fall headfirst into a relationship. But she seems happy, and Crank is... well, he's a typical biker boyfriend. Possessive, over-protective, and completely wrapped around Quinn's little finger.

"Speaking of Crank... he didn't happen to mention what my wayward boyfriends might be doing today, did he?"

"Even if he knew, he wouldn't tell me. Bro code and all that." She rolls her eyes.

"Yeah, I guess. I just hate surprises." I've had enough of those to last me a lifetime.

"I still can't believe Wes turned down the football scholarship," Quinn says.

"Things change." I shrug. "People change."

The trip to Colton was amazing. We hung out with the team and toured the campus and town. But when it was time to leave, Wes made his choice, and it wasn't the Colts.

"So you're both going to apply and do the regular college thing?"

"That's the plan. It's close enough to commute back and forth, or we can get a place in Colton and split our time. We haven't worked out all the details."

Quinn studies me, a faint smile playing on her lips.

"What?" I ask.

"You're so different, Sadie. "It's like they light you up inside. It looks good on you."

"They're it for me," I say with complete confidence.

"I get it now," she agrees, "what it's like when you find your soulmate."

But I didn't find my soulmate.

I found three.

And I'm never letting go.

Ever.

Rhett

I sit on my bike in the school parking lot as all the students begin to emerge from a day full of boredom and monotony.

Although, I must admit that I do have a newfound enjoyment of school with Sadie always being close by. I'm also rather fond of the girls' bathroom that Dane was always going on about.

I totally get the fascination now.

Fuck, watching Sadie take my cock while we both should have been in class before we left for Colton a few weeks ago was fucking insane.

Reaching down, I give my jeans a tug to make space for my growing cock, my eyes locked on the main entrance where I know she's going to emerge from.

I only have to wait another two minutes before her dark hair catches the winter sun. And just like I'm expecting, she doesn't look even a little bit excited to see me. Her face twists in irritation, her full lips pursing in anger.

I can't help but smile at her as she approaches with Quinn at her side.

I'm not surprised when the rumble of another engine vibrates through me and Crank pulls in beside me to pick up his girl.

Who knew that good little Quinn Renshaw could actually pull the stick out of her ass for long enough to fall for a biker.

He's good for her, though. Even I can see that. And the feeling is entirely mutual, because Crank looks at her like she's his entire fucking world. That's a feeling I know all too well.

Quinn bounces over to her man, jumping into his arms and slamming her lips down on his, whereas my girl just comes to a stop in front of me and places her hands on her hips, her brow quirked as she waits for an explanation for our absence today.

She'll be lucky. I'm not telling her anything yet.

"Get on, princess."

"No," she sasses, holding firm.

"Get on or I'll put you on there myself."

"You don't get to lie to me, Rhett. None of you do. That's not what we agr—"

"Get the fuck on the bike, Sadie Ray. Stop being a brat."

A growl of frustration rumbles in her chest, her lips parting to argue, but she doesn't find any words. "This better be fucking good, or I'm castrating you all."

A deep chuckle erupts from my throat. "No, you won't. You love our cocks too much to ever harm them."

"Do you always have to be fucking right?" she snaps, pulling her helmet on and wrapping her arms around my middle.

Having her behind me, holding onto me as if I'm her everything, is something I know I'm never going to get used to.

"Trust us, princess."

"Whatever. Get on with it, Savage."

I give Crank a nod, aware that we're going to be seeing them in only a few hours, and I take off, heading in the opposite direction to what Sadie is expecting.

Her grip on me tightens and I laugh to myself as I think about the confusion that's written over her face right now.

The ride isn't overly long, and in no time, we're following the signs that point toward Red Ridge. She doesn't relax, though, because we're not heading for the clubhouse. We're heading somewhere she's never been before.

Something flutters in my belly. I try to shove it down, but I can't. I also can't keep lying to myself.

I'm fucking nervous, dammit.

We've gone out on a bit of a whim with this plan. But when Dane found the place online, none of us could deny that it would be perfect and that our girl would love it. Hiding it from her will probably be something we regret for the rest of our lives, but I'll more than take whatever punishment Sadie deems suitable for this little surprise.

She thinks we're lying to her, and while, yeah, we might have been hiding shit, this is nothing like anything she's been mad at us for keeping from her in the past.

I take a left turn and pull off the main road, up a street that only has one thing at the end.

A house.

"What the hell is this?" Sadie asks the second I pull the bike to a stop beside two others.

"This?" I ask, keeping my expression blank while my insides are having a riot.

Fuck. I really want her to like this.

Reaching for her hand, I give her little choice about linking her fingers with mine and tug her toward the huge front door.

"Rhett?" she warns, clearly not happy about this.

"Just wait."

We come to a stop at the front door and I pull her into my body. Her brows pinch when she looks up at me. "Are you... are you nervous, Savage?" she asks, guessing correctly.

I can't help but laugh. "Can't get anything past you, can I, princess?"

Reaching up, she cups my cheeks and stares into my eyes. "Nope. So now is the time to start fessing up."

Reaching into my back pocket, I pull out a single key attached to a fluffy pink heart.

"Cute."

"It's yours."

Understanding starts to flicker through her eyes. "M-mine?"

"Yep. Try it."

Hesitantly, she pushes the key into the lock and twists. "Rhett, what is this?"

I press my hand to the dark wood and swing it open the second it's unlocked to reveal Dane and Wes standing in the hallway.

"Surprise," they sing, both with shit-eating grins on their faces.

"W-what?"

Pressing my hand to the small of her back, I gently push her inside, and we all surround her.

"Welcome home, princess," Dane says eagerly. It's not lost on me that this is his first real family home. I can only imagine what it means to him.

The thought actually chokes me up a little, not that I'll ever admit that to anyone.

"T-this is..."

"This is ours." He throws his arms out wide, gesturing to the huge open-plan living and kitchen space behind us, plus the insane view across the lake.

"Oh my God. You guys bought a house?"

"Do you like it?" Wes asks.

"I-I... I love it, but I'm a little blindsided right now."

"Come on, let's give you a tour," Dane says, bouncing on the balls of his feet like a little kid in a toy shop.

"Okay," she agrees, taking both of their hands and allowing them to lead her through the house.

Our house.

Resting my hip against the wall, I watch the three of

them as they explore. Sadie looks about ready to explode with excitement.

"Want to see the best part?" Dane asks.

I laugh, not expecting him to have waited this long to show her what he's talking about.

They lead her toward the stairs, and I fall into step behind them and all the way to the master bedroom.

This place has enough room that we can all have some space if we want it, but the best part, as Dane put it, is definitely Sadie's new room.

"Oh my God," she squeals when Wes opens the door.

The far end of the room has floor-to-ceiling windows looking out over the lake and trees in the distance, but the most striking thing is most definitely the enormous bed in the center of the room, complete with pink sheets and more pillows than four people will ever need in their lives. There's even a fucking sloth stuffed toy in the middle.

"This is insane. You bought us a house?" Sadie repeats in total disbelief. "And this bed... Where the hell did you find one this big?"

"You know us, Sadie, girl. We're pretty resourceful when we want to be."

"I'm mean... this is utterly crazy."

"No," Dane states. "What's crazy is that you're not already naked and in the middle of that thing."

He lifts her clean off her feet and throws her onto the bed.

"Oh yeah?" she asks seductively, giving us each a lust-filled look.

We each take a step forward like lions stalking our prey.

"Come on then, boys. Time to break this baby in."

River

"Hey, you." Quinn nudges my shoulder as she steps up beside me. We're at my brother's new house. Well, Sadie, my brother, Dane, and Wes's new place.

They bought her a house.

A freaking house.

I mean, I'm happy for them, but I can't help the pang of jealousy I feel.

They're so happy, laughing and joking with everyone who came. Ray and Victoria. Micky and Dee. Pike and Rosita. And Jax. Crank and some of the other Red Ridge crew are here too, crammed into the yard, drinking and celebrating. It's chilly, but the guys set up a gazebo to grill under and the scent of the barbecue and firepit fills the air.

"You're quiet tonight," she adds when I don't offer her more than a weak smile.

"I'm fine."

"River, come on. You think we don't know something is going on with you."

"It's nothing." Besides, tonight is a celebration. I don't want to dampen the mood with my issues.

As if he hears my thoughts, Jax steps into my line of sight.

Damn him.

His mouth tips in a small, uncertain smile, but I don't return it. I can't. Not when he broke my heart in two, sleeping with that club whore a few weeks back.

I'd been ready to put myself out there and tell him exactly how I felt... only to watch him get shit-face with some woman with fake boobs and bottle blonde hair and then leave with her.

It was like having my heart ripped in two. All those weeks he spent with me, protecting me, being my friend.

Tears prick the backs of my eyes, but I blink them away.

He doesn't deserve any more of them.

"He really hurt you, didn't he?" Quinn asks.

"It doesn't matter." I push the words past my lips.

"Riv, Quinn, get over here," Sadie calls, and reluctantly I follow Quinn over to them.

"I still can't believe this place," she says. "Tell me again how you afforded it."

The guys share a look, and Sadie frowns. "What?"

"So, your dad might have had something to do with it."

"He *what*? He helped you buy me a house?" She starts scanning the crowd for him.

"Relax, Sadie, girl." Dane takes a long pull on his beer. "At least with you gone, he doesn't have to worry about getting down and dirty with Victoria."

"Seriously, Stray," Wes grimaces. "That's my mom you're talking about."

"Yeah, don't be a dick," Rhett adds. "Besides, River still lives there."

Everyone looks at me and my cheeks heat. As if I need a reminder that Sadie has moved out and once again, I'm all alone.

"I'm going to go inside and get a drink," I murmur.

As I move past them, Sadie and Quinn call after me, but I don't stop. And thankfully, no one follows me.

I walk straight through the big, open-plan kitchen and down the hall toward the bathroom. But another voice stops me in my tracks.

"River."

I inhale a shuddering breath, my eyes shuttering as I turn slowly to meet Jax. "What do you want?"

"Please, just hear me out."

"I already told you, I want nothing to do with you."

He steps forward. "River, I—"

"No, Jax. No. You don't get to do that. You don't get to stand there and pretend you care. Not when you..." I force myself to take a deep breath. "Do you know what? It doesn't even matter. We weren't together. We weren't anything, so feel free to go fuck whoever you want."

Spinning on my heel, I hurry down the hall and around the corner. Tears stream down my face as I reach for the door. It swings open, and Diesel appears.

God, can this night get any worse?

"R-River?" He gawks at me, scrubbing a hand down his face. "I... I didn't expect to see you here."

I snort. "Seriously? You do know Rhett is my brother, right?"

His expression darkens. "I just... What's wrong?" He finally notices my blotchy, tear-stained face.

"Nothing," I clip out. "I need to use the bathroom."

"Y-yeah, of course." He watches me with a strange look on his face as we switch places.

"Okay, you can go now."

"Are you sure you're okay?"

I will be when you leave.

"I'm fine."

I slip into the bathroom, about to close the door, but

400

Diesel says, "About what happened at the party... I'm sorry, River."

The Halloween party.

In a moment of drunken madness, I'd kissed him.

I just wanted to feel something other than the gnawing ache inside me.

I wanted someone to want me back.

And Diesel was nice and kind, and he had a good heart.

He also liked his girls more mature. His words, not mine.

Feeling something snap inside me, I meet his tortured gaze and narrow my eyes with contempt. "Forget I ever kissed you, because I know I will." I slam the door in his face and crumple against it.

Jax.

Diesel.

They can both go to hell, as far as I'm concerned.

I'm done with guys.

Especially bikers who will steal your heart, only to break it without a second thought.

River's story starts in RUIN.
PRE-ORDER NOW

DELICIOUSLY DARK ROMANCE

Two angsty romance lovers writing dark heroes and the feisty girls who bring them to their knees.

SIGN UP NOW
To receive news of our releases straight to your inbox.

Want to hang out with us?
Come and join CAITLYN'S DAREDEVILS group on Facebook.

TAUNT HER

SNEAK PEEK

Ace

I look around at the only home I've ever known and feel conflicted. It's a shithole, but it's our shithole—the only place I and my brothers have ever called home. And if I wasn't convinced that this move would benefit them, it wouldn't be happening.

They throw their bags into the trunk of their heap-of-shit car without a word. Dread sits heavy in my stomach as I move on autopilot, as if we aren't about to leave our home. The feeling isn't an unusual one, nor is the fury that fills my veins on a daily basis.

Our uncle should have been here ten minutes ago to take us away to start our new life in Sterling Bay. Maybe he's decided we're not worth it after all. Chance would be a fine fucking thing.

I'm just about to tell them to give up and go back

inside when the crunching of gravel by the trailer park entrance hits my ears.

Fucking great.

A black town car with equally blacked-out windows comes to stop in front of the three of us.

"I hope he's not planning on staying long, that thing'll be on bricks in minutes," Conner mutters, his eyes locked on the driver's door.

We haven't seen our uncle in years, not since he left us with our shit show of a mother. It seems family only matters when his hand has been forced by the state.

I'd have quite happily been my brothers' guardian for a year, but apparently an eighteen-year-old with a rap sheet like mine isn't a responsible enough adult to look after others.

The door opens and I lean to the side to get my first look at the man who abandoned us to this life instead of fighting for his family, but the guy who stands isn't one I recognize.

"Who the fuck are you?" I bark, much to the guy's irritation if the widening of his eyes is anything to go by.

"I'm your uncle's driver. He sent me to pick you up."

"Fucking brilliant." The laugh that accompanies my words is anything but amused.

"If you'd like to put your bags in the trunk, I'll take you home."

Home. *This* is my home.

My body tenses, my fists curling at my sides, as I step up to the man. He already looks totally intimidated by his surroundings, and I delight in him taking one step back as I approach. Slamming the door as I go, I stop him from an easy escape should he feel he needs it.

No motherfucker, you've probably not dealt with anyone like me before.

The scent of his expensive aftershave fills my nose, and it only makes me want to hurt the privileged asshole that much more.

"Let's get a few things straight." I don't stop until I'm right in his face, so close I see the fear in his eyes. Now *that's* something I can work with, something I can feed off like a fucking leech. "Firstly, that place you're meant to be taking us to is not our home. It'll never be our home. And second, we're not getting in this fancy-ass fucking car. Where the hell is James? I thought he was coming to collect us."

"He's been called out on business."

This is a fucking joke. First he demands we move into his pretentious mansion—blackmails me into it when he knows it's the last place in the world I want to live—and then the motherfucker can't even be bothered to turn up himself. He's probably too good for this place. No wonder he looked down his nose at us all those years ago and turned his back as fast as he could.

"He will be home later to greet you."

I stare at him, no emotion on my face and a storm brewing in my eyes.

"If you could just get in and—"

"Un-fucking-likely. We can make our own way."

I told James as much when he instigated this whole thing in the first place, but he insisted. Probably because he doesn't want my brothers' rust bucket sitting in his fancy driveway and bringing the tone of the area down.

"I really don't think—"

"I don't give a fuck what you think, *Jeeves.*"

All the blood that was left in his face from when he first stepped out of the car drains away, and he swallows nervously.

"D-do you want to f-follow me then?"

"Marvelous, Jeeves. What a fantastic plan," I mock, mimicking his posh British accent.

The second I take a step back, he scrambles into the car as quick as he can. Fucking pussy.

"I can't believe he sent a car," Conner mumbles as my brothers join me, and together we watch the town car roll slowly down the dirt track.

"Really?" I balk. "James isn't our savior, Con. You think he'd even be taking us in if it weren't for the court deciding I'm no good..." I swallow the rest of the words. Of course, no one would trust me with my brothers. Apparently, the fact that I've raised both of them since we were just kids doesn't matter.

My chest tightens.

"It'll be okay, Ace." My brother squeezes my shoulder. "A fresh start could be just what we need."

"Yeah, whatever." I shrug him off. "We should probably get going." There's nothing left for us here.

Conner gives me a weak smile before following Cole to their car. It's an ancient Ford they somehow manage to keep running despite the fact that it should have been scrapped at least ten years ago. Cole doesn't even spare our trailer a backward glance as he climbs inside and guns the engine. I'll need to keep my eye on him; he's always been a quiet kid, but lately he's been even more brooding.

They follow Jeeves' lead before I throw my leg over my bike and rev the engine. The vibrations instantly help to cool me off. The anticipation that I'll soon be flying down the coastal road helps to push my ever building anger over this fucked-up situation down a little more.

I gun the engine once both the town car and my brothers have disappeared from sight and take one last look at this place. It's dark and dingy, like Hell on Earth. But it's our home... *was* our home. We're moving. Heading over the border to the rich side of town. Like we're ever going to fucking fit in there.

Dust and gravel fly up behind me as I speed off to find my brothers' taillights somewhere up ahead. We know roughly where James lives, but I've no idea which of the insanely pretentious houses actually belongs to him. Probably the biggest one, knowing that pretentious stuck-up prick.

I catch them just before the road opens up and the bright blue sea appears in the distance. I guess that's one good thing about where we're going: the girls on the beach. It's just a shame they're all going to talk like Jeeves, as if they've got a spoon permanently stuck in their pouty mouths.

"Fucking hell," I mutter to myself as I follow the two cars up a long ass driveway. It's not until the very last moment that the actual house appears. It's a huge place on a hill overlooking the ocean. The kind of house I've only ever seen images of in magazines, or on the TV when the piece of shit worked.

Images of the parties we can have here start to fill my mind. Maybe this place won't be so bad after all. I can get off my face and attempt to fuck some rich chick looking to take a walk on the wild side... in every room of the house.

Parking between my brothers' car and a flashy Mercedes, I throw my leg over my bike and head in the direction I just watched Jeeves walk into the house. He obviously thought against helping with our belongings. Wise man. He's learning quickly.

With our bags in hand, we climb the stairs to the double front door. It's a damn sight different to the one on our trailer that swelled up so bad in the summer we had to crawl out through a window, and that allowed the wind and rain to come inside during any storms.

"Holy crap," Conner gasps as we walk into the entrance hall of all entrance halls. I swear to fucking god that the only house I've seen quite this lavish is the Playboy mansion. I'm half expecting scantily-clad women to pour through the doors for a welcome party at any moment.

Sadly, the only person who emerges from one of the many doorways is Jeeves.

"Would you like a tour?"

"Or a fucking map," Conner mutters. Cole, however, stands totally mute and looking bored out of his skull. I know he's taking everything in, though. It's how his brain works.

"Just point us in the direction of our rooms. I'm sure we can figure the rest out ourselves. We might be from a trailer park, but we're far from stupid."

"I'm well aware of that. I'm William, by the way."

"I would say it was nice to meet you, Jeeves," I spit, curling my lip in disgust, "but in all honesty, it wasn't."

"Right, well. You can get to your rooms via this staircase, but you do have your own at the other end of the house. If you'd like to follow me."

For once, the three of us do as we're told and trail behind him until he comes to a stop at a slightly less audacious staircase, although it's still much grander than any I've seen before.

"At the top you'll find four rooms. Each has a fully stocked en suite, but if you need anything extra please speak to Ellen. You can usually find her in the kitchen, which is directly behind the main staircase, and she'll see you have everything you need."

"How about an ounce of weed and a few bottles of vodka?"

He stares at me as if I'm going to laugh at my own joke. It's not a fucking joke. I'm going to need that and then some if I'm meant to live here.

It's only a year. You can do this for a year for your brothers.

"If that's all, I'll leave you to find your feet." He spins on his heels and fucks off as fast as his legs will carry him.

"Shall we do this shit then?" Conner asks as we all stand like statues at the bottom of the stairs.

"Fuck it." I move first, but they're not far behind me.

I take the furthest door from the stairs, and the one I'm fairly sure will have the best view. I might be here for them, but they can fuck off if they think they're getting it.

"Fucking hell," I mutter, walking onto the insanely spongy cream carpet and looking around at my new digs. This one room alone is about double the size of our trailer.

I dump my bag on the window seat and look out at the ocean beyond, exactly as I'd hoped. Staring out at the perfect postcard view, I hope its calmness will somehow transfer into me. No such luck, because when I turn and take in the room around me, the need to smash it up is all-consuming.

I don't want to fucking be here.

I want my old life. My shitty trailer. My state school and dead-end opportunities.

Pulling my cell from my pocket, I sync it with the speakers I find on the sideboard and turn it up as loud as it'll go. This house might be a mansion, but I'll make sure Uncle fucking James knows we've arrived.

Retrieving the packet of smokes from my bag, I pull one out and place it between my lips before falling down onto my bed. I can only assume there's a no smoking rule in a place like this. I smile as I light up and blow smoke right into the center of the room.

I didn't follow any rules before, so like fuck am I about to start.

I can't hear anything over the sound of my music, so it's not until the door opens that I realize someone wants me. Looking up, I expect to find my brothers, but instead Uncle James stands before me in his sharp three-piece suit, slicked-back hair and clean-shaven face.

"What do you want?" I bark, turning away from him and lighting up once again.

"I was coming to see how you were settling in, but I see you've already made yourself at home."

"What the fuck?" I seethe when the cigarette is plucked from my lips, seconds before it's flicked out the window.

He pulls up the front of his perfectly pressed pants before sitting down on the edge of my bed. If he's trying to look authoritative, then he needs to try fucking harder.

"A few house rules are in order, I think."

I scoff but allow him to continue so he can list his challenges, because you can bet your sweet ass I'm going to breaking each and every one just to piss him off.

"No smoking in the house. You want to kill yourself with those death sticks, then you do so outside. You will not bring any drugs or drink into this house. If you want friends here, you can use the pool house. I've set it up as a den of sorts for the three of you. That's your domain."

"So we can smoke, drink, and do drugs in there?"

"No. There will be no parties, no girls, nothing that will cause any trouble of any kind."

"If you're not looking for trouble, then you invited the wrong guys to come and live with you."

"You are no longer in Sterling Heights." He frowns. "Things are different around here. I think it might be important for you to remember that."

"Whatever."

"School starts in two weeks. Your uniforms are already in your closets. I suggest you familiarize yourself with the place before the hard work starts, because there is no way you're not graduating this year," he jibes, knowing full well that I fucked up what should have been my senior year last year. Not my fault that someone had to earn some goddamn money to support my brothers.

I look to the other side of the room as if his mere presence is boring me.

"Dinner will be served in an hour. I expect you all to be cleaned and dressed appropriately." I see his gaze from out of the corner of my eye drop to my ripped jeans and oil-stained shirt. "My girlfriend and her daughter are coming to welcome you to town, and I shouldn't need to tell you that you will be nice to both of them."

Well, doesn't that sound like a fucking fun way to spend our first night in Sterling Bay? A nice, cozy family meal with the man who only wanted us when we had no parents left in this world.

He makes out like he wasn't aware of what our lives were like.

He's a fucking liar.

"An hour. I've already warned your brothers. We'll be waiting."

I do shower and change—not because he told me to, but because I fucking stink, and to be honest, I can't deny that the rainfall shower in my en suite wasn't appealing. It was a shit load better than the open pipe we had in the trailer.

Wearing a different pair of ripped jeans and a slightly cleaner shirt, I step out into the hall at exactly the same time both Cole and Conner do. They're dressed similarly to me; it seems they took Uncle's warning about as seriously as I did.

The sounds of voices direct the three of us toward the dining room. My curiosity as to what hides behind each door we pass is high, but I don't look. I don't want to seem like I care, because I really fucking don't, I'm just intrigued as to why a man who's always lived alone needs so many fucking rooms.

As we join them, all conversation stops and three heads turn our way. I know our uncle is here but don't pay him any mind. The brunette, however, captures my imagination quite nicely.

He might have warned me about no girls already, but he didn't mention one who clearly already spends time here.

He walks over and wraps his arm around both the

brunette and her mother. "Ace, Cole, Conner..." He grins like the cat who got the cream, and I fucking hate it. "This is Sarah, my girlfriend, and Remi, her daughter."

DOWNLOAD TAUNT HER to continue reading Remi and Ace's story now.

Printed in Great Britain
by Amazon

68617498R00251